MW00622985

A VERY WOODSY MURDER

Books by Ellen Byron

A VERY WOODSY MURDER

Books by Ellen Byron writing as Maria DiRico

HERE COMES THE BODY

LONG ISLAND ICED TINA

IT'S BEGINNING TO LOOK A LOT LIKE MURDER

FOUR PARTIES AND A FUNERAL

THE WITLESS PROTECTION PROGRAM

Published by Kensington Publishing Corp.

A VERY WOODSY MURDER

A GOLDEN MOTEL MYSTERY

Ellen BYRON

Kensington Publishing Corp.
www.kensingtonbooks.com

KENSINGTON BOOKS are published by

Kensington Publishing Corp.
900 Third Avenue
New York, NY 10022

All Kensington titles, imprints, and distributed lines are available at special quantity discounts for bulk purchases for sales promotion, premiums, fund-raising, educational, or institutional use. Special book excerpts or customized printings can also be created to fit specific needs. For details, write or phone the office of the Kensington Special Sales Manager: Attn. Special Sales Department, Kensington Publishing Corp., 900 Third Avenue, New York, NY 10022. Phone: 1-800-221-2647.

Library of Congress Control Number: 2024934890

KENSINGTON and the KENSINGTON COZIES teapot logo Reg. U.S. Pat. & TM Off.

ISBN: 978-1-4967-4535-4

First Kensington Hardcover Edition: August 2024

ISBN: 978-1-4967-4537-8 (ebook)

10 9 8 7 6 5 4 3 2 1

Printed in the United States of America

Who's Who

At the Golden Motel
Dee Stern: sitcom writer turned budding motelier
Jeff Cornetta: data analyst turned budding motelier
Ma'am: handywoman who lives off the grid in the
    backwoods with her husband
Mister Ma'am: Ma'am's mate
Michael Adam Baker: a motel guest
Nugget: Dee's hound, adopted from the estate of the
    Golden's late owner, Jasper Gormley

In Foundgold
Elmira Williker: owner of Williker's All-in-One General
    Store, which has been in her family since the Gold
    Rush
Serena Finlay-Katz: ethereal charcuterie artist married to
    a big Hollywood agent
Callan Katz: Serena's husband, who's basically up in
    Foundgold on the weekends
Marisa Young: Callan's ambitious assistant
Emmy: Serena and Callan's infant daughter
Oscar: Serena's tiny dog
Huck, aka Hunk: drop-dead gorgeous firefighter on the
    Cal Fire inmate crew

In Goldsgone
Verity Donner Gillespie: proprietor of Goldsgone
    Mercantile and Emporium, who runs the town
Jonas Jones: real estate agent
Liza Chen: restauranteur

Shawn Radinsky: personal trainer
Brian Oakhurst: a contractor
Millie Oakhurst: Brian's mother, who works part-time at the mercantile
Owen Mudd Jr.: local jeweler

Law Enforcement
Raul Aguilar: deputy sheriff at the Goldsgone substation of the county sheriff agency
Tom O'Bryant: chief district ranger, Majestic National Park

Los Angeles
Sam Stern: Dee's dad, a voice actor
Mindy Baruch: TV writer
R.J. Morrin: TV writer
Pria Hart: Michael's ex-girlfriend

CHAPTER 1

Dee watched her best friend check out the potential gold mine across the narrow country road from them. She couldn't tell what he was thinking, which made her nervous. Patience was not Dee's strong suit—and with the high stakes of her current situation, waiting for a response from Jeff was torture.

Jeff shifted position. Dee's hopes rose. But . . . nothing. The only sound came from the rustling of leaves by a spring breeze and the caw of a hawk circling above them in a brilliant blue sky.

Unable to take it anymore, Dee gave up on patience. "Jeff, *please*. I really want to know what you think."

More silence. Then . . . "It's definitely cool," he acknowledged. "And the setting *is* spectacular."

He squinted. Dee couldn't tell if it was to get a different perspective or the beginning of a frown.

"I get impulse buys," he said. "I really do. That's how I wound up with a case of anti-balding cream from a deal I saw on TV." Jeff touched a hand to his tight copper curls. "Do you think it's working?" he asked, hopeful but insecure.

"Yes," Dee said. It wasn't a complete lie. Jeff's curly ginger hairline did seem to be receding at a slightly slower pace.

"Awesome," he said, relieved. "Anyway, like I was saying, I do get impulse buys. But . . . a motel?"

"Not just any motel. This one."

Dee made an expansive gesture toward the worn, yet charming, rustic mid-century lodging in front of them: the Golden Motel, the lone hostelry in the tiny village of Foundgold, California.

The motel was nestled amidst a grove of pine trees at the foot of the Sierra Nevada mountains and the southernmost tip of Gold Rush Country. Behind it loomed the incomparable beauty of Majestic National Park, whose entrance was a mere few miles up the winding two-lane road fronting the motel.

Built in the early 1940s, the property consisted of a quaint, single-story redwood lodge containing ten guest rooms. A one-bedroom apartment, which counted as living quarters for the motel owner, was attached to the small, low-slung lodge's lobby and lounge. Ten cozy cabins, also of redwood, were scattered in the woods behind the lodge. A pool shaped like a gold nugget claimed the western edge of the property, but instead of water, decaying pine needles filled its bottom. A large neon sign sporting another gold nugget advertised the motel's name in bright yellow. Or would have if some of its lights weren't out.

"You really want to buy this place?" Jeff asked.

"Yes. It's a motel that feels like a hug."

He gave her a skeptical look and Dee hastened to explain.

"It gives off this really warm, cozy vibe." She gazed at the Golden as two squirrels skittered up the giant ponderosa pine standing guard in the grass oval at the center of the motel's graveled circular drive. "You know how miserable I've been lately."

Jeff's expression softened. "You've been through a lot."

Dee responded with a grateful smile. "I only drove up to Majestic to get out of L.A. for a weekend. I wanted a simple, pretty place where I could think about how to get my life back on track." She motioned to their surroundings. "I can't believe I've lived in California my whole life and never been here. It's so beautiful. And peaceful. You know my feeling of burnout?" Dee waved her hands in the air as if waving away bad spirits. "*Gone.*"

"Peaceful? That's a switch. You always said you were a city girl and the country creeped you out with all the quiet and dark."

"I know. I didn't appreciate it until now."

Jeff gestured to the motel. "How'd you find this place?"

"I drove in the north end of the park, but I drove out the south end. I rounded the bend and there it was. The For Sale sign was like a sign to *me.*" She tapped her chest. "It's the one-eighty career change I've been looking for."

"Career change or running away?" Jeff sounded dubious. "I'd hate to see you make a huge decision like this for the wrong reasons."

Dee knew her friend's concerns were well-intentioned. And not far off the mark. Her mother's unexpected death, the end of her second marriage, a career downturn—it all added up to her very own "annus horribilis," to quote the late queen of England.

"What about your job?" Jeff asked.

"This hiatus showed me I need to move on. Every time I think about going back to work when it's over, I get a sick feeling here." Dee formed two fists and placed them on her stomach. "*Duh!* is a kids' sitcom, which I could live with. But it's a bad one. The job is just as hard as when I worked on network and streaming shows, but the pay is half, the staff hates being there, and the writing is terrible. Even my own."

The expression "what goes up must come down" was never more appropriate than when applied to a Hollywood career. Ever since breaking into television in her mid-twenties as a writer-producer, Dee had scored jobs on decent, workhorse sitcoms that garnered viewers, but not accolades. Without an award-winning hit credit to take to the bank, as she aged out of being the latest shiny object, job opportunities went from few to nonexistent. After a year of unemployment, the sole offer she'd received during the recent staffing season was from *Duh!*, a cheesy sitcom for kids about tween superheroes attending a middle school on New York's Long Island.

"I was going to tough it out, I really was," she continued. "Work my butt off to write and produce the best scripts I could. But then I found out that when I turn forty in December, I'm eligible for the union's career longevity committee. And that pushed me over the edge."

"Longevity sounds like it's a good thing."

Dee shook her head so emphatically that the ponytail corralling her thick chestnut hair whipped her in the face. She rubbed her cheek. "It's not. It's the opposite. It's a euphemism for 'too old to hire.'"

"How can writers be too old at forty?" Jeff wondered.

Dee shrugged. "It's Hollywood. Everyone's too old. I know a writer who made her six-year-old lie about mommy's age on a kindergarten school project. Another friend knocked five years off her dad's age in his obituary to make herself younger."

Jeff looked appalled as he took this in. "Ouch. But being in tech, I guess I'm not one to talk. They started calling me 'the old guy' when I turned thirty."

Dee put her hands on Jeff's shoulders and looked him in the eye. Since he was almost a foot taller than her five-two height, this required neck-craning on her part. "That's why I want you to make a lifestyle change with me. You're always complaining about how expensive the Bay Area is and how you're over being a systems analyst and want to do something more creative. If you come into business with me, you can do two creative things: We'll work together to transform the Golden into a motel everyone wants to visit, and you can set up a business as a freelance web designer and app creator. You've wanted to do that for forever. Now you'll have the time."

Dee could see Jeff was conflicted, which she considered progress. He hesitated. "The thing is, we don't know anything about the hospitality business. I don't even make my own bed. I don't know how, which is going to make it a little tough to make the beds for"—he silently counted the rooms in the motel—"ten guest rooms and however many cabins."

"I've been watching videos by motel owners and signed up for some online classes. I'll teach you what I learn. And once the Golden starts generating income, we'll hire a room comfort specialist. I just made that up as a better name for housekeepers. Do you like it?"

"I do."

"You see? We'll be job creators. And hospitality innovators."

Jeff gave a snort. "Innovators. Nice way of saying amateurs."

"Yes. But we do have useful skill sets. You have your

creative side, but you also have the tech talent to turn the Golden into a smart motel with a vintage feel but state-of-the-art everything. And if there's one thing fifteen years of working in writers' rooms has taught me, it's how to deal with personalities, from nice to horrible. So I can manage guests. And we can brainstorm on marketing."

Jeff pondered this. "What are the guest rooms like?"

Dee, excited, did a little bounce up and down, her sneakers leaving indents in the wet, mossy ground beneath her feet. "Wait until you see them. They're totally mid-century woodsy time capsules."

A pinecone dropped off the tree above them and beaned Jeff. "Ow!" He winced and rubbed his head.

"You'll live. Come on." Dee darted across the street. Jeff followed, massaging where the pinecone made contact.

The two traipsed through overgrown brush to the window of a guest room. A broken venetian blind hung askew, allowing a glimpse inside. The walls and ceiling were covered with knotty pine paneling. The centerpiece of the room was a double bed with a western-style carved and whitewashed oak headboard. Matching nightstands adorned each side of the bed, and a red-plaid quilt topped it. A desk of the same oak design claimed one corner of the room, while a club chair upholstered in forest green Naugahyde sat across from it. A rag rug covered a small section of the wood floor. Lamps with bases made of stacked horseshoes graced the desk and both nightstands.

"You're right," Jeff said, awed. "It's like time just stopped in the forties or fifties. Whenever this place was built."

"In 1941, over eighty years ago. People all over the country are buying mid-century motels like this and restoring them. I want to breathe life back into the Golden and make it a must-visit destination. And I want to do it with you."

Jeff closed his eyes. He inhaled a deep breath of the fresh mountain air, scented by the omnipresent pine trees. Then his eyes popped open. "The bathrooms. Have you seen them? If the plumbing's bad—"

"The plumbing's good."

"Are they dated?"

"Yes, but in a cool way. Cleaned up and with fresh linens, they'll look great. Same with the bedrooms."

Jeff stroked his chin stubble. "If it goes well," he said, "we could expand. There are probably motels like this all over the state. The country."

"Yes. Exactly." Dee pressed her lips together to contain a swell of emotion, then released them. "I follow this social-media site called R.I.P. Mid-Century. It shows before-and-after photos of places like this, the 'after' being when they've been abandoned. It breaks my heart. I don't want that to happen to the Golden. It needs us. And we need it."

Jeff gave his head an amused shake. "You've always been a rescuer."

He gazed at the Golden, brow furrowed. Once again, Dee waited.

"Okay," Jeff finally said. "I'm in."

Dee let out a happy shriek, startling the squirrels in the ponderosa pine, who chittered a scolding. "Yes! Whoohoo! I'll call the selling agent. It's a probate sale through the state, since the owner died without a will or heirs. I know they'll be thrilled to unload it, so we can negotiate a good deal. Then we can go over every inch of the place and work up a list of the three *R*'s—Repair, Restore, Replace."

Jeff gave her an affectionate grin. "Did you make that up too?"

"I did," she said with pride.

A loud buzzing drew their attention to the motel neon sign. The letters G, E, and N sputtered, then completely burned out. "I guess we'll soon be the proud owners of the OLD motel," Jeff said, his tone wry.

"That will go on the list under Repairs."

Jeff raised an eyebrow. "Why do I have the feeling we're going to be looking at some very long lists?"

"Getting the Golden up and running will definitely be a challenge," Dee admitted. "But with Team You and Me, I know we can work through every obstacle we come up against."

"I like your optimism," Jeff said. "Hopefully, my accountant will share it."

He headed back to his car, careful to avoid low-hanging pinecones. Dee gave the guest room interior a parting glance. She was about to return to her own car when she heard what sounded like leaves crunching under footsteps.

Dee froze. Her heart thumped as she listened for sound again. It came, only slightly more distant, like it was moving away from her. She relaxed slightly. *Probably an animal. Nothing to be scared of. I'm perfectly safe here in the country. Perfectly, perfectly safe.*

But as she made a quick jog up to the road, she couldn't shake the feeling she might be wrong about that.

CHAPTER 2

With Jeff on board—although his accountant, not so much—Dee managed to quickly close the deal for the Golden, making them the proud possessors of twenty-two rusty old keys: twenty for the guest rooms and cabins, one for the main office and lobby, and one for the owner's apartment, where Dee would reside. Jeff chose the one-bedroom cabin closest to the motel as his new home. Tiny as it was, it beat the single bedroom he'd been renting in a San Francisco home for a jaw-dropping amount of money.

Dee had rented out her Studio City condo fully furnished, so she welcomed the furniture that came with her new digs, all of which were in the same woodsy style as the guest rooms. Her living space was comprised of a bedroom and bathroom, down a short hall from the main room, a large open space housing the living, dining, and kitchen area. The ancient avocado stove looked like an accident waiting to happen, but proved functional. Even better, Foundgold served up unexpectedly strong Wi-Fi, which was coming in handy as she sat working on her laptop at the living room's oak desk, researching the discouraging cost of repairing the neon sign, as well as the Golden's pool.

The room was warm. Her tortoiseshell glasses began a slide down the damp bridge of her nose, and she pushed them back. She rested her feet on one of several ancient trunks filled with the late owner's belongings, which had come with the property. Dee hoped a thorough search of the trunks would unearth historic relics she could sell on the internet to help fund the motel venture.

"I hate how much it's going to cost to deal with the pool, but we don't have a choice," she said to Jeff, who was splayed out on the green Naugahyde sofa, working from his phone. "We have to make it a top priority. Aside from the fact it's in terrible shape, the condition it's in right now makes the Golden look abandoned. We could fix up every room in the motel and people would still drive right by."

"That won't be a problem," Jeff said. "I crunched the numbers for what it would cost to get all the rooms ready to go and forget a big grand opening. With the cost of new mattresses, air conditioners, linens, mini fridges, and microwaves for each room, we'll have to rehab and book them one by one. And do all the cleaning and maintenance ourselves for longer than we originally thought. We'll still have to live off our savings for a couple of months, but it's our only option."

Dee nodded, swallowing her anxiety. She'd brought Jeff along for this ride and owed him a positive attitude. "Not a problem. And I'll have more income from my tenant's rent in a few weeks."

"Uh-huh," Jeff said, half-listening, focused on his phone. "Ooh, I like her." He roused himself from the couch and padded over to Dee in his bare feet. "What do you think? Swipe left or right?"

Dee took his phone and glanced at the bleached blonde on Jeff's screen pouting for the camera. "Duck-lips-enhanced-with-fillers selfie. Swipe left. You really do have questionable taste in women."

"I married you, didn't I?"

"Proving my point," Dee said with a chortle. She and Jeff had met, instantly fallen in love, and impulsively married at the end of their senior year at UCLA. Three months into their ill-fated marriage, they were forced to admit it was an epic fail. But the short union had resulted in a lifelong friendship, for which they'd be forever grateful.

Dee handed the phone back to Jeff. "There's no point in connecting with her anyway. Now that you've moved here, you're geographically undesirable."

"Argh." Jeff plopped down on the couch, which emitted a flatulent creak. "Living here is going to seriously cramp my dating life. Where do we meet people?"

"Not in Foundgold, that's for sure. The Welcome sign said the population was sixty-eight, and I think that's optimistic. Maybe in Goldsgone? There's way more going on there."

"I don't get it," Jeff said. "You'd think it would be the reverse. That a place called Foundgold would be way more prosperous than a town with the depressing name of Goldsgone."

"The lady at the general store explained it to me. Once miners found gold, they left. But the ones who didn't find it wound up broke. They didn't have the option of leaving, so they had to make their town a decent place to live. Then someone realized they could market the fact it looks pretty much exactly like it did a hundred and fifty years ago, and a tourist trap was born." Dee snapped her laptop shut. "A trap I want to tap into for future guests."

She rose to her feet and stretched. Her worn T-shirt, decorated with the logo from *Thanks a Latte*, a failed sitcom about baristas she'd worked on, popped out of her jeans and she tucked it back in. "Speaking of the general store, I'm going to head over there and pick up something for dinner."

She removed a leash from the hook, where it hung by the front door, and motioned to a mutt, who'd been sleeping at her feet. Dee had happily adopted Nugget, the pet pup of the late motel owner, Jasper Gormley. Her furry new friend was a midsize mix of beagle and terrier, with a touch of basset hound, and a possible dose of Doberman. One ear folded over itself, while the other stuck straight up. A doggy smile or yawn revealed a broken canine tooth, leading Jeff to joke Nugget had incurred the damage in a bar fight. The dog's age was anyone's guess.

The mutt rose to his feet. Seeing the leash, he gave an appreciative bark and nuzzled Dee's calf as she clipped the lead to his collar. She gave him an affectionate pet. "That's my boy. You want anything besides dinner and a six-pack of IPA?" She addressed the question to Jeff.

He shook his head. "Be careful. There was another bear sighting." He put down his phone. "Which reminds me, the one thing we do have to pony up for ASAP is security cameras, at least for here and my cabin and our first guest room. I'll hunt some down on the internet I can install myself. The kind with a phone app that'll alert us to any visitors of the ursine persuasion."

Dee shuddered. She hadn't given much thought to bears prior to purchasing the Golden and couldn't say with confidence she would have gone through with the deal if she had. *What's that old saying?* She tried to remember, and then it came to her: *Hindsight is twenty-twenty vision.*

She wondered if black bears had good eyesight. And if there was any way to decrease the appeal of her and Nugget as potential snacks.

* * *

Foundgold was a postcard-perfect collection of nineteenth-century and early-twentieth-century homes nestled in the hills of a pine forest undulating upward from the winding two-lane road that led past the Golden. Like the motel, the homes were built from local redwood and ranged from log cabins to bungalows whose porches were made of stone scooped out of the countryside's creek and streams, one of which meandered its lovely way north into the Sierras.

Williker's All-in-One General Store stretched out along the road like an expanded wooden telescope. The building was a haphazard blend of additions in different architectural styles, each one representing the time period when it was added to the original building. A faded plaque marked the center section as dating back to the 1849 Gold Rush and was built of the same stone used on Foundgold homes.

Dee parked her Honda Civic, picked up a couple of reusable grocery bags resting on the passenger seat, and exited the car with Nugget. She and her furry friend strolled past the store's two gas station pumps and up a ramp to the store's entrance.

What began as a nineteenth-century one-room store catering to a gold miner's needs had grown into an enterprise that earned the added appellation of "All-in-One." But the original rustic space still retained its status as a general store. Items on the well-stocked old wooden shelves ran the gamut of essentials, showcasing everything from canned goods to paper goods. Freezer and refrigerator cases lining the walls offered such a wide range of local beers and wines it led Dee to assume imbibing was the primary form of entertainment for locals—and probably for tourists on their way to Majestic.

The store also featured a hefty display of souvenirs, most of which celebrated the national park, although Dee did notice an enameled key chain shaped like a gold nugget that was emblazoned with the proclamation, "I Found-gold!" The east end of the All-in-One contained a café and a bar, which also served a wide range of coffee drinks. A post office and laundromat were housed in the west end.

Dee had only met proprietor Elmira Williker once, and their brief interaction had been limited to subjects like whether the Golden's septic tank would buckle under the weight of two-ply toilet paper. Elmira, a sturdy woman in her mid-forties who gave off the vibe of not being some-one you wanted to mess with, had been courteous, but aloof, with Dee. The nascent motelier attributed this to a general wariness on the part of locals to Angeleno inter-lopers who'd discovered the region during the pandemic lockdown and driven up housing costs.

Determined to break through the shop owner's reserve, Dee greeted her with an extremely cheery "Good morning!"

Elmira responded with a taciturn nod. Then she saw Nugget, who was busy sniffing the worn old wooden floor for errant snacks, and a warm smile replaced the wariness. "Nugget? Old buddy, is that you?"

Nugget glanced up. He barked an affirmative and wagged his tail. Elmira came out from behind the long wooden cash register counter and went to him. She bent down and stroked his head.

"He was being boarded at the shelter," Dee said. "As soon as the deal closed, I brought him home."

"Good. We weren't sure what the new owners would do. We were worried about him."

Dee wasn't sure if this was a royal "we" or if Elmira was speaking for the whole village. Knowing that the shopkeeper was the mayor of Foundgold, Dee assumed it was the latter. "Well, the new owners being me and my friend Jeff, you don't have to worry anymore. I've always wanted a pet, but when I was a kid, my mother had severe allergies. And then when I was working in TV, my hours were endless, which wasn't fair to an animal—or a human for that matter."

"We all miss old Jasper, but no one more 'n this guy, huh, fella?" Elmira ruffled Nugget's fur. "Jasper's family went back far as mine in Foundgold."

"Your ancestors were miners?"

"Started that way. Yes, there were Black miners. People are like this when they hear that." Elmira mimed shock, then rolled her eyes. "My great-greats figured out they'd make more selling to miners than mining, so they started this place."

Nugget whimpered and pawed Elmira. "I know what you want." She stood up and went to the counter, where she extracted a desiccated long brown stick from a jar next to the register. She brought it back to Nugget, who responded with ecstatic yelps. He devoured the stick. "Venison jerky," she explained to Dee. "I'll give you a dozen of 'em. Housewarming present. You'll like 'em too."

"Thank you so much," Dee said, knowing she was about as likely to eat venison jerky as she was to play quarterback for an NFL team. "That's so kind of you. I plead guilty to stereotypes of the country. I was always afraid some guy with no teeth and an ax would jump out from behind a tree and start chasing me."

"Oh, he died years ago."

Dee's eyes widened.

Elmira shot her a look. "I'm joking."

"Oh," Dee said, embarrassed. "Ha. Sure. Good one." She paused. "It's just . . . I've heard what sounds like footsteps in the woods a few times."

Elmira returned to her position behind the register. "That's probably just Stoney."

"Stoney?" Dee repeated.

"The bear. Some fellas running an illegal pot farm gave him the nickname. He got into some edibles they were tinkering with and let's just say he was one blissed-out bear. Play on the name Smokey."

"Right. Got that. About that pot farm . . ."

"Gone. Feds broke up that operation." Seeing the expression on Dee's face, Elmira added, "For real. Not a joke."

"Phew." Dee took a large bag of pretzels from a rack of snacks and placed it in one of her grocery bags. "I was starting to think I was safer in Los Angeles."

Elmira pulled a large container of jerky from under the counter and refilled the jar. "There are days you might be," she said, not making Dee feel better. "Things can get crazy at the national parks, like Majestic, during the summer. You know what they call Yosemite during peak times? 'Yo-seme-city.' Because the park's got all the same problems and crimes as a city when the population explodes with tourists."

A loud beep came from the building's west end, startling Dee. Elmira wiped her hands on her butcher's apron. "My laundry's ready. If anyone comes in, tell them I'll be right back and not to steal nothing, because I know where they live. Oh, and don't leave without some of my homemade berry hand pies." She gestured to a small bakery case on the counter with pride. "Made 'em myself. Baking's my hobby, even though I lost my sense of taste a while ago, thanks to a virus."

Elmira headed toward the laundromat section of the store, leaving Dee to mull over the disconcerting tidbits she'd picked up from Elmira. Bears, illegal marijuana farms, national parks where summer simmered with danger. "What have I gotten myself into?" she murmured to

Nugget, who had finished his jerky stick and was licking his front paws for any tidbits he missed.

Feeling the need for a comforting snack, Dee helped herself to one of Elmira's hand pies. She took a bite and gagged. The dough was dry, made from old, stale flour, and the filling had turned. Dee desperately searched for a trash can, finally locating one behind the counter. But before she could spit out the noxious ingredients, Elmira emerged from the back, carrying a full laundry bin. "I'll fold between customers." She saw the half-eaten pie in Dee's hand and gave an approving smile. "You picked up a pie. What do you think?"

Dee managed to swallow the offending mouthful. "Yum," she weakly lied. "I'll take a dozen."

While Dee finished shopping, Nugget went through another jerky stick. She left the store on friendly terms with Elmira, even if it cost her the worst pastries she'd ever tasted.

Dee was about to drive off, when her cell rang. She answered the call and Jeff's voice boomed through the car speakers.

"I have great news!" he declared.

"You found a lower bid to repair the pool?" Dee clasped her hands together in silent prayer.

"God, no. But"—Jeff took a theatrical pause—"I've been working on the Golden website. I put up a beta version—and we got our first booking!"

Dee transitioned from praying to clapping. "Whoohoo! That's fantastic. I hope not too soon. We don't even have one room ready."

"No worries, he's not coming until Friday. Gives us a couple of days to get a room ready to go. You get credit for this reservation, because he says he knows you."

"Yay me." Dee grinned and gave herself an imaginary pat on the back. "Who?"

"A writer named Michael Adam Baker."

Dee's grin disappeared. She got a sick feeling in the pit of her stomach, not helped by remnants of Elmira's abysmal pastries.

"He said he heard about the Golden through the writers' grapevine and thought it would be a great place to hunker down and write his new pilot. How cool is that?"

"So cool," Dee said, hoping the dread she felt didn't color her response.

"If he loves it here, and he will, we can get a testimonial and use it to generate writers' retreats. Fill the whole Golden in one shot, once all the rooms are up and running. I'm telling you, the mind blows at the possibilities." Jeff paused. "Dee? Hello? You still there?"

"Yes, sorry. I was about to leave Williker's. Be home in five. Michael Adam Baker, huh? *Wow.*"

Dee hung up before Jeff could respond. She didn't have the heart to tell him Michael Adam Baker was the most devious, backstabbing writer she'd ever worked with. And considering some of the writing staffs she'd been on, that was saying something.

CHAPTER 3

Once home, Jeff insisted on celebrating their first booking with a toast. "This is good," Dee said, sipping the cabernet sauvignon Jeff had poured into the Mason jars they'd found in a cabinet and sanitized. "Did you get it at Williker's?"

Jeff shook his head. "No, at a gas station off the 101 on the way here the other night. Only in California does a gas station convenience store have a better selection than most wine shops in the rest of the country." He topped off her jar. "Now, tell me why I'm getting this extremely disappointing reaction to my big news."

"I'm excited," Dee protested.

Jeff made a face. "Gimme a break. How well do we know each other? Tell me the truth. What's the story with this guy?"

Dee sighed. "Fine. Here's the story. We worked together on my very first TV job. I never even told you about it, because it went by so quickly. It was called *On the John.*"

"I don't wanna know what that show was about."

"It was about exactly what you think it would be about—a plumber named John. It was picked up by the network with a six-episode order and joined the elite club of shows canceled after only one episode aired. I was a staff writer on the show. The lowest level."

Jeff rested his long legs on the green Naugahyde side chair that matched the couch. "I love how in Hollywood the only writer on a TV staff who's actually called a writer is at the bottom of the food chain. Everyone else has some kind of producer title."

"Agree it's ridiculous, and back to Michael. He was a story editor, which was only one level above me. He was a good-looking guy and kind of a flirt, but he was incredibly threatened and competitive. He always made a point of shooting down my joke and story pitches. On the positive side, it taught me to fight for anything I really believed in, which came in handy on future shows." She looked down at her jar. "I'm sure Michael bad-mouthed me to Mark the showrunner, because Mark never hired me again, even though he hired other writers from the *John* staff, including Michael himself."

"Wow. This Baker guy sounds like a primo jerk. I was already leaning toward not liking him for the three-name thing. Pree-tentious. I'll write him we're not open yet and don't know when we will be."

Jeff started to rise. Dee put out a hand to stop him. "No. I'm being overly sensitive. It was a while ago. My first show, his second. We were both scared of being left without a job in the musical-chairs game that's staffing season. And I don't have actual proof he bad-mouthed me." She scrunched her face, conflicted, then came to a decision. "Let him come. I think it'll be fine."

Jeff looked at her with concern. "Are you sure?"

"Yes. A hundred percent." Dee delivered this with confidence, fighting back a pesky hint of hesitation.

* * *

Since their inaugural guest requested a quiet cabin, Dee and Jeff chose to spiff up the one farthest from the main lodge and the road. But first, Dee suggested they round up the prints hanging in all the guest rooms and transport them to her apartment so she could clean and ready them for rehanging in her free time. "I recognize this artist," she said to Jeff as they lugged a half dozen into her living room.

"You should. It's Kristof Honestadt. He spent most of his career in the nineteenth century painting images of Majestic National Park. He's a legend."

"I'm sure he'd be honored to know I saw one of his paintings on a souvenir cigarette lighter at Williker's." Dee put down her framed prints, resting them against a leg of the dining-room table. "Not this one, though." She studied the print, at least as much of it as she could see under the decades of grime that had built up on the frame's protective glass. Her face lit up. "Oh, wow. I just realized something. This is the view of Majestic from behind the Golden. Before it was built, of course. It's like our very own Honestadt."

Jeff studied the print. "I wonder where the original painting is. Remind me to research that. I can find a way to work it into our website."

"Put it on the list of to-dos." Dee headed to the kitchen area. She pulled a pair of rubber gloves out of a bucket of cleaning supplies and snapped them on. "Right now, it's Operation Clean Michael Adam Baker's Cabin."

The next eight hours were a grueling whirl of scrubbing, scraping, repairing, and hauling. Dee painstakingly replaced broken grout in the bathroom's mid-century mint-green tiles, while Jeff lugged out the cabin's old mattress, replacing it with a brand-new one. It was well into night-time when the exhausted duo agreed they'd made enough progress for one day and would finish in the morning.

They trudged back to Dee's place and washed up. Dee picked up one of the Honestadt prints. "Why don't I work on cleaning this for Michael's room, and you go pick up dinner at Williker's? Pick up some of Elmira's pastries too. They're too god-awful to eat, but she'll love us for buying them."

"Maybe they're really good and we don't know it because we're not used to all the fresh ingredients out here in the country." Jeff pulled his car fob from his back jeans pocket. "My car could use a charge. I'll plug it into the outdoor socket on the side of the lodge for a few minutes, and then take off."

Jeff headed out. Dee retrieved a rag that had once been a T-shirt from *The Blues Family,* an animated series she'd worked on about a musical family that happened to be various shades of blue. She dabbed cleaner on the rag and began rubbing off the dirt on the frame's glass. As she worked, she flashed on a memory from *On the John.* Michael, showrunner Mark, and another male writer had gone into the men's room together. A few minutes later, they came out high-fiving each other, having solved a story problem. On the surface, it was a minor moment, but for Dee, it was a telling one. *How do women writers compete with the male bond of a urinal?* she'd wondered. She never did come up with an answer.

Forget the past, Dee admonished herself. *Eyes on the present.* She rubbed at the glass until it gleamed. "Nice job, you," she told her reflection with a grin. "Let's put this in a safe place."

She stood up and was about to lay the print on the

table, when the room suddenly went dark. "What the—"
She stumbled toward the front door and threw it open.
Dark as it was inside her apartment, it was pitch black
outside. "Jeff! Jeff? Are you okay? There's a blackout!"

"I'm fine," Jeff yelled to her. "It's the mid-century
wiring here. It can't support a car charge."

Dee stepped back inside, almost tripping over a snoozing Nugget as she negotiated her way through the apartment. She felt around the dining table until she found her
cell phone. She turned on the phone's flashlight and reversed course, negotiating a path out of the apartment to
Jeff.

"My bad, I should have thought of that before I plugged
in," he said, typing quickly on his phone. "I'm doing a
search on how to get the electricity up and running again."

"Okay." Dee did a slow turn, taking in their surroundings. What was bucolic in daylight now seemed ominous
and threatening. "I didn't know how dark it can get out
here in the country. It's, like, *really*, really dark."

"I watched a show online about the Salem witch trials,"
Jeff said, still typing. "Historians think a lot of the Puri-
tans' superstitions can be attributed to their fears of the
super-dark nights three hundred years ago. Like this."

"Thanks for not making me feel better."

A rhythmic crunching sound came from the woods, like
heavy feet tromping over sticks and dead leaves. "Oh, my
God," Dee said, panicked. "It's Stoney."

"Who?" Jeff asked, confused.

"The bear."

Dee held her phone flashlight up to the direction of the
sound. The tree branches parted, and a being emerged
from the woods. Not a bear—a man. His scraggly gray
hair hung below his shoulders. His clothes were worn be-

yond recognition. He carried a large ax he swung back and forth as he loped toward Dee and Jeff.

"It's the man with no teeth and an ax!" Dee screamed.

"What are you talking about?" Jeff said, eyes still on his phone. "You're crazier than a Puritan."

Dee elbowed him. He looked up and froze. His mouth opened and shut, but no words came out.

The screen door burst open, and Nugget flew out of the apartment. He charged toward the man and jumped on him. The man picked up the dog.

"No!" Dee yelled.

She ran to save Nugget, but stopped short. The dog's tail wagged with the vigor of windshield wipers during a heavy storm. He alternated happy barks with licking the stranger's face. The man laughed a hearty laugh, revealing a perfect set of teeth. "Nugs, my old friend. Good to see ya."

"That Nugget?"

The shorthand question came from a disembodied woman's voice. There was more crunching of undergrowth, and a woman appeared behind the man. Like him, she had scraggly gray hair and wore shapeless, worn clothes more akin to sacks. In fact, under the bright flashlight, Dee made out markings indicating the garment was constructed from actual feed sacks.

The couple took turns showering Nugget with affection; then the man spoke. "We're your neighbors. We got a cabin in the woods behind you. We saw the Golden's lights go out and thought you might need a hand. This is Ma'am." He gestured fondly to the woman, who was throwing sticks to a euphoric Nugget. "And I'm Mister Ma'am."

"Hi," Dee said, trying to calm her rapidly beating heart. "Nice to meet you. I'm Dee, and this is my friend Jeff."

She motioned to the techie, who'd joined her. "We're the new owners."

"And thanks for the offer," Jeff said. He held up his phone. "But I found a couple of training videos, and as long as the battery charge on my phone doesn't run out, I think at least one of these will help me figure out how to—"

Every light in the Golden suddenly came to life, almost blinding Dee and Jeff. Ma'am sauntered back to them, Nugget at her heels. "Ya overloaded the circuit breaker. I flipped it back on. Breaker's by room 10. But I wouldn't be charging your vehicle here. It'll happen again. There's a charging station by the Unitarian church in Goldsgone."

"Good to know," Jeff said.

Dee managed not to laugh at how mortified he sounded. "Thank you so much. It's great to know we have such nice neighbors."

Mister responded with a big smile, once again displaying a set of gleaming white choppers. The sight triggered a memory for Dee, but it flew out of her mind before she could land on it.

"If you need us," Ma'am said, "just ring the bell. That's how Jasper got in touch when he needed to."

The woman pointed to a giant triangular bell, the kind Dee associated with calling ranch hands to dinner on old Western movies and TV shows. The triangle dangled low from a hook at the far end of the lodge and Jeff had banged his head on it at least twice thus far. "Thanks," Dee said. "We appreciate that."

The four said their goodbyes and the Ma'ams disappeared back into the woods, lugging the discarded mattress from Michael's cabin as a thank-you present. Dee stared after them. "It's so weird. Mister Ma'am really does look familiar to me."

Jeff scoffed. "That's the dark night talking." They turned toward the lodge. "I've got enough of a charge on my car to get to Goldsgone. I'll grab us something to eat there while I top it off there. We should make it an early night. Your frenemy Michael will be here tomorrow afternoon and we need to finish fixing up his cabin."

"Right," Dee said by rote. Her mind was elsewhere. Despite Jeff's scoffing, she was absolutely sure she recognized Mister Ma'am.

But from where?

CHAPTER 4

The next day, Dee added the final touches to Michael's cabin—a gold nugget–shaped bar of soap from the All-in-One's souvenir section—just as a black Porsche Carrera with tinted windows pulled into the Golden's circular driveway.

She was greeting the motel's first guest on her own, because Jeff had an impromptu meeting in San Francisco with a potential client for his new content creation business. He'd expressed concern about leaving Dee to deal with her former nemesis without him, but she assured him she'd be fine. Now, watching Michael Adam Baker emerge from his six-figure sports car, a surge of doubt overwhelmed Dee. But she fought it back, plastered on her best motelier smile, and waved to him.

"Michael. Hi."

He responded with a mock salute. "Dee. Deester."

"Welcome to the Golden Motel, where we hope you'll make memories as precious as gold." Hearing this out loud for the first time, Dee winced. "We're still working on our slogan."

"It's cute." Dee knew he was lying, but appreciated the support.

Michael took off his sunglasses and put them in the inside pocket of his black leather bomber jacket. He walked toward Dee and held out his arms for a friendly hug. "Everyone in town is talking about you. Remember Mark from *On the John?* We're still in touch, and when I told him where I was going, he said, 'Dee got out? Tell her congrats and I'm jealous.'"

Dee found it hard to believe that a man who was paid like a Saudi prince to basically come up with fart jokes envied her career change, but she kept the skepticism to herself. "He wouldn't be if he saw what it's going to cost us to repair the pool," she half-joked.

"Don't worry. We'll get the motel on the map, and you'll be able to resurface the pool in actual gold." Michael walked a few steps back to his car and popped the trunk. He removed a high-end carry-on suitcase. Dee noticed a studio logo placed discreetly on the suitcase's front corner. The suitcase was the kind of swag studios only gifted to the highest echelon of writer-producers.

Feeling guilty for shirking her hospitality duties, she joined Michael at his car. "Let me help you with your luggage."

"No need. I got it." He pulled out a leather laptop case sporting the logo of a different studio from the one decorating his carry-on. "I'll stick everything in my room; then I want a tour of the whole place."

"Sure."

While they made small talk on the short stroll to Michael's lodgings, Dee subtly took inventory of the writer. He was a few years younger than she was, and still handsome, but his face was more lined than she remembered, and his blond hair was flecked with white. He'd dodged the weight gain that came with the sedentary lifestyle of a writers' room, unlike Dee, who fought a constant battle against the twenty pounds she'd put on over the course of her career. Dee attributed Michael's lean frame to the fact he'd spent the last few years on overall deals that stressed development over staffing jobs, giving him control over his own schedule. She'd expected their conversation to revolve around gossip about their mutual acquaintances and was pleasantly surprised that Michael was far more interested in her current motel adventure than rehashing the past.

They arrived at Michael's cabin. Butterflies swarmed in Dee's stomach as she led him inside, but to her relief, he seemed genuinely enthusiastic about the space. He deposited his belongings in the bedroom, and they left for what Dee assumed would be a brief tour of the property, given that except for his cabin, the rest of the Golden was a work in progress. But Michael insisted on scoping out every inch of the property, even peeking into the windows of each guest room. "Good bones," he said, peering into a room in the main lodge. "The whole vintage thing still seems to be popular, so that's in your favor. Looks like you're missing some artwork, though."

"The frames are filthy, so I'm cleaning them up. I live in the old owner's quarters."

Michael stepped back from the window. "Jasper Gormley was an odd guy. At least that's what the gas station attendant told me when I stopped to fill up." He checked his smartwatch. "I almost forgot, I've got an online meeting with an exec. I gotta go. Hey, if you need an assist around here—doing laundry, cleaning frames, walking Nugget—let me know." He flashed a grin. "I'm always looking for ways to procrastinate."

Dee returned the grin. "I can relate."

They parted ways. Happy that the reunion with Michael had gone so well, Dee practically skipped back to her place. She treated herself to a spirited game of fetch with Nugget, had a bite to eat, then opted to spend a few hours going through one of Jasper Gormley's old trunks instead of cleaning another print frame. She was delighted to discover a collection of ephemera and gadgets dating back to the founding of Foundgold. Land deeds, a century-old map, photos, and even daguerreotypes of the late owners' ancestors and friends—while Dee doubted the collection had monetary value, she considered its historical significance priceless.

Debating what to do with the memorabilia, Dee had a brainstorm. Excited, she grabbed her car keys. She knew exactly to whom she should pitch her idea.

"Hello there!" Elmira's greetings had grown increasingly warm with each pastry purchase on the part of Dee or Michael. She gestured to the bakery case with a come-hither expression. "I made chocolate espresso scones. You know you want one."

"*One?!*" Dee exclaimed, knowing the lousy taste would belie the scone's delicious name. "I'll take a dozen. We have our first guest. I'll serve them to him with breakfast." She crossed her fingers behind her back. "So I had an idea I wanted to run by you."

"Shoot." Elmira began boxing the scones. "Oops, I shouldn't say that. Lotta guns around here. People could take it literally."

"I've been going through Mr. Gormley's trunks and they're a treasure trove of historical items. I know Foundgold has a hard time competing with Goldsgone for tourists. What if the town's tourism board put together a Foundgold Historical Trail?"

Elmira snorted. "I love how you think we have a tourism board."

"You don't?" The news disappointed Dee. But she refused to let it quash her enthusiasm. "Then I'll start one. I'll set a meeting, make flyers, and distribute them to every household in town. Which shouldn't be too hard, since there are only about fifty of them."

"Good for you." Elmira sealed the bakery box. "I think it's a wonderful idea. Why don't you hold the meeting here, in the café! I'll donate baked goods."

"Yay," Dee said weakly.

The general store door opened, and Michael stepped inside. Dee gave him a friendly wave. His response came as a surprise. He seemed taken aback to see her. "Hi. I didn't expect to run into you."

"It's my favorite store in town," she said, wondering why he seemed so uncomfortable. "And that's not because it's the only store in town." She leaned an elbow on the counter and whispered to Elmira, "That's our guest."

"Really." The store owner pursed her lips.

"If I'd known you'd needed anything, I would have picked it up for you," Dee said to Michael.

"That's okay. I had a good writing day, so I'm rewarding myself with a six-pack of Sierra Nevada." Michael nodded to Elmira. "Hey."

"Hello," she replied, her tone terse. "How have you been?"

"Not bad. You?"

"Can't complain."

Dee raised an eyebrow. The exchange, while close to monosyllabic, indicated Elmira and Michael knew each other. *What exactly is going on here?*

Michael grabbed a six-pack. He plunked down a twenty-dollar bill on the counter. "Keep the change."

"Absolutely not."

There was an awkward pause as Elmira rang up the

purchase and counted out what she owed Michael. He thanked her and then, in an obvious attempt to recover, tossed a casual "see you back at the Golden" to Dee and left the store.

Dee faced Elmira. "Is it my imagination or do you know Michael?"

The terse expression returned. "I do. You know the nice houses on the lake between here and Goldsgone?"

"Golden Lake Cottages. Which is a bit of a misnomer, since the houses are way nicer than cottages."

"Yes. Michael's family owned one and he spent summers there. After his parents divorced, he moved up from the San Fernando Valley and finished his last two years of high school in Goldsgone." Her expression darkened. "He was a big smack face."

Dee reacted to the hostility in Elmira's voice. "Wow. That's kind of harsh. He was just a kid."

"Sorry. I'll put it another way. He was a *little* smack face." She checked a calendar on the wall behind her. "Why don't we hold the board meeting tomorrow night?"

"Sure," Dee said, recognizing a change of subject when she heard one. "But are we giving people enough notice?"

"I think so. We're between seasons, so it's not like anyone's got anything better to do right now."

"Sounds like a plan. I'll get Jeff to make a flyer tonight."

A timer sounded. "That's my scones," Elmira said, back to her friendly self. "Good thing I made a second batch, seeing as how you bought out the first. Watch the register for me?"

"Sure."

Elmira disappeared into the back. Dee made sure she was gone, then whipped out her cell phone. She texted Jeff: **Can u talk?**

He gave the question a thumbs-up and she called him.

"I need you to make me a flyer I can print out tonight, but I'll get to that in a minute."

"How did it go with Michael?"

"Between him and me, fine. But here's the weird part." She detailed what she'd witnessed between Elmira and the writer, along with Elmira's disparaging take on him. "He never said a word about having almost grown up here. He acted like everything was new to him. You'd think he would have said *something* about his connection to the area."

"Huh." Jeff thought for a moment. "Well . . . maybe he doesn't have great memories from it."

"Then why would he come stay with us?"

"Cheap rates?"

Dee frowned. "No. Although I'm sure that didn't hurt. Something's going on. Something funky. I can feel it."

"Uh-oh."

"What?"

"Your storyteller's kicking in."

"No, it's not," Dee said, defensive.

"Yes, it is. You're doing that thing where you turn a small situation into a big deal. Next come the plot points. Look, Dee, this guy Michael heard about the Golden. It brought back memories, some bad, some good. Maybe he decided it was fate that a writer he knew bought a motel in an area where he had a special connection. Who knows? But he's under no obligation to tell you his backstory, as you like to call it."

"You're right. My bad. And thanks."

"No problem. So tell me what this flyer is for."

The All-in-One's rustic theme extended to its café, with sturdy, utilitarian oak two-top and four-top tables planted on a solid pine floor. But the café also featured a show-stopper: Running the length of the back wall was the most elaborate bar Dee had ever seen. Curlicues, cherubs, and rosettes carved from walnut covered every inch of it. Carved Doric columns three feet high framed a huge mirror gilded in gold that at the moment reflected Dee's anxious expression back to her.

Elmira's "treats" sat untouched on the bar counter. Dee wished she could blame it on their lack of gustatory appeal. Instead, the blame lay with the empty room meant to host the tourism meeting.

Dee checked her watch. The meeting was due to start in three minutes. "Do people usually run late around here?" she said to Elmira, who was putting up a pot of coffee behind the bar. "Is that a country thing?"

"Sure," Elmira said with much sympathy.

The All-in-One front door opened and Dee perked up. Ma'am and Mister Ma'am marched down the length of the general store to the café. "The flyer said there was free food," Ma'am declared, skipping the niceties.

"Savory and sweet," Elmira said with pride. "Cheese biscuits and tea cakes."

"Lucky us," Mister said with forced heartiness.

The door opened again. A wraith of a young blond woman pushing a baby carriage and wearing a baby sling came toward them. Beautiful to the point of being ethereal, she didn't walk so much as float. Years in show business had taught Dee to know a trophy wife when she saw one, and the apparition was definitely a trophy wife. The vision confirmed this when she introduced herself in a soft voice as "Serena Finlay-Katz. I'm so happy you've moved to Foundgold. Elmira told me you're a TV writer. Do you know my husband, Callan Katz?"

"Not personally." But it was impossible not to know of one of L.A.'s most simultaneously hated and admired agents, who'd earned the nickname "Killer Katz" for breaking the will of many business affairs executives in his quest to wring every possible dime out of them for his clients.

"It's why we got great Wi-Fi," Elmira said. "When they moved up here during the pandemic, he needed a good connection for his Zooms, so he pulled some strings. He's here mostly on weekends now, but we got superspeed internet 24/7/365."

Dee was about to respond, when a bark came from Serena's baby sling. A Morkie stuck out its small head and Serena petted it. "What's in the carriage?" Dee, taken aback, asked Elmira, sotto voce.

"A baby. Emmy," Elmira whispered back to her. "The dog is Oscar. You never know who's where, so it's always best to check."

The Ma'ams greeted Serena with almost tearful joy. A moment later, Dee learned why. The general store door slammed open. A brunette in her twenties dressed in business attire stomped toward them. She carried a huge wooden cutting board covered with an array of meats, cheeses, and dried fruits. She dropped the board on the bar counter with a thud and stomped back the way she came, slamming the door shut behind her. "My husband's assistant," Serena said. "Marisa Young. She doesn't like me."

The Ma'ams descended on the board. "Serena, you outdid yourself," Mister said with a mouth full of prosciutto.

Serena responded with a small curtsy. "Thank you so much, Mister." She favored Dee with a smile formed by rosebud lips. "I'm a charcuterie artist. Some people create works of art with paint or pastels. I create them with foodstuffs."

"Nice," Dee said, her sympathies with the assistant. She checked her watch again. "I'll give it another five minutes before we start. People may be running late."

"They're not." Ma'am carried a plate piled high with charcuterie to a table. "Summer people aren't here yet and the rest of us gave up competing with Goldsgone for tourists a long time ago. But go ahead and tell us about this trail idea of yours."

"Right," Dee said, utterly deflated. "Okay. I, uh . . ." She fumbled with her phone, then began reading. "'What is the buried treasure of Foundgold? It's no longer actual gold. It's history. When I began going through the late Jasper Gormley's belongings, I discovered a wealth of historic artifacts . . .'"

Pitching an idea destined to fail was excruciating, but Dee powered through, sharing her vision of creating a trail leading from one historic Foundgold site to another, culminating with a small museum and gift shop—Elmira's favorite addition to the proposal—in the All-in-One. Finally, blessedly, she was done.

To her shock, Serena jumped to her feet, applauding, earning an annoyed bark from the Morkie. "It's a fantastic idea. Brava!"

"It's good," Ma'am acknowledged. "But I wish you luck pulling it off. Elmira, could me and the mister get some to-go boxes?"

While the Ma'ams concentrated on boxing up a food haul, Serena pushed her carriage to Dee. Dee glanced inside to check out the baby. An adorable little being, around ten months old, cooed at her and batted literal baby blue eyes.

"I love the thought of a history trail in Foundgold," Serena said. "I'll do whatever I can to make it happen."

"Thank you so much," Dee said, grateful for the enthusiasm.

"Also," Serena added as she simultaneously bounced the baby in the carriage and dog in the baby sling, "I want to talk to you about charcuterie options at the Golden. I think a breakfast theme would be unique. No one in Goldsgone—they're your biggest competitor—is doing it. And if you're doing a happy hour for guests, a charcuterie board is *perfect*."

Dee's positive impression of Serena instantly trended downward. *She's only sucking up because she sees me as a future client,* she thought, disappointed. "Thank you, but I don't think charcuterie fits into our vision of the Golden."

After a few minutes of obligatory small talk, Dee said her goodbyes, then left the café and trudged to her car. The meeting couldn't be labeled anything but a complete dud. She fought back tears and regrets on the drive home, but couldn't avoid feeling dispirited.

She parked on the side lot by her motel apartment. Even with power fully restored to the Golden, the woods surrounding it were deep and ominously dark. Dee hurried to her front door. As she leaned down to put her key in the lock, the front door slowly swung open.

"Uh-oh," Dee murmured.

Frightened, she peeked inside . . .

. . . and let out a scream as the shadow of a man loomed over her.

CHAPTER 5

Michael stepped into the light. "Dee, I'm so sorry." He couldn't have sounded more contrite. "I needed another roll of toilet paper, so I came by to ask you for it. When I knocked, the door opened. You might want to get a more secure door. I think the hinges on this one have corroded. I didn't mean to scare you."

"Nugget, shush, boy. It's okay." Dee's scream had triggered a round of barking from where the dog still lay supine. "I'm the one who should be apologizing. Not stocking a guest room with enough toilet paper is a rookie innkeeper's mistake. Did you find more?" Michael shook his head.

"I'll get it for you."

Dee went to the pantry, which also served as a second supply closet to the supply room located in the lodge. She retrieved a four-pack of toilet paper and handed it to Michael with an apologetic smile. "My bad. If you need anything else, text me. Jeff and I want our first guest review to be a good one."

Michael gave her one of his now-signature mock salutes. "No worries on that score, Madame Innkeeper." He departed with his stash.

Dee texted Jeff a reminder that they both should confirm the TP status in a guest room before marking it as available. Her adrenaline still pumping from the unexpected fright, she sat down at the dining-room table and booted up her laptop. It was time to check out the tourism competitions.

She entered a search for "Goldsgone Tourism" and a website titled visitgoldsgone.com popped up at the top of the page. She clicked on it and found herself viewing an appealing site trumpeting the vacation delights of the neighboring town. The site was cleverly designed to look like a nineteenth-century sepia-toned newspaper titled the *Goldsgone Gazette,* but loaded with up-to-date color photos and chockful of upcoming events and travel tips. Inspired, Dee made a note of the tourism director's name. She'd visit her in the morning and pitch a joint promotional venture between the two towns.

Nugget rose to his feet. He loped over to the doggy door and exited to an enclosed dog run attached to the house. He reappeared a few minutes later and headed for the bedroom. The events of the day caught up with Dee. She gave a weary yawn, closed her computer, and started for the bedroom. Her phone pinged a text. She checked and saw Jeff had written back to her: **There was a four-pack in his room. Trust me on this.**

Discomfited, Dee pondered this development. Did Michael lie to her? If so, what was he doing in her living quarters? Then again, maybe he burned through the toilet paper already provided. *When a man needs TP, he needs TP.* If she wasn't supposed to question a guest's backstory, she certainly wasn't about to question their bathroom habits.

* * *

Standing outside the Goldsgone Mercantile and Emporium the next morning, Dee touched up her lipstick. What to wear had been an hourlong internal debate. Her wardrobe consisted of T-shirts, jeans, athleisure wear, and a couple of business casual outfits for shoot nights, the evenings some of the shows she worked on filmed in front of a live audience. For an impromptu meeting with the town's tourism director, which further research had shown to be a volunteer position, one look felt too casual, the other too formal.

She'd finally gone with crisp black jeans and a taupe silk button-down shirt. For an extra dollop of good luck, she adorned the shirt with a simple but stunning gold starburst brooch inherited from her beloved late mother. Black ankle booties added two inches of height to her frame. *Then again, maybe I should have dressed like a frontier woman,* she thought as a woman walked by wearing nineteenth-century prairie garb. Everyone who worked in Goldsgone seemed to embrace the cosplay of promoting their historic mining town by dressing like time stopped in 1849.

The store was housed in a 150-year-old stucco-and-red-brick building. Large multipaned sash windows sat on either side of double doors decorated with beveled isinglass decorative inserts. A metal awning ran along the front, offering protection from inclement weather, more likely in winter than the current spring season. Carved into the stucco above the entrance was 1852—the year of the building's birth.

A family of three entered the store. Dee took a breath to calm her nerves and followed them inside, entering under a banner that read in an old typescript: A GOLD MINE OF GIFTS FOR ALL AGES!

Dee took in the shop's interior and immediately concluded that stepping into the Goldsgone Mercantile and Emporium was about as close to entering a time tunnel as a human being could get. Wooden shelves lined every wall from floor to ceiling, filled with souvenirs meant to evoke a bygone century. Glass display cases displaying a wide range of penny candy ran down the shop's center, creating aisles on either side. Calico bonnets, ranging in size from adult to infant, hung from hooks running along the edges of the display cases. Harmonica music sounded from wireless speakers disguised as miniature cracker barrels. Dee sniffed the scent permeating the air. *It smells like root beer, but not quite. Is that . . . sarsaparilla?*

She glanced around the shop for her target, Verity Gillespie. A tall, lean saleswoman hovering somewhere around Medicare age approached Dee. She was dressed in standard Goldsgone pioneer garb of long gingham dress, white apron, and eyelet lace–trimmed bonnet, and had the weathered skin of someone with a disdain for sunblock.

"Welcome to the Mercantile and Emporium," she greeted Dee with a beneficent smile. "Can I help you shop for some necessities and vittles?"

"Thank you," Dee said, giving the woman points for working the word "vittles" into modern conversation. "I'm not shopping . . . today." She added the last word to make sure she didn't turn off the saleswoman, whose face had fallen upon hearing "not shopping."

"I dropped by to talk to Verity Gillespie—"

"Verity *Donner* Gillespie," the woman interrupted to correct her.

"Right. Is she around?"

"She's over there."

The saleswoman pointed to where the family Dee had followed inside stood. They appeared to be cornered by a zaftig woman a few years older than Dee. The woman wore a nineteenth-century dress, but hers was tighter than any Dee had seen in town, hugging a figure that was more saloon girl than schoolmarm. She wore her mass of blond hair wound into a loose bun on top of her head.

The woman Dee assumed to be Verity gestured to a shelf of books with hands sporting incongruously long, fake nails. "This whole shelf is filled with the children's books on the history of California. Everything a fourth grader needs to beat out the other kids in class." She bent over, coming eye to eye with the young girl in the family, who looked terrified. Her father put his arms around her in a protective embrace. "We also got everything you need to make the best model of a mission your teacher's ever seen."

"We—we—we don't make those," the girl stammered.

The girl's mother stepped in to help out her daughter. "Our school system banned them. They're considered culturally insensitive."

The hard squint of Verity's eyes indicated she'd like to have a word with the family's school system. She grabbed a coloring book and thrust it in the girl's hands. "Then I recommend this wonderful coloring book. And a tin of a hundred twenty-four crayons." She pulled a heavy tin from a shelf. "The school doesn't need to know you're *coloring* a mission, now does it?" She said this in a whisper, putting a finger to her lips.

The father took the tin and escaped with wife and child to the sales counter. Verity stood up. She looked down and noticed Dee. Sensing another mark, she graced her with a wide smile. "Why, hello there. What can I do ya for?"

"Hi." Dee extended her hand. "I'm Dee Stern. I just moved to the area."

"Well, welcome, Dee Stern." Verity extended her hand to shake, and Dee noticed each long, index-finger fingernail sported a painted wagon wheel with a rhinestone as the wheel hub. "I'm Verity Donner—yes, *that* Donner—Gillespie. What brings you to town?"

"I'm the new co-owner of the Golden Motel." Dee said this with pride. She was surprised to see Verity tense up, but continued with her pitch. "I've come up with an idea for a Foundgold Historical Trail, which the town is really excited about," she said, embellishing reality a smidge. "But I think making it a Foundgold-Goldsgone Historical Trail would create an even better tourist draw, with benefits to both towns. I know you're the tourism director in Goldsgone, so I want to run the idea by you to see if we can work together on it."

"No."

"No?" Verity's instant, harsh response took Dee aback.

"Ugh, I'm sorry, that was so rude." Verity placed a manicured hand on her heart and gave Dee an apologetic look. "It's just . . . you should know you're not the first person from Foundgold to try to cash in on our town's popularity. Frankly, it gets wearing. I do mention Foundgold on our own website—"

"Actually, you don't. I did a search."

"And I'm afraid that's the best we can do." Verity finished her sentence as if Dee never spoke. "Best of luck with the Golden."

Dee didn't miss the insincerity in Verity's sign-off.

The shop owner left Dee to descend on a new customer. Dee tamped down her annoyance at being dismissed. She wandered the store for a bit, trying to come up with a new approach to entice the tourism director. She stopped at the sales counter. On the wall behind it, a row of headshots hung below a placard anointing it the GOLDSGONE WALL OF FAME. Smirking back at Dee, front and center in the row, was a headshot of Michael Adam Baker. Her spirits rose. She'd found a possible in.

She waited until Verity finished strong-arming the customer into purchasing an overpriced water bottle decorated with yet another Honestadt reprint, then pointed to the photo. "I know someone on your Wall of Fame. Michael Adam Baker. I'm a sitcom writer too. We worked together on a show."

"Really?"

"Yes," Dee said, buoyed by the woman's flip from dismissive to impressed. "We're good friends," she continued, stretching the truth to meet the moment. "Such good friends that he's supporting the Golden by being my very first guest there."

Verity's positive response evaporated. She stared at Dee with a mix of dismay and resentment. "That's impossible. He always stays with me when he visits Goldsgone. He's a local hero. Why would he stay at a dump, I mean place, like the Golden when he could stay at my 'incredibly charming Victorian B and B'? And I'm not just saying that, I'm quoting an online review."

Dee forced a smile. "I'm sure he's only staying with me right now to support my career change. Believe me, my business partner, Jeff, and I could use all the support we can get. If you could help us in any way, like coming in on the historical trail, it would be amazing. An honor." Sensing Verity had an outsized ego, Dee laid it on thick and then opted to finish with a silly joke. "Throw us a bone, esteemed tourism director." She winked. "See what I did there? Donner Party? Bone?"

Verity gaped at her, horrified. "I see what you did and it's awful. How can you make fun of my ancestors like that? They were *people*. What happened to the Donners was a tragedy, not a joke."

"I'm so sorry," Dee said, mortified by her faux pas. "I was nervous, and I make dumb, lame jokes when I'm nervous. Incredibly stupid, on my part."

The store's saleswoman, who'd been lurking behind the counter, glared at Dee. "That was a terrible thing to say. You've upset Verity. I think you should leave."

"Yes. Yes, of course."

Verity strode to the shop's door and pulled it open. Dee, feeling abashed, slumped out of the store. As she passed the tourism director, she heard the woman mutter under her breath, "Citiot."

Dee paused. She drew herself up to her full height of five feet and almost two inches and summoned up a show of dignity. "It's too bad my extremely sincere apology wasn't enough. It's also too bad we can't work together to make Foundgold and Goldsgone the best historical tourism destination in the state. I guess I'll have to do that by myself. And *only* for Foundgold. Oh, and by the way, 'Mercantile' and 'Emporium' are redundant. They're synonyms. So . . . ha!"

Her goal of a dramatic exit was stymied by a collision with a barrel hosting a display of vintage postcard reproductions. "Ow! Sorry." She fell to her knees and gathered up the postcards, which had gone flying in various directions. As she rearranged the display under the glare of Verity and her sales associate, a mortified Dee thought that Michael Adam Baker's booking was turning out to be more of a curse than a blessing.

A second thought occurred to her. *Did Michael do this on purpose? Is he setting me up to fail? Could he still be that competitive?*

Dee dismissed the train of thought, labeling it paranoia. But as she finally made her way out of the store, she couldn't shake the sense there was something off about the writer's visit.

CHAPTER 6

Fuming from her run-in with "Yes-that-Donner"—Dee's new nickname for Verity Gillespie—she almost missed noticing Jeff's car, which confirmed he'd returned from his sojourn to San Fran. Dee found him cleaning and waxing a desk in one of the motel's guest rooms.

"We're citiots." She said this glumly and flopped onto the room's bed, generating creaks and groans from the springs of the soon-to-be-replaced mattress.

Jeff shot her a look. "We're what-iots?"

"Citiots. Like 'idiots,' but with a *c*. That's the nickname country people have for us. At least in Goldsgone."

"Oh, *really*." Jeff gestured to the desk. "Would a citiot be able to do this?"

"Wax a piece of furniture? Probably." Dee sat up. "I pitched my historic trail idea to Verity Gillespie, and it did not go well." She filled Jeff in on her ill-fated exchange with the tourism director. "But the gorgon did make one good point. I get what you said about Michael being under no pressure to tell us about his past in the area. But why is he staying at the Golden instead of Verity's incredibly perfect B and B? She's not exaggerating. I looked it up on my phone."

She passed her phone to Jeff. He scrolled through a gallery of photos. "Wow. I gotta say, she earned that five-star rating."

"It's like a Victorian dollhouse you see at a museum."

"With modern touches." Jeff handed Dee's phone back to her. "I've never seen a hot tub designed to look like a wishing well. That's some serious extra. But in a good way."

"Like I was saying, why would Michael—" Her cell pinged a text. "It's him."

Jeff cast a nervous glance at the door. "Do you think he heard us talking about him?"

Dee jumped up from the bed. "No. The toilet in his room won't stop running and he thinks it's going to over-flow."

Jeff dropped his waxing rag and grabbed his phone. "I'll search for a tutorial."

"No time!"

Jeff held up his phone triumphantly. "Found one!" He pressed Play. "Ugh, it's in German."

Dee ran out of the motel room to the triangle dangling from the far corner of the lodge. Panicked, she banged on it for what felt forever.

"You can stop."

"Agh!" Startled, Dee turned to see Ma'am. With her shapeless dress, long gray hair, and silent steps, she resem-bled an apparition.

Ma'am gestured to the triangle. "You rang. What's up?"

"A plumbing issue with our guest. The toilet."

"Got it."

Ma'am went to the supply room located in the middle of the motel rooms. She pushed aside the ancient industrial vacuum cleaner and dug around. Eventually she emerged, holding a plunger, and followed Dee to Michael's cabin.

The writer stood on the steps outside the cabin, holding an open laptop. "Good timing. It's getting dicey in there."

"Gimme five minutes."

Ma'am disappeared into the cabin, leaving Michael and Dee. There was an awkward beat of silence as Dee debated the best way to bring up what she'd learned from Verity. "Sorry your writing day got interrupted."

Michael snapped his computer shut, as if he forgot it was open. "No worries. I needed a break."

"Been there," Dee said with a commiserating writer's nod. "Oh, this morning I met someone who knows you. Verity Gillespie."

"Verity. Ha." Michael grinned. "I bet she *never* mentioned she's descended from the Donner family."

"Ha." Dee forced a chuckle. "She mentioned she was hurt you're not staying with her."

"Oh, man." Michael rolled his eyes and shook his head. "I was so glad there was another option up here besides her place. I mean, it's great and all. But she is *a lot.* Too much."

Having gotten a heavy dose of Verity, this rang true for Dee. "I can see that. She made me nervous, so I overcompensated with a bad joke and wound up making a terrible impression."

Michael lifted a corner of his mouth in a conspiratorial half smile. The expression created a dimple in his left cheek Dee castigated herself for noticing. "So," he said, "what was the joke?"

Dee winced as she repeated it, but he chuckled. "Good one. A little cheap. Puns always are. But solid."

"Thanks," Dee said, preening slightly. She'd forgotten how good it felt getting respect from a peer. Even for a bad joke from a possibly sketchy guest.

Ma'am exited the cabin. She held her tools in one hand and a plastic bag in the other. "You're good to go."

"You think she meant that literally?" Michael said to Dee under his breath. She stifled a laugh. "Thanks. The Golden gets an extra star for prompt and courteous service." He disappeared into his cabin.

Dee and Ma'am started the walk back to the motel. "You're a lifesaver," Dee said to the woman.

"All I ask is you pay me in cash." Ma'am handed Dee the plastic bag. "There was a leak in the sink, and I fixed that too, but not before it did a number on this." Dee looked inside the bag and saw a soggy four-pack of toilet paper. "Leave it in the sun to dry and it'll be good as new. In the meantime, your guest has a spare."

"Uh-huh," Dee said, hiding her horror at the thought of sun-dried toilet paper. Then she stopped in her tracks. "Wait. Are you saying Michael has another four-pack in his bathroom?"

"Yup. Barely touched."

Ma'am veered off into the woods, leaving a steaming-mad Dee. She knew now Jeff was right: He *had* stocked Michael's room with the necessary guest supplies. Which meant the writer lied to her when she caught him in her apartment.

Dee deposited the ruined toilet paper in one of the motel's bearproof trash containers, then marched to her car, determined to uncover exactly what Michael Adam Baker was up to. Because she was now positive he was up to something.

* * *

In Hollywood, there was rarely a better source for gossip than a high-powered agent. Luckily for Dee, Foundgold had Callan Katz, Serena's husband, who came up to the rural outpost on most weekends. Dee learned from Elmira that after a midmorning job he always stopped by the All-in-One's café for coffee, so she timed a visit within the range of his arrival.

The minute Dee stepped into the store, Elmira greeted her with a friendly wave, saying, "I've got homemade lemon bars—a tasty treat for your guests."

"I'll take six," Dee said. She took a moment to fantasize about using them to torture the truth out of Michael, then asked, "Is Callan here?"

Elmira gestured toward the café area. "Down there, drinking a cappuccino made from rare beans he imports for himself, has me grind with a special grinder and store in a mini fridge he's provided that's calibrated to the exact specificities of the rare beans." Elmira's dry recitation told Dee what the proprietor thought of Callan's grandiose coffee arrangement.

Dee walked down the wide sloping planks that led to the café area. Callan sat at one of its small tables, air pods in, typing away on his cell phone. In his early forties, he had the sculpted look of a man with access to L.A.'s best and most expensive personal trainers. With his high-end exercise togs, stylish stubble, and black hair cut to the latest trend, he projected the self-satisfied confidence that came with being one of the best in a notoriously cutthroat business.

She waited until Callan was done typing, and was about to introduce herself, when he said, "Hi, Dee."

"You know me?" she asked, surprised.

"Dee Stern, first job *On the John,* last job *Duh!,* ten

years of jobs in between, some on workhorse shows, some on six-and-out, and a pilot that never made it past script."

"The network president loved it, but they fired him in the middle of the season and brought in a guy who didn't want female-driven shows." Dee cringed at her own defensive reaction, which was met with a skeptical expression from Callan. She forced herself to focus on the reason she was there. "If you don't mind, I need to ask you something."

The agent sighed. "I knew this was coming the minute I heard you bought that sad motel. No, I'm not taking on any new clients."

"It's not a sad motel," Dee said, ticked off, "and I'm not interested in having you represent me. I'm out of the business."

Callan gave a derisive snort. "*Please.* The only people out of the business are people who couldn't get into it in the first place, or can't get *back* in."

"You have foam on your nose."

Callan wiped his nose with a napkin decorated with the store's logo and slogan, *You Foundgold!* "Fine. You don't want to 'get back in the business.' "

Dee congratulated herself at maintaining self-control in the face of Callan's air quotes. The agent took a sip of his designer coffee drink. "Talk to me."

"We have a writer staying with us, Michael Adam Baker. We worked together on *John,* but I wondered if you know anything more recent about him. It would help me as his host." She added the last sentence to cover why she was nosing around.

"I know a lot about him, because he happens to be a former client. He's been doing kids' animation and was trying to get back into adult television, but all his pitches bombed. He went back to the kids' space, but his pitches bombed there too. He sent me something new to read, but I was on the road coming here and couldn't get to it. He blew up, and that was that." He eyed his drink with distaste. "My coffee's getting cold."

"Thanks, Callan," Dee said, knowing a hint when she heard one. "You've been a big help."

Dee returned to the store checkout counter to retrieve her lemon bars. She found Callan's wife, Serena, waiting for her, baby sling and carriage in tow. The charcuterie artist greeted her with a delicate smile. "Dee, I'm glad I ran into you."

"Hi. I was just talking to your husband." As she spoke, Dee took a dog biscuit out of the container Elmira kept on the counter for free treats. She held it in front of the baby sling. "Here, Oscar . . ." Baby Emmy stuck her head out of the sling. "Oops." Dee pulled her hand back. A bark came from the baby carriage. Dee dropped the biscuit inside the carriage and crunching replaced the barks.

"I came up with graphics of breakfast charcuterie boards that I'd love to send you," Serena said.

"My partner, Jeff, put up a beta of our website," Dee said, polite but noncommittal. "You can email them to me through the contact page."

"Yay! Also . . ." Serena lowered her voice. "I was in the paper goods section and heard what Callan said about Michael Adam Baker. I clean out Callan's inbox for him and I think I can find whatever material Michael emailed, if it would help you."

"Really?" Dee's respect for Serena climbed several notches. "That would be great. But . . . it is a violation of privacy."

Serena's pretty face darkened. "I don't care. I never

liked Michael. At parties, he always did that thing to me some people do when they're stuck talking to the wives of important people."

Serena mimed being a bored party attendee scanning over Dee's head for someone more important to talk to, behavior Dee recognized and related to. She'd been the recipient of The Scan herself from people who didn't rate her as worthy of their time.

"I'll take whatever you got," Dee said. "Let's exchange numbers."

With Serena's promise to let her know by morning if she located Michael's email, Dee returned to the Golden. As she wiped down picture frame after frame, she replayed her conversation with Callan. Being fired was a blow to any agent, but particularly to one with the outsized ego of a Callan, and Dee allowed herself a brief but satisfying bit of schadenfreude.

Still . . . there had been a warning sign in Callan's explanation of not having the time to read whatever material Michael had sent him. If Michael was a star client, Callan would have stopped in the middle of the freeway to read it. The fact he didn't meant Michael Adam Baker was starting the inevitable slide down writer-career mountain.

Dee slept fitfully, knowing morning would bring an aye or a nay re: Michael's material from Serena. She woke up early and immediately checked her phone. It showed a text from Serena, along with an attachment.

Jeff was on his computer when Dee burst into his cabin. "I was going to call you," he said. "We got an email from someone named Serena Finlay-Katz with photos of breakfast charcuterie boards she's pitching. They're pretty cool. I think we should consider trying them out." He eyed Dee, who was steaming mad. "But we can put a pin in that. What's wrong?"

"This." Dee, furious, waved her phone in the air. "I found out what that pond scum Michael Adam Baker is up to. He's stealing my new life and career here at the Golden as a premise for a pilot!"

CHAPTER 7

Jeff stared at her, stunned. *"What?"*

She thrust the phone into her friend's hand. "Here. Read the scene he wrote. It's my life. It's me. Even the dialogue."

Jeff opened the file and skimmed it. "Wow . . . sonuva . . ." Equally furious, he rose from his chair. "You're right. It's you. The whole premise is about a burned-out sitcom writer who buys an old motel in Gold Rush Country. And the writing stinks." He read from the scene. " 'Come on, Mrs. Donner, throw me a bone.' " He looked up from the phone, appalled. "That's a terrible joke. I don't blame you for being upset. The guy's a hack."

"That's not why I'm upset! And that god-awful joke is mine. He stole everything about my new life, including that."

Jeff's eyes narrowed. "I'm gonna kill this guy. He's not gonna get away with this."

Determined, he hurried to the door. Dee blocked his way. "No. I love you for caring so much, but I need to handle this."

Jeff, frustrated, balled up his hands into fists. "You're my best friend. I can't let him do this to you."

"Don't worry. He won't."

Dee slammed out of Jeff's cabin and ran down the path to Michael's. She banged on his door with all her might. "Hey, jerk! Open up! *Now!*" She kept pounding, but no one answered. Finally she gave up. Rubbing her sore fists, she bent down by the room's front window. She managed to get enough of a glimpse into the cabin to see the unscrupulous writer's belongings were still there.

She marched to the parking lot. Michael's car was gone. She had a feeling where he might be, so she ran to her apartment, grabbed her own car keys, and headed for the All-in-One.

Dee pulled into the general store's parking lot and hit the brakes. There was a chill in the early-morning air, but Dee, hot with anger, didn't feel it.

She pushed open the store's doors and marched inside, down the sloping aisle to the café. A short line of customers waited for coffee from Elmira and Heloise, who worked part-time at Williker's All-in-One General Store. The line included locals, a few rangers from Majestic National Park—and Michael Adam Baker. Dee stormed up to him. "Thief!"

The others in line exchanged looks and discreetly put distance between themselves and Michael. He held up his hands and stared at Dee with an expression of dismay.

"Whoa. I have no idea what you're talking about."

Dee held up her cell phone, open to Michael's scene. "*This*. We need to talk. *Now*."

"Okay. Fine. Sorry." He addressed the apology to the others in line, not so subtly twirling a finger by his ear in the international sign of "cuckoo."

Dee suppressed the urge to throttle him. She took the sleeve of his hoodie and yanked him in the direction of the parking lot.

Once outside, Dee lit into the writer with full force. "How dare you show up at my motel acting like all you want to do is support my new venture, when you were really plotting to steal my life for a pilot!"

Out of sight from anyone else, Michael dropped the self-effacing–victim act. "Not my problem, babe. You can't copyright an idea."

"Don't you *dare* 'babe' me," Dee said through gritted teeth. "You have no right to do this. It's *my* life. I'm the only one who should ever write about it."

"I thought you were out of the business," Michael said with a sneer.

"I am, but maybe someday I won't be. I don't know." Feeling put on the defensive, Dee repeated, "But it's *my* life, and it's *my* choice."

Michael shrugged. "I don't know why you're freaking out so much. Your ex already based a whole show on you."

Dee winced. The comment touched a nerve. Ian Akerman, her second husband, was a struggling television drama writer when they married. His envy of her success ate away at their relationship until they finally divorced. After the breakup, Ian channeled his jealousy into a sci-fi drama pilot called *Vengeance: Year 3004* about a heroic space force commander fighting back against his evil ex-wife, Lee Flern.

As Dee's writing career sputtered out, Ian's took off. *Vengeance* was a massive streaming hit, recently picked up for four additional seasons.

She scowled at Michael, wishing she could shoot daggers at him with her eyes, like Lee Flern could. "This is completely different. Ian's series may have been inspired by our marriage, but that's it. It's set in a dystopian future and doesn't resemble real life at all. You're full-on stealing. If you pitch whatever piece of drek you come up with anywhere, I'll sue you."

Michael gave a derisive snort. "Like I said, you can't copyright an idea, and since you've already admitted you haven't *written* anything about your life, that's what we're talking about here. A notion. Besides, who are you gonna hire as your lawyer? Some local yokel? I'm guessing all your money's sunk into the Golden, so that's all you can afford, if you can even afford that." He taunted her with a second salute. "Good luck, 'Lee.'"

Michael hopped into his Porsche and roared out of the parking lot, kicking up a cloud of dust that enveloped Dee. "I hope Stoney the bear finds you and eats you!" she screamed after him.

Choking from the dust, Dee turned to go back inside the All-in-One, almost colliding with a ranger heading back to his truck with a container of coffee. She found Elmira waiting for her.

"We heard everything," Elmira said. "Pluses and minuses of poor insulation in these old places."

Dee coughed up more dust. "Can I get some wa-wa-wa—" Unable to control her emotions any longer, she burst into tears.

Elmira put a comforting arm around her shoulder. "Let's get you some water and a free coffee drink."

She led Dee to the café and sat her at a table. Patrons at other tables eyed her with sympathy. Heloise came from behind the coffee bar, holding a large ceramic cup. "Here. Our biggest cappuccino." She leaned in and whispered, "I used Callan Katz's coffee beans. Don't tell him."

Dee managed a smile. "I won't."

Elmira fetched a glass of water and paper towel. She wet the towel and handed it to Dee, who wiped dirt and tears from her face. "Thank you."

"Anytime." Elmira placed a hand on Dee's. "That Michael Adam Baker was a bad bet back in the day and he's a bad bet now. But don't you worry. Us 'local yokels' got your back. Right?"

Her customers responded with a chorus of "Right" and "You bet," along with a few scatological names for the duplicitous writer-producer.

Comforted by the support, but still shaken, Dee decided she wasn't ready to return to the Golden. After thanking everyone at the All-in-One for their kindness, she drove past the motel to a dirt road barely visible from the main road. She turned onto the secondary road and parked in front of a trailhead.

Dee followed the trail, which took a slow, steady climb through the forest. She emerged from the dense thicket of trees into a valley. A meadow lay before her, green grass and wildflowers gently swaying from a slight breeze. In the middle of the meadow was a small, pristine lake reflecting the striking granite outcrops of the Sierra Nevada mountains rising above it. Dee had stumbled upon the hike on her first visit to Foundgold. The spectacular scenery was what inspired her to trade the city for the country. Now it provided a refuge.

She sat on the grass and drank in the beauty around her, listening to the song of chirping birds and the occasional woodland creature scurrying by. The bucolic setting brought a sense of calm to Dee, allowing her to analyze Michael's actions more objectively.

Based on her conversation with Callan Katz, she knew

the scheming writer's own career was in trouble. He didn't even have an agent at the moment. He could write about her life all he wanted, but there was no guarantee he'd sell the pilot, or if he did sell it, the pilot would be produced. She'd written half-a-dozen pilots herself that were currently collecting e-dust as files on her computer.

I still hate Michael with the passion of a thousand white-hot suns, she thought. *But he's way less of a threat.*

Dee rose from her spot. She hiked back to her car and made the short drive back to the Golden, where she headed straight to Michael's cabin. She gave the door a purposeful rap. He opened the door, holding an ice pack to his right eye with his free hand. "I want you gone," Dee said, her tone terse and determined. "You're no longer welcome as a guest at the Golden."

"I'll leave when I'm ready to leave." He dropped the hand holding the ice pack, revealing a swollen, blackened eye. "I paid for tonight, so I'm here until at least the morning. Maybe longer. And I'd be a good host if I were you. You wouldn't want your first online review to be a crappy one." He slammed the door on Dee.

Her sense of calm shattered, Dee stomped away, heaping curses on Michael Adam Baker.

"Dee!"

Jeff waved from the doorway of his cabin, then strode over to her. "I was worried about you. I drove over to the All-in-One. Elmira told me what had happened. I came back and had a little talk with our guest."

Dee eyed her friend's left hand. His knuckles were raw. "You did more than talk, I'm guessing."

Jeff massaged his hand. "Whatever I did, the SOB deserved. He's not gonna win, Dee. Trust me on this." He hugged her.

"Ach. Can't breathe."

"Sorry."

Jeff released her. She managed a fond smile. "Thank you. For being there for me. There's nothing we can do about Michael now, so let's put all our energy into getting more guest rooms ready. We need to attract a better class of clientele." She added the last line in a halfhearted attempt at humor.

"I'll work on the rooms," Jeff said. "You do whatever you need to do to take care of yourself."

Dee decided to take Jeff's advice. She took Nugget on a long walk, then spent a few hours cleaning more frames, a mindless task that proved relaxing. She didn't have much of an appetite, so after a dinner that was mostly liquid—as in lots of wine—she passed out early.

Unfortunately, science proved correct in its claim that alcohol was not a sleep aid and Dee woke up after only a few hours. She lay on her back staring at a water stain on the ceiling she hadn't noticed before, mentally adding it to the Golden's endless list of repairs.

She tried going back to sleep, but the comfort she'd found in dismissing Baker as a threat had evaporated. The only thing worse than a competitive writer was a desperate writer. *Michael could be stealing my life for a script right now*, Dee thought, incensed.

She toyed with a few fantasies of Baker meeting an ugly demise, then landed on a fate worse than death for a comedy writer: a terrible script reading. Dee pictured him sweating as every joke he wrote fell flat, met with silence instead of laughs. Reveling in the thought of the deceitful writer enduring this torture, she finally drifted off.

She awoke to the sound of the old-fashioned call bell in

the Golden lobby that announced a guest's arrival. Startled, she called out, "Be right there." She threw on clothes, gave her hair a quick brush, and popped a mint.

She strolled into the lobby through the door that connected it with her apartment. A couple around her age waited on the other side of the pine-paneled reservations counter.

"Hi," the man said. "We decided to take a spur-of-the-moment trip to Majestic, but they're booked up."

"We weren't expecting that so early in the season," the woman said. "We stopped at this cute little general store and the owner recommended your place. She said it's a mid-century time capsule you're restoring. We're big fans of that."

God bless Elmira, who is my new BFF. "Wonderful." Dee gave them her sunniest smile. "We have one recently refurbished guest room in the main building ready for guests. We also have a cabin that a guest recently checked out of." She said a prayer she was right, and that Michael Adam Baker was gone from the motel and her life.

The couple debated; then the woman said, "The motel is so sweet and charming. We'll take the room there."

"Fantastic." Dee began typing the reservation into the website system Jeff had set up. "Let me book the reservation, then I'll take your credit card and a form of ID."

"Do you, by any chance, have a wine-and-cheese hour?" the woman asked. "I saw you have a picnic table in the grove of woods by the motel. It would be lovely to sit out there with a glass of wine and enjoy nature."

"Oh, yes," Dee said, regretting she'd gotten off course in planning the Golden's amenities and making a mental grocery list for the All-in-One. "It starts at"—the triangle bell began ringing, to Dee's bewilderment; she ignored it— "five and goes until . . ." The ringing continued, with increased urgency. "Sounds like someone's having fun with our old-timey bell," she said, faking a laugh. "Let me text my partner. He can show you to your room."

She shot Jeff a text: **We have guests! And are u ringing that g-d- bell??**

There was no response. "You know what, I'll show you there myself."

She led the couple outside, where she saw Mister Ma'am banging the triangle. "Be right with you," she called to him, adding with emphasis, "You *can stop ringing*!"

She deposited the couple in their guest room and after assuring them she could be reached by text to handle any and all of their needs, she hurried to Mister Ma'am.

"What's going on?" she asked, not bothering to hide her annoyance. "It's been a rough couple of days and you're giving me a headache with that thing."

"It's about to get worse," Mister said with alarming bluntness. "I was out chopping in the woods behind the cabins, about where your property bumps up against the Majestic. And I came across something bad. A body."

Dee gasped. "Oh, my God."

The older man gave her a somber look. "Pretty sure you know the guy."

Dee thought of the text she'd sent Jeff, which remained unanswered. A feeling of nausea welled up and she fought to control it. "Take me to him."

She followed the backwoodsman through the brush, pushing aside branches that scraped against her as they hiked deeper into the forest. Mister Ma'am came to a stop. "There."

Dee closed her eyes. She clutched her heart and inhaled

a big, shuddering breath. Steeling herself, she opened her eyes . . . and gasped again.

Michael Adam Baker, clad in his expensive black leather bomber jacket, lay sprawled face down on the ground. Blood dripped from a gaping wound on the back of his head.

CHAPTER 8

For a dizzying moment, Dee felt like she'd stepped into the middle of a production shot. But this wasn't the movies. It wasn't TV. It was real life.

And Michael Adam Baker was really dead.

After emergency texts to 911 and to Jeff on Dee's part, she and Mister waited in silence with the body of the late writer for what felt like hours, but turned out to be only ten minutes.

They heard the sound of someone running through the woods. Seconds later, Jeff appeared, out of breath from more exertion than the techie was used to. "Sorry I didn't get here sooner. I was trying to talk Yes-*that*-Donner Gillespie into working with you on the historical trail and only just checked my messages." His face paled at the sight of Michael's body. "Oh, man. I can't believe I'm saying this about him, but poor guy. What happened?"

"Don't know." Mister rubbed the stubble on his chin as he contemplated the question. "Coulda been a bear."

"It's my fault," Dee said, shaking like a leaf. "I cursed him. I yelled that I hoped a bear ate him. And now one killed him."

"Dee, I love you like a sister, but that's cuckoo-crazy talk." Jeff said this with compassion.

More crunching of underbrush came from the forest. Tree branches parted and a young man dressed like a nineteenth-century sheriff emerged. "Oh, great," Dee said, aggravated. "There's some kind of cosplay event going on. Just what we need."

"That's not a costume," Mister said. "It's Deputy Sheriff Raul Aguilar from the Goldsgone substation of the county sheriff agency. The county thinks it makes tourists more relaxed if law enforcement looks as period as everyone else working in Goldsgone. Hey, Raul."

"Hey, Mister." The sheriff, who appeared to be in his late twenties, eyed Michael Adam Baker. He circled the writer's body, studying it from every angle. He did the same with the surrounding area. "You didn't touch anything? Move anything?"

"No," Dee said. "We've just been standing here. I'm Dee Stern, by the way. And this is Jeff Cornetta, my business partner."

Jeff extended a hand to the sheriff and the two men shook. "The rumors are true," Jeff said. "Two citiots bought the Golden, and we're them."

This brought a glimmer of a smile to the sheriff's face, so brief that Dee almost missed it. She and the others watched as Aguilar slowly and carefully scoured the area around Baker's body.

"We think a bear got him," Dee said, trying to be helpful. "I don't know what he was doing in this part of the property, though. Maybe the bear dragged him here?"

The sheriff shook his head. "This was no bear attack."

Dee stared at him, bewildered and more than a little scared. "If it wasn't a bear, then what—"

She didn't get to finish her question. Several park rangers emerged from the woods, led by a stocky middle-aged ranger, who was red-faced and wheezing from the brief hike to the body.

Deputy Sheriff Aguilar acknowledged him with a curt nod. "Chief District Ranger O'Bryant."

The older man dismissed the greeting with an annoyed wave of the hand. "What's the deal, Aguilar?" He managed to get this out between huffs and puffs of breath. He gestured to Baker's body. "Why are you calling national park rangers for a local crime? We got a whole dang park to police."

"I asked you to come because of this."

Aguilar pointed to the late writer, and for the first time, Dee noticed part of a broken chain-link fence lying under his body. O'Bryant trudged over. He took in the scene and scowled. "Sonuva—"

"Since he's half on national park property, I have to bring you in on the investigation." The Goldsgone sheriff didn't sound happy about this.

"Garland, Mendoza," O'Bryant barked at his subordinates. "Tape off the crime scene. And get an investigative unit up here."

"They can work with county CSI," Aguilar said. "The unit's on their way here from West Camp."

O'Bryant gave a grunt of displeasure. Now that he was on board with the investigation, he seemed disinclined to surrender any control of it.

"I'm Jeff Cornetta, and this is my business partner, Dee Stern," Jeff said, taking the lead on introductions this time. "We're the new owners of the Golden Motel. The vic—Mr. Baker was our guest."

"He was, huh? Not getting off to a great start, are ya? I never heard of the previous owner hosting a dead guest."

Dee whimpered, drawing O'Bryant's attention, much to her regret. He squinted as if trying to place her. "You look familiar."

Dee flashed on the angry exchange she'd had with Michael Adam Baker in the All-in-One parking lot and the reason why she looked familiar to the ranger dawned on her. Unfortunately, whispers between O'Bryant and his underlings indicated they'd also remembered where they'd seen her before.

"Williker's," O'Bryant said. "You were having a fight with a guy." He pointed to the prostrate body splayed on the ground. "That guy."

"I wouldn't call it a fight," a nervous Dee tap-danced. "More like an exchange of words."

The chief ranger glowered at her. "You yelled that you hoped Stoney the bear ate him. We don't take threats like that lightly around here."

"It wasn't a threat," Dee defended herself. "It's not like I can control what a bear does or doesn't eat."

O'Bryant shot her a look. Then he folded his arms across his chest and studied Baker's body. "I'd say it was a bad fall, but—"

"The injury is to the back of his head," Aguilar said.

"Which is what I was about to point out," O'Bryant said, annoyed at being interrupted.

"My money's on this as the murder weapon." Aguilar gestured to a heavy, rectangular rock about the size of a large shoebox. A corner of it was covered with a reddish-brown sticky substance. Realizing this was probably blood, Dee suddenly felt queasy.

"We'll see what the coroner has to say about that, Wyatt Earp," O'Bryant said.

Dee could see Aguilar steam at the crack and felt for the sheriff. It couldn't be fun doing such a serious job dressed like an extra from a TV Western. "If it's okay, we had new guests check in today and I should see how they're doing," she told the law enforcement officers.

"I'll need to interview you." Raul and O'Bryant said this simultaneously. They glared at each other.

"Why don't you start with me?" Mister suggested. Dee, who'd forgotten he was there, started at the sound of his voice. His rough-hewn clothes made him blend in with the background, which Dee assumed was intentional on the part of the backwoodsman. "I'm the one who found the body," he continued. "Dee didn't see him till I fetched her."

"Thank you," a grateful Dee said. She made her escape from the crime scene before the ranger and sheriff had a chance to object.

Dee raced to her apartment. She opened the fridge and pulled out a chilled bottle of expensive Napa sparkling wine she'd been saving to celebrate the first time she and Jeff lit up the Golden's NO VACANCY sign. But with a parking lot full of law enforcement vehicles, she figured the beverage would be put to better use buttering up their current guests.

She hurried from her apartment to the motel and gave the guests' door a friendly rap. No one answered. "Hello," she called in a chipper voice. "It's Dee, your host. I have a welcome gift for you." Again, there was no response.

She noticed the blinds were up a few inches and peeked into the room. Her heart fell. It was untouched. The Golden's guests hadn't even stayed long enough to sit on the bed.

Dispirited, Dee dragged herself to the motel lobby. The couple's room key sat atop a piece of paper on the reservations counter. She hung the key in the cabinet with the other room keys, all of which were sadly still in place, and read the note: *We decided to try our luck in the park. Thanks anyway!*

Liars, Dee thought glumly. *You probably just checked into Yes-that-Donner's perfect Victorian B and B.*

Dee heard the lobby door swing open. She turned, hoping to see either new guests or the couple's return, having had second thoughts about their hasty departure. Her hopes were dashed at the sight of Deputy Sheriff Aguilar and Ranger O'Bryant. The latter officer crooked a finger at her. "Your turn."

When Dee wrote for a short-lived sitcom called *Law and Orfa*—a show featuring a sassy comedienne named Orfa Eckert playing an equally sassy detective—she'd penned a hilarious scene between Eckert and a panicked, sweating suspect who was innocent and happened to be in the wrong place at the wrong time.

Living this out in real life proved not to be funny at all.

Aguilar and O'Bryant sat on the couch opposite Dee, firing one question after another at her.

"What was your history with the victim?"

"What prompted your argument in the All-in-One parking lot?"

"What happened after the argument?"

"Where were you in the hours following the argument up until the discovery of the victim?"

The only saving grace was that the two officers seemed more interested in competing with each other than in any of Dee's responses. She wasn't even sure they heard them. Having exhausted themselves after an hour of this, the officers called a wary truce. They excused Dee and called in Jeff.

While her hapless partner was subjected to Aguilar and O'Bryant's firing line of questions, Dee took Nugget for a walk. This proved to be more of a saunter, since the dog was at the stage of life where a half hour of sniffing leaves and other animals' droppings was exercise enough for him.

As they strolled, Dee mulled over the morning's traumatic events. She wondered if she'd ever recover from the sight of Michael Adam Baker's lifeless body, made even worse by the assumption he was murdered. She had good cause to hate the scheming writer. Yet she couldn't imagine her fury escalating to the point where she killed him.

How did he drive someone to cross that line? she wondered. *And what kind of person would actually cross it?*

Dee maneuvered Nugget away from a particularly nasty pile of droppings and they loped along the trail behind the motel back to her apartment in time to see Aguilar and O'Bryant heading to their respective law enforcement vehicles. She waited until they pulled out of the parking lot, then went inside.

A glum Jeff sat on a kitchen barstool; he held a bag of frozen broccoli to his bruised knuckles. "Greetings, fellow suspect. That was fun, huh? As in *not fun* at all."

Dee eyed him with worry. "We are suspects, aren't we?"

"Oh, absolutely. They'd be terrible at their jobs if we weren't. I was one step away from telling them I wouldn't say another word without a lawyer present. But I didn't want to tick them off, so instead I kept my answers short and factual and sent them the links to the security cameras for your place and Michael's cabin. Too bad I never got around to putting up a camera at my own cabin. That'll teach me for being all, 'The country doesn't scare me; I'll get to it when I get to it.'"

Dee stood on her tippy-toes to open the cabinet where she kept doggy treats out of perpetually hungry Nugget's eyeline. She extracted a dog biscuit shaped like a fire hydrant and fed it to the eager mutt.

"I'm so sorry. This is all my fault. I talked you into going into business with me. Michael came here because of me—"

"Stop." Jeff gestured to her with the broccoli bag. "I'm an adult and responsible for my life choices, like coming in on the Golden with you. And this whole thing with Baker—"

"Less of a thing. More of a murder."

"Mur—you know what, I'm gonna stick with *thing*. This whole thing doesn't negate the fact that creating a writers' retreat package is a great marketing idea."

"As long as we're not running the Golden from jail."

"Oh, I can't go to jail. I'm a ginger. You know that'll make me a target." Jeff popped up from the barstool and returned the broccoli bag to the freezer. "If you want a piece of good news, we have three reservations for next weekend."

"Yay for that," Dee said, her spirits perking up infinitesimally. "We can get a few more rooms ready for guests instead of doom scrolling on how to make bail." She shuddered. "I could use a day drink. Want to join me on a run to the All-in-One?"

"You have no idea how much."

On the short drive to the general store, Dee made a point of not discussing anything related to Michael Adam Baker's murder. She could tell that despite his flippant attitude, Jeff was scared. His altercation with the writer had been physical, not verbal like hers. She guessed that positioned him slightly above her as the prime suspect.

The two parked and entered the All-in-One, making their way through the general store aisles to the café and bar. Both areas were packed, which Dee found unusual for a midafternoon weekday. As she and Jeff approached, all eyes turned to them, and the buzz of conversation stopped.

"I guess that old saw about news traveling fast in a small town is true," Jeff said to Dee.

"Uh-huh." She delivered this like a ventriloquist, a big fake smile plastered on her face. She waved to the patrons. "Hi, everyone. Nice to see you and we didn't kill our guest."

This generated the hoped-for response, an embarrassed chorus of "Of course not" and "We didn't think that." The buzz of conversation returned, with Dee under no illusion that the chatter was about anything other than Michael's murder and the role she and Jeff may or may not have played in it.

The two bellied up to the bar and put in their orders with Elmira: white wine for her, whiskey for him. "You poor things," Elmira said, refusing payment for the drinks. "That Michael Adam Baker brings nothing but trouble." She corrected herself. "Brought. We'll have to refer to him in past tense now."

She shook her head sadly. Jeff downed his drink and held out his glass. "I'll take another."

"Pace yourself," Dee warned. She took a sip of wine. "Law enforcement is all over the case," she said to Elmira. "Local and national, counting rangers as national. Deputy Sheriff Aguilar and Chief Ranger O'Bryant."

Elmira raised an eyebrow. "Them two? Hard to imagine either of them giving the other ground."

"It's definitely a you-know-what–measuring contest," Dee said. "But they can measure away while we prep for guests. We've got a few reservations coming up."

"Add those to the list of things to talk about in past tense." Jeff, depressed, held up his phone. "Canceled. All of them."

"What?" Dee took his phone. She glanced at and released a frustrated groan. "Ugh. I can't believe this. Why would they all suddenly cancel like that?"

Elmira, who'd been reading something on her own phone, looked up. Her expression telegraphed she wasn't going to deliver good news. "I got an idea why."

She handed her phone to Dee, which was open to a *Goldsgone Gazette* e-blast. The sensationalistic subject line read in all caps: *LOCAL LEGEND LOSES LIFE IN MURDER MOTEL!!!*

Dee knocked back her wine and held the empty glass out to Elmira. "I'll take another."

CHAPTER 9

Over the next few days, Goldsgone grieved the loss of their somewhat-native son with an intensity that made Dee and Jeff dread running errands in the town. Since Michael Adam Baker died on at least half-private property, depriving mourners of a public shrine, they turned the picturesque town square gazebo into one. A poster-sized headshot of the late sitcom writer sat on an easel, surrounded by a carpet of flower bouquets.

"There was less of a fuss when the retired pope died," Dee muttered, taking in the growing memorial.

Having run out of furniture wax and not trusting online delivery, where rural two-day service was more of a wish than a reality, she'd worked up the courage for a run to the Goldsgone hardware store. This meant braving stink eye from the locals, which was somehow creepier coming from people dressed like characters out of *Westworld*. "It's innocent until proven guilty, bub," she shot back at the village blacksmith, who fake-sneezed the word "mur-derer" as he walked past her.

Head held high, Dee marched up the front steps of Goldsgone Feed and Hardware, housed in yet another of the town's historic brick single-story storefronts. The store exhibited the timeless chaos and clutter of the average hardware store, which overwhelmed Dee in the non-fake Western world. She hunted up and down the aisles for furniture wax with little success.

Giving up on finding it herself, she tried to flag down a sales associate. He made a point of ignoring her. Annoyed, she followed him down an aisle.

"Excuse me. Excuse me. *Helloooo!*" She cut in front of the associate, making contact unavoidable, and enjoyed the brief triumph. "I'm looking for Howard Feed-N-Wax."

He gazed at her with contempt. "We're out."

Dee folded her arms in front of her chest and returned his contemptuous look. "You weren't out when I called an hour ago."

"Sorry," the man said with a shrug.

"You need to get your eyes checked, Hamish," a male voice said, "because I see three bottles right up there."

Dee pivoted to see a tall, good-looking man a few years her senior pointing to the top shelf of the display. He reached up and corralled the bottles.

"How many do you need?" he asked Dee with a warm smile.

"I'll take them all," she said, grateful for the stranger's kindness.

He turned over the bottles to her. "I'll walk you to the register to make sure you don't run into any other problems."

"My hero," she said, hoping to sound a little, but not too, flirtatious. "I'm Dee Stern. My friend and I are the notorious new owners of the Golden Motel. If you'd like to take this opportunity to scowl at me and accuse me of murder, I give you permission. You earned it with these." She indicated the bottles.

The man chuckled. "Jonas Jones, and pass. My cousin

Elmira only has good things to say about you and your friend."

"You're Elmira's cousin?" Dee lit up. "We love her."

"She's good people. I trust her judgment a hundred percent. And"—he lowered his voice—"knowing the victim, I'm guessing he finally pushed someone too far."

Dee stared at him. She hadn't expected to hear a negative comment about the late writer in a place that treated him like a deity. "You're the first person I've met in Goldsgone who's not a member of the Michael Adam Baker fan club."

"There are a few of us. But we keep a low profile."

They reached the cash register. Dee placed her bottles on the counter, appreciating the fact Jonas hovered over her to ensure the cashier didn't try to thwart the transaction. Dee paid for her purchase and stuffed the bottles into her tote bag. Jonas held the door open for her, and as she left, she couldn't resist calling back to the judgmental sales associate, "Thank you *so* much for your assistance." She pointed to him with both hands. "I want every customer here to know that this man went out of his way to help Dee Stern of the Murder Motel. Bye-yee!"

Jonas applauded as Dee made a grand exit from the store. "Brava," he said, laughing.

She bowed, taking a mock curtain call. "Thank you, thank you very much. Throw money, not flowers." She straightened up. "But seriously, this 'murder motel' rap is terrible for business. If things don't pick up at the Golden, I'll definitely need a part-time job, if not full-time." She glanced at the scenic village street. "But Lord knows it won't be in Goldsgone."

"If it comes to that, and I hope for your sake it won't, I'm sure you'd be able to find something in West Camp," Jonas said, referring to the Gold County seat. He took out his wallet and removed a business card. He handed the card to Dee. "I'm a real estate agent. I handle properties all over the county. If you and your partner decide running the Golden isn't for you, give me a call. I'm sure I can find new owners."

"Oh. Okay." Dee took the card. "Well . . . nice meeting you. And thanks again for your help in there." She motioned to the store.

"No problem. You need more wax, you got my number."

Jonas strode down the street and Dee watched him go. *So much for a non-transactional exchange,* she thought, disappointed. She stuck the business card in the back pocket of her jeans and started for her car. As she walked, she considered her conversation with Jonas. He'd said something that struck her as important. *What was it?* She suddenly remembered and stopped in her tracks.

"Finally!" she blurted the word, earning confused looks from passersby. Dee was too absorbed in her own thoughts to care. Jonas had said Baker *finally* pushed someone too far, indicating the writer had a history of taking advantage of people, like he planned to do with Dee. This meant there were other suspects in Baker's murder besides her and Jeff.

Here's hoping Aguilar and O'Bryant come to the same conclusion, she thought as she drove off.

Once back at the Golden, Dee immersed herself in waxing furniture to the point where for a few hours she even forgot about the demise of Michael Adam Baker. That ended with a rap on the door from Deputy Sheriff Aguilar. He tipped his cowboy hat to her, and they exchanged brief greetings.

"I'd like to talk to you and your partner."

"Okay." Dee's heart thumped like the big drum in a

marching band. She hoped the sheriff couldn't hear it. "I'll text Jeff." She quickly did so. "He'll meet us in my apartment."

She pulled the motel room door closed and, with the young sheriff, followed the walkway lining the front of the motel.

"Do we need to wait for Ranger O'Bryant?"

"No. He's busy at the park. Someone called in a missing hiker." As she spotted the mischievous glint in Aguilar's eye, it wasn't hard for Dee to guess who the caller might have been, and her opinion of Aguilar rose exponentially.

Jeff met them outside Dee's living quarters. Like Dee, he made an effort to remain calm, but the shaking hand he extended to Aguilar gave him away. To the sheriff's credit, he pretended not to notice and responded with a sympathetic smile.

They went into Dee's living quarters. After declining an offer of water, Aguilar took the seat opposite the couch, allowing Dee and Jeff to sit next to each other.

"We have some new information regarding your guest's murder. Based on the fact I observed evidence of facial rigor mortis on the victim when we showed up at the crime scene, which was around eight-thirty a.m., Harry Liu, the sheriff coroner, puts the time of death somewhere between one-thirty and three-thirty in the morning. We've examined the security camera footage from this location and the victim's cabin." Aguilar addressed Dee. "There's no evidence of you leaving your living premises during the hours of eleven p.m. and seven-thirty a.m."

"So I'm not a suspect anymore?" *Please let that be a rhetorical question where I'm posing a fact as a question, please . . .*

"For now." The sheriff's answer was not reassuring.

Aguilar turned his attention to Jeff. "Security footage

from the camera installed at the cabin shows an argument between you and the victim, resulting in an assault on your part."

"It's a lame defense to say he asked for it, isn't it?" Jeff posed this weakly.

"Yes, but in your interview, you admitted to striking the victim, so the footage confirmed what you already told us."

"Phew." Jeff sagged with relief. "Then it also confirmed I left right after that."

"I'm afraid not."

Jeff, stunned, sat up straight. "What do you mean? How could it record one thing and not the other?"

"The camera went dead. The rechargeable battery ran out of juice and the model doesn't come with a backup battery."

The techie let out an anguished groan. "I can't believe this. They were out of the security brand I used here, so I went with a different one. I didn't check to see if a backup battery was included." He slapped himself on the head. "Dummy! Dummy, dummy, dummy."

"Stop." Dee grabbed his hand and placed it in his lap. "It's not your fault. We were on overload; we were doing way too much. Things fell through the cracks. I could have double-checked the system, but I didn't."

"Thanks, but no. This is on me."

Jeff dropped his head in his hands. Dee rubbed his back, trying to console him. She faced Aguilar. "We're not the only suspects, you know." She was angry about what felt like tunnel vision on the part of the investigators. "Baker was a lying, cheating SOB."

"Not helping yourself," Jeff said, sotto voce, speaking in a singsongy voice.

"He had a history in this area, and I know for a fact there are people who did not belong to the weird cult that developed around him." She relayed what Jonas Jones had said about Baker.

"As a lifelong resident of Goldsgone, I'm aware there are people in town who had issues with him," Aguilar said. "I'll be exploring every angle."

Dee frowned. "You said 'I.' Not 'we,' as in you and the chief district ranger. I have a feeling that wasn't a Freudian slip."

"Good instincts," Aguilar said with a rueful half smile that quickly faded. "O'Bryant's father and grandfather were Majestic National Park rangers. He was born and raised in the park and is what we call a 'green blood.' He's always throwing this around. He thinks it makes him better than the rest of us. It kills him he's not even higher up the ranger food chain and is always angling to score points with his superiors. Solving your guest's murder fast would do that."

"Eff him." Angry as Dee was, she didn't go full-on profane, unsure how the sheriff would react. "I'm not a murderer, and neither is Jeff. He doesn't even kill bugs. When I scream, 'Agh! Spider!' he runs in and traps it, then releases it outside."

"Spiders don't get the respect they deserve," Jeff said. "They're an invaluable part of the ecosystem."

"There's no evidence you clocked a spider," Aguilar said. "But there is security footage showing you took a fist to a guy who wound up dead just hours later. And that's ammunition to a guy like O'Bryant." The sheriff stood up, then fell back into his chair. "Dang spurs. One caught on your rug." He reached down and separated the two. "Sorry. I think the rug's okay."

He departed. Dee realized she'd been clenching her jaw during his entire visit and unclenched it. "I did not have 'murder suspect' on this year's vision board. Then again, I didn't have 'buy an old motel in the country' on it either. I think I'm wasting my time with those boards."

"You'll be fine," Jeff said. "And I'm glad, because I love you and someone needs to survive this disaster and run the Golden." He ran his hands through his hair. "I'm supposed to go back to the city tomorrow. My new client's a chef who opened his first restaurant and I'm photographing his creations for the website I've built for him. If he loves it, he'll recommend me to his friends. Restaurants would be a great client base for me. But now I'm scared I'll get arrested for leaving town."

"You won't. The police can't tell you not to leave town anymore. At least that's what it said in the mystery book someone left at the car wash."

"I can't leave you here alone," Jeff said, adamant.

"Yes, you can." She put a hand on each of Jeff's arms and pulled him to his feet. "Elmira's only a little ways down the road. And I've got Nugget for protection."

"I thought he was part of the rug and almost stepped on him," Jeff said, glancing down at the perpetually sleeping hound. "Dee, someone was murdered on our property. Well, the Majestic's too, but mostly ours. You can't be here by yourself. It's too dangerous."

"I'll be fine. I believe, one hundred percent, this wasn't a random killing. I keep going back to what Jonas Jones, the guy I met at the hardware store, said. Michael 'finally pushed someone too far.'" A look of fierce determination crossed Dee's face. "And if the police won't do it, then I'm going to find out exactly who it was."

CHAPTER 10

It took much more effort on Dee's part, but she finally convinced Jeff she wasn't in danger and he left for San Francisco in the morning, albeit reluctantly. As soon as he was gone, she made the quick drive to the All-in-One.

She found Elmira pulling a load of sheets out of the store's laundromat dryer, which she then dumped on top of a rolling laundry bin already brimming with towels. Dee eyed the load. "That's a lot of linens."

"Not mine." Elmira opened the door of the second dryer and pulled out an even bigger load. "Serena's. Her super-fancy, super-expensive dryer died for about the third time this year, so I'm helping her out."

"That's nice of you."

"I left out the part where she's paying me a hefty chunk of change to do it." Elmira caught a towel before it fell to the floor, which in this part of the store was a linoleum so old it looked like it dated back to linoleum's invention.

"I have to talk to you about something," Dee said. "I can help you fold while we talk."

"Deal."

Dee took one end of a pale gray flat sheet and Elmira

took the other. "Ooh." She closed her eyes and stroked her cheek with a corner of the sheet. "I wonder what the highest thread count is. Because whatever it is, these sheets are it."

"I wouldn't know," Elmira said. "I buy mine at the Odd Lots store in West Camp. So you can 'count' me out of thread count talk."

"Touché," Dee said, abashed. "No, it's a lot more serious than that. You know the police suspect us of Michael's murder."

"I lay that at the feet of Tom O'Bryant, a pompous blowhard if there ever was one. I don't believe it for a Foundgold minute."

"Thank you." Dee cleared her throat to contain her emotions and continued. "Michael spent a lot of time around here and I know he's like a local folk hero, but I'm sure he made enemies too. I mean, you didn't like him, right?"

"No, I did not." Elmira gave Dee a hard look. "I also didn't kill him."

"Oh, I know," Dee hastened to reassure her. "But you've spent your whole life in Foundgold and Goldsgone. And I'm sure you pick up a lot of gossip at the All-in-One. Between us—well, you, me, and Jeff, because he's really in deep suspect doo-doo, but no one else, I swear—can you think of anyone else who might have wanted Michael dea . . . not with us anymore?"

Elmira gave a snort. "You know those machines at the grocery store where you have to take a number when the deli counter gets too crowded? One of those'd come in handy for making a line of people who probably did a happy dance when they heard he's gone to his Maker." They finished folding the sheet and moved on to another. "Offhand, there's Shawn Radinsky. He was Michael's best friend until they had a falling-out over something. I don't know what, but if you saw the look on Shawn's face whenever Michael's name came up, you best believe it was bad. Shawn's a personal trainer at the gym in Goldsgone."

"Goldsgone has a personal trainer?" Dee repeated, surprised.

"We got a few around here. We also got indoor plumbin' and those newfangled horseless carriages." Elmira delivered this with much side eye.

"Sorry," Dee said. Embarrassed, she resolved to monitor herself for country-folks-as-hicks stereotypes.

After folding the second sheet, the women moved on to towels as Elmira resumed listing possible murder suspects. "There's Liza Chen, Michael's girlfriend until she found out he was cheating on her, and not for the first time. And Brian Oakhurst. His mom, Millie, was an English teacher at the high school and Michael's mentor. You could see how much Brian resented his own mother going on more about Michael than her own son. Also, my cousin Jonas was friends with Michael, but something happened between them."

"I met Jonas today." Dee didn't elaborate. She wanted to hear Elmira's unfiltered reaction.

"*Him.*" Elmira scowled and snapped her towel. "That man's an operator."

"I had a feeling," Dee said, disappointed to have her negative instincts confirmed. "Do you have any idea what went down between him and Michael?"

Elmira shook her head. "Nuh-uh. I'll nose around my family and see what I can dig up. It won't be easy. Half my relatives aren't talking to the other half, most of the time."

"Whatever you come up with would be great."

Elmira held up another laundry item. "The dreaded fitted sheet. Dare we?"

Dee grinned. "Oh, we totally dare."

Elmira tossed her one end of the sheet. It landed on Dee's head. As she tried to extricate herself, she heard the tinkling of a baby carriage mobile, followed by the sound of Serena Finlay-Katz's soft voice. "Thank you for stocking the organic baby food, Elmira. And dog food. Heloise rang me up. Emmy and Oscar's little tum-tums will appreciate it."

"Long as you keep buying it, no problem."

"I'm leaving for home, but before I go, I thought I'd make sure everything is okay with the laundry."

"It's going fine, especially since I have a helper."

Dee lowered the sheet's elastic corner. "Hi, Serena."

To Dee's surprise, Serena's jaw dropped, and her porcelain skin turned slightly green. "Dee. Hey . . . hi, I didn't expect . . . Thanks for helping Elmira. Bye." She did a one-eighty and practically ran from the laundry area. An annoyed bark came from Oscar, confirming he was the one being bounced around in Serena's baby sling.

Dee and Elmira stared after her. "That was strange," the store owner said.

"Very." Dee furrowed her brow, trying to imagine what triggered Serena's discomfited reaction at the sight of her. A possible reason dawned on her. "I think I know why. And I feel terrible."

She tossed the sheet to Elmira and made a dash through the All-in-One to catch Serena before she left. She found the charcuterie artist taking care of her charges. She'd buckled Emmy into her car seat and was currently clicking a safety harness into place around Oscar. "Serena, I'm so sorry if sending me Michael's script got you in trouble with Callan."

"Callan doesn't know I did that." Serena snapped the dog harness in place and jumped into the driver's seat of her high-end SUV. "I need to go. I'm experimenting with a way to make a butter charcuterie board that isn't a health hazard and it's already been out a couple of hours."

Serena threw the car into reverse and would have roared out of the parking lot, had she been driving a gas-powered vehicle instead of her almost-silent hybrid.

Puzzled, Dee returned to the All-in-One. She saw Elmira had given up on folding the fitted sheet, instead opting to wrap it around itself in a sort of bundle. "Do you want to try folding it again?"

Elmira shook her head. "Nah. If Serena's got a problem with it, she can hand it over to her husband's witchy assistant. But I doubt she'll care. Serena's okay, especially for a pretty, wealthy, entitled white woman." She tossed a small knitted blue sweater to Dee, who wasn't sure if it belonged to the Katz baby or dog. "Were you right about what's bothering her?"

Dee shook her head. "No, and I really want to know. If I did something wrong that I don't know about, I want to fix it. I can't afford to make any more enemies around here, especially since I can practically count the entire town of Goldsgone as one."

Elmira fixed a sympathetic look on the struggling motelier. "I'm sure it's nothing serious. But if you want to get to the bottom of it, you might try working Callan's assistant, Marisa. She can't stand being up here and really hates being used as an errand girl for the Katzes. I bet she'd be happy to share any gossip she's overheard."

"Good idea. All I have to do is come up with a way to 'accidentally' run into her."

"I got you covered on that." Elmira gestured to a garment carrier hanging from a hook. "Callan's tux. I had it cleaned for him. Marisa should be by soon to pick it up."

Dee gave her friend a grateful smile. "You da best, Elmira."

Rather than return to the Golden and risk missing Marisa, Dee stuck around the All-in-One. She bought a coffee and an Elmira homemade blondie she pretended to eat. When she snuck out to drop it in the store dumpster, she noticed it landed next to a handful of other trashed blondies.

Her patience was rewarded when a black early-model Tesla pulled into the parking lot. Callan's assistant got out of the car, her face displaying its chronic expression of resentment. She slammed the car door shut and marched toward the store entrance, her inappropriate black suede pumps with four-inch heels leaving a trail of tiny indents in the ground.

She flung the doors open and Dee darted in after her. "Marisa, hi. I'm Dee Stern, the new owner of the Golden Motel. Can I talk to you for a minute?"

Marisa used a perfectly manicured index finger to press a button on her smartwatch. "You've got exactly a minute."

"That was more of a figure of speech," Dee said, inwardly spewing vitriol at the assistant's attitude.

"Fine. You get two minutes. Three if you buy me a latte to go."

"Deal."

They headed to the café, where Dee purchased lattes for each of them. She joined Marisa at a café table. "I'm guessing you heard about what happened to Michael Adam Baker."

Marisa responded with an eye roll and a flip of her sleek, shoulder-length bob. "Idiot."

Dee's eyes widened. This wasn't remotely the reaction she expected. "I'm sorry, what?"

Marisa leaned forward, a vindictive gleam in her eyes. "Cone of silence. Totally between us."

Dee raised one hand and placed the other on the table. "I swear on a story bible."

"Michael Adam Baker came over to Callan's for a meeting. They got into a huge argument. And Michael *ended up firing Callan*." She said this with utter disbelief. "Can you believe it? Firing, like, the best agent in Hollywood? Callan was so ticked off. He just began screaming, 'Who do you think you are? Nobody fires Callan Katz, especially a lowlife like you!' It got ugly."

"Really." Dee managed not to show her elation. She knew Michael fired Callan, but his furious reaction tagged him as a suspect in the writer's murder.

"Uh-huh," Marisa said with a vigorous nod. "Callan wasn't exaggerating. People would kill to be represented by him." Dee winced, but Marisa didn't notice her poor choice of words. "His clients do amazing. It's too bad you never signed with him. You'd be living in the Palisades or Brentwood instead of stuck in the boonies out here."

"Poor me," Dee said in an acerbic tone Marisa didn't pick up on.

The assistant's phone alarm rang. "Time's up." Marisa turned off the alarm and rose. "I have to grab Callan's backup tux and bring it down to him in L.A."

"*Backup* tux?" Dee, bemused, shook her head. "I pretty much grew up in the business and I never heard of that before."

Marisa gave her a patronizing, almost pitying smile. "Probably because it's an A-list thing."

Dee managed not to snap a comeback at the assistant

and her superiority complex. Marisa started toward the laundromat, her spike heels clicking on the wooden floor. Dee trailed her. "His other tux was almost ruined at a fundraiser a couple of nights ago," Marisa explained. "Callan tried to break up a fight between a Real Housewife he represents and one of the others, who tried to smash a bottle of red wine over Callan's client's head. They all ended up covered with wine."

"Yikes. Um . . . when exactly did this happen?"

Just as Dee feared, Marisa named the night of Baker's murder. "It was all over the internet," Marisa said with relish, bringing to mind the classic adage that there was no such thing as bad publicity.

Marisa retrieved her boss's backup tux without so much as a thank-you to Elmira and zipped off to L.A. Relieved of folding duty by Elmira, Dee returned to the Golden.

She popped the tab on a can of sparkling water, sat down at her desk, and typed "Fundraiser Callan Katz Real Housewives" into her computer's search bar. Pages of posts and photos documenting the altercation popped up, providing the agent with an airtight alibi. Not only was Callan at the event, he signed the housewife who instigated the blowup as a client, bragging that he knew a "breakout beeyotch" when he saw one.

Crestfallen, Dee rose from her desk and treated herself to some comfort food: mint chocolate chip ice cream from the freezer. She pondered her next move as she ate a serving. Knowing people in the business, Dee was sure Michael firing Callan was preceded by much complaining about his agent to anyone who would listen. She placed the ice cream back in the freezer and typed "writeorwrong.io" into the search bar. The private site was a refuge for fellow screenwriters and TV writers. Dee belonged, but hadn't visited it in months, since quitting *Duh!* happily deprived her of the need to vent about the miserable experience.

Michael Adam Baker, on the other hand, had been very active on the site up until the day he died. And every single comment slammed Callan Katz. There were even two long threads where Baker talked two promising young writers out of accepting offers of representation from the agent.

Dee sat back in her chair. A thought occurred to her. Callan might have an alibi for the time of Michael Adam Baker's murder, but what about his wife? Dee doubted being a "charcuterie artist" was a high-paying gig. Serena needed her husband's income to propel her status from dabbler to influencer. And Michael Adam Baker was on a mission to destroy Katz's reputation, with collateral damage to his salary.

Dee knew Serena disliked Baker. She had access to Callan's computer, which meant she might have come across emails or messages indicating Baker was starting to have some success chipping away at her husband's career.

Was Serena's strange behavior around Dee motivated by feeling guilty for committing murder on motel property?

CHAPTER 11

Dee was trying to come up with a way to manipulate
Serena into incriminating herself, when her phone
rang with a video call. She answered and Jeff's face appeared on her screen. "Have you heard anything else from
the sheriff or ranger?" he asked.

"No."

"Neither have I. That's good. It means we're not in their
crosshairs. Or"—his expression of relief morphed into
worry—"it means they're gathering the evidence they need
to arrest us. And that's bad. Look at this." He bent forward and his curly red hair filled the screen. "I'm losing
more hair. The anti-balding crème isn't working. It can't
fight back against the stress."

"Jeff, hon, your hair is fine. It looks exactly like it did
the day we bought the Golden. I'm as jealous of it now as
I've always been."

He lifted his head. "I can always tell when you're
lying."

"Which means you can always tell when I'm not."

"Truth." Jeff relaxed and the two friends shared a
smile. "Since law enforcement isn't breathing down our

neck, I think I'll stay in the city for another day. Maybe two. You okay with that?"

Dee nodded. "I may have found another suspect."

"Really?" Jeff brightened. "Who?"

"Serena Finlay-Katz."

"No way." He shook his head. "She's too pretty."

Dee reacted with outrage. "What?! That's the most sexist thing you've ever said. I'm ashamed of you. How do you know anyway? You've never met her."

"Yes, I have. At the All-in-One when I made a beer run. I gitchy-gitchy-gooed her baby sling and it turned out I was making baby noises to a dog. But before you go all feminist activist on me, I'll explain. Serena is thin and blond and beautiful. She's also, what, in her early thirties? From everything you've told me about Hollywood, she's basically the younger version of every middle-aged agent or CEO's current wife."

Dee reluctantly acknowledged Jeff was right, so he continued.

"So, if Callan's career went south, she'd still walk away with a big settlement. And score plenty of interest from anyone in the town's top tier who's looking to trade in wife number one for a new model."

"Especially from his agent competitors," Dee said. "They're brutal. I can absolutely see one of them trying to outdo Callan by marrying his ex-wife and giving her an even better life."

"Exactly."

Dee tapped her index finger against her chin as she thought about this. "Still . . . I do get Serena loves Callan. And they have a child. And a dog who's like a child. She could have confronted Michael to protect her family, and he could have pushed her over the edge. I wish we knew her well enough to make a judgment call on her homicidal tendencies."

"The solution to that is, get to know her better. Set up a one-on-one with Serena. Tell her you're interested in her charcuterie."

Dee groaned. "Ugh, that stuff is so pretentious. Where I come from, we call it food. Or if I'm on a set, craft services."

"Lower your nose from the air to a non-snob level, friend. The proposal she sent me is worth considering. I'll forward it to you. It's your in with Serena, especially if you add some generally sucking up about being in awe of how she works her magic with cheese and cold cuts."

Dee walked over to the refrigerator and pulled out another can of sparkling water, buying a few minutes before surrendering her unfounded resistance to what she had to admit was a good idea. "Fine. Forward what she sent. I'll look at it and set up a time to meet with her."

Dee pulled a stool up to the kitchen bar. She checked her laptop to see Jeff had already sent her the file from Serena. Dee opened it and scrolled through the photos attached to the proposal. Two represented different takes on breakfast boards and two featured platters appropriate for a wine-and-cheese happy hour. Dee had to admit they were tempting to the point of making her hungry.

She texted Serena about setting up a meeting to discuss the possibility of working together and instantly received a reply: **YAY!!!!!!!!!!!!!! How's now? Emmy and Oscar napping!**

The response included a link with instructions to the Callan-Katz home, which was located on Mirror Lake, one of the many lakes in the region. Dee gave the response a thumbs-up and texted back a yes.

The drive from the Golden to Mirror Lake proved short

and scenic, like all the drives in the area. Dee made a left off the main road onto an unexpectedly wide side road. The road's sparkling tar gave off the unpleasant smell that telegraphed it was only recently paved. The road ended in a cul-de-sac of new homes whose log cabin exteriors were a wan attempt to disguise their true status as McMansions.

Dee parked in the driveway of one of the cul-de-sac's older homes, "older" meaning its construction dated back at most a few years. The Callan-Katz cabin was a massive two-story assemblage of logs and stone surrounded by pine trees and set on the uppermost point of the cul-de-sac to capture distant views of the Sierras. Dee climbed the steps leading to the home's massive two-story double front door, arriving at it slightly out of breath. She was about to ring the bell, when Serena flung one of the doors open. She wore a filmy beige maxidress and delicate leather thong sandals in a complementary neutral shade. She held up her phone. "I saw you coming on the doorbell app. You should have texted from the driveway. I would have let you in through the garage so you could use the elevator."

"Next time," Dee said, hoping there wouldn't be one.

Serena hugged her. "I'm so happy you're interested in my proposal. I made a couple of sample boards. Come."

She led Dee through a two-story foyer and almost comically large dining room into an expansive great room furnished in a rich person's idea of rustic cabin décor. At the far end of the great room—and the end was indeed far from the great room's entrance—sat an open kitchen that almost matched its neighboring room in size.

Serena gestured to a china platter shaped like an egg sitting on the kitchen island's granite countertop. Mini bagels, croissants, and pastries shared the platter with a variety of condiments and cut fresh fruit. "I made a small version of what I pitched to Jeff as a possible breakfast board for your guests," Serena said. "It's basically what you'd serve as a continental breakfast, and the cost is about the same. But the layout will make guests think it's much fancier than that. A trick of the eye." Serena gestured to her own crystal-blue orbs and winked.

"Impressive," Dee said, completely sincere.

"I source everything I can from independent farmers, butchers, and bakers all over California." Serena handed her a plate. "Here. Try it. I'll get the sample wine-and-cheese board I put together."

She pulled open the door on one of the kitchen's two state-of-the-art refrigerators. Dee helped herself to a chocolate mini croissant and took a bite. She almost swooned. "This is amazing. Definitely not from Elmira. I love her, but her pastries not so much."

"Poor Elmira. No one has the heart to tell her how bad her baking is." Serena removed a wooden serving board covered with plastic wrap, and laden with an array of high-end meat, cheeses, nuts, and dried fruits, and placed it next to the breakfast board.

Dee inhaled the heady combination of flavors. *Focus, Delilah Annabel Stern!* her inner voice reproached. *You're here to investigate, not nosh! Put down the incredibly delicious croissant, ignore the hand-carved prosciutto, and get to work!*

"Serena, I'm so impressed. I don't know how you can pull off such . . . artistry." Serena's porcelain complexion blushed a becoming pink, confirming she was buying Dee's flattery.

Emboldened, Dee added, "Especially with the pressure you're under."

"Pressure?" Serena sounded puzzled and a little wary.

"Yes. You know, with Michael Adam Baker firing Callan and bad-mouthing him and . . ." Dee's confidence began to wither. "I mean, it could affect his reputation and relationships with clients and . . . you know. That would be bad."

And you know what else is bad? Me at investigating. Ugh.

Serena stopped laying out flatware for the new board. She narrowed her eyes at Dee. "You're not here because you're interested in my business, are you? Or even being friends."

Mortified, Dee turned an unflattering beet red. "It's just that you acted so strangely with me at the All-in-One. Like you were hiding something. And I thought, you know, that maybe—"

"You'd come here and try to sneak out of me whatever I was hiding?"

Serena glowered at Dee, who noted the angry expression didn't detract from the charcuterie artist's general beauty.

"Yes," Dee said, giving up all pretext for her visit. "A guest we all have a connection to—Callan, me, you—was murdered. You and I barely know each other. I didn't feel comfortable just coming out and asking you what was going on."

"That's too bad." Serena's expression transitioned from anger to sadness. "But I guess I get it." She fiddled with the napkins she'd been arranging. "The reason I was acting strange is I overheard Michael fire Callan, and Callan did *not* take it well. Then Michael was killed, and you and Callan know a lot of the same people, and I got scared."

"That I might start a rumor about Callan being the one who killed Michael?"

Serena gave a slight nod. Tears bubbled over lower eyelids and dripped down her cheeks. Dee couldn't help noting that Serena even looked pretty crying, as opposed to the blotchy, swollen-lidded face that beset Dee when she blubbered.

"For the record," Dee said, "I would never do that. Agents and clients break up all the time. Believe me, I've burned through enough of them to know."

"I know. But this was different. Callan discovered Michael. He nurtured and guided his career. He was furious when he found out Michael was blaming his career problems on him. The only reason Michael got work at all lately was because of Callan's agenting, so he took it more personally than I've ever heard him take a falling-out with a client. So . . . when I heard Michael had been murdered . . ."

She trailed off and stared down at the charcuterie, unable to make eye contact with Dee. Dee's suspicions turned to sympathy for the woman's anguish.

"Serena, you don't have to worry about Callan. He has an alibi."

The agent's wife looked up. "He does?"

"Yes. He was at a fundraiser the night Michael was killed. There was a fight between a couple of Real Housewives—"

"Isn't there always," Serena said, her tone wry.

Dee extracted her cell phone from her pocket. She thumbed a search, then turned the phone toward Serena, displaying photos of Callan trying to break up the fight. "There. You see?"

Serena, her fears allayed, released a breath. "I had no idea. Thank you."

"Glad I could help."

Dee put the phone back in her pocket. She found it curious and a little poignant that Serena didn't know her own husband's schedule. He hadn't bothered to tell her, and she hadn't bothered to ask. Or perhaps Serena had given up asking, which Dee suspected was the case. It provided her with a clearer understanding of Serena's drive to forge a path separate from Callan's and be more than arm candy for an agent. Dee's respect for the charcuterie artist increased multifold.

Serena began peeling back the plastic protecting the delicacies on the wine-and-cheese board. "That husband of mine never misses a photo op," she said with a rueful shake of her head.

Dee snuck a slice of prosciutto, which almost melted in her mouth. "I read he signed the housewife who started the fight with his client."

"I'm sure he did. I know his game plan by heart. He signed a new client, made a grand gesture of a huge donation to whatever org sponsored the event, and cut out of the place."

Dee stopped chewing the second slice of prosciutto she'd snitched. Serena had just inadvertently cut the legs out from under her husband's alibi. Or was it an accident? Callan seemed to lead a second life that barely included his wife, if at all. Maybe putting a lie to his alibi was Serena's passive-aggressive way of enacting revenge. Or if Serena had snapped and killed Michael, maybe she realized that alibiing her husband put more of a light on her as a suspect? Which scenario was it? Serena's insouciant personality made all of them conceivable.

A thought suddenly occurred to Dee. She resumed chewing and assumed a casual air.

"Were you ever an actress?"

"Yes." Serena appeared thrown by the capricious question. "That's how Callan and I met."

Of course, Dee thought. In Hollywood, being an agent beat dating apps by miles. But Serena's previous career made everything she said regarding Michael's murder suspect, in Dee's opinion. She had no way of knowing whether the former performer was acting or not.

She tried another tack. "It must be hard being here alone while Callan's down in L.A. at parties. I mean, I assume you were alone here that night. Of the event. And Michael's murder."

Serena froze. She stared at Dee, the expression on her face reflecting anger and hurt. "Oh, my goddess. You think I killed Michael."

"No! No, no, no." Dee cursed herself for once again underestimating Serena.

Serena didn't respond. She rewrapped the wine-and-cheese board, then did the same with the breakfast platter. She faced Dee. "I think you should go."

Dee hefted herself from the kitchen stool, feeling terrible. "I don't know what to say except that I'm really sorry, Serena. Having our very first guest murdered"—she held up her hands in a gesture of helplessness—"I'm not myself."

Serena pursed her lips and gave a slight nod, which Dee hoped indicated forgiveness.

"I'll head out. I can take the samples for Jeff."

Serena pulled open the refrigerator door. She placed the platter and board inside the fridge, closed the door, and turned to Dee. "Just go."

Chastened, Dee found her way out of the house. There was no offer of using the elevator for her departure. As she climbed the endless stairs to ground level, she brooded about ruining one of the few potential friendships she might make in tiny Foundgold. But as she drove out of the cul-de-sac, she vowed to trade her personal feelings for an objective take on what she'd learned about Serena Finlay-Katz and Callan Katz. Both had reason to hate Michael. And both had weak alibis.

Meaning both were strong suspects in Michael Adam Baker's murder.

CHAPTER 12

By the time Dee returned to the Golden, night had fallen. Still, she managed to text Deputy Sheriff Aguilar as she strode to her apartment, guided by the light her phone shed.

She was almost at her front door when a shadowy figure in a hoodie suddenly appeared out of nowhere and blocked her path.

Dee froze, too scared to even scream. She held up her hands like someone being robbed at gunpoint. The light from her phone revealed the mysterious figure to be Jeff.

Dee dropped her arms. Furious, she yelled, "What are you doing, scaring me like that?! You look like the Unabomber."

She swatted at him. Jeff hopped back and forth to avoid her. "I look like every techie in the Bay Area. But my bad. I didn't mean to scare you."

Dee stopped swatting him. "I should have figured it was you. But I'm scared of everything these days. What are you doing here anyway? I thought you weren't due back until tomorrow."

Jeff grimaced. "That was the original plan. But Ranger

O'Bryant wants to talk to me again in the morning. Like most Americans, I've learned everything about law enforcement from what I've seen on TV, and if there's one thing I learned from all the *Law and Order* reruns I watched on my computer last night, no good comes from a second interview with the police."

Any annoyance Dee felt toward her friend melted away. "Come inside," she said with sympathy. "I'll nuke us dinner."

The friends entered Dee's place, pushing aside the clutter from a trunk she was going through and avoiding the stack of motel room artwork she'd yet to clean. Dee removed a low-cal frozen fettuccine alfredo from the freezer. While she heated it up in the microwave, she filled Jeff in on her ill-fated visit to Serena.

"Thoughts?" she asked, handing him the now-unfrozen meal.

He studied the pasta. "This needs something. Can you nuke some broccoli to add to it?"

"I was talking about Serena and Callan. But yes." She extracted a bag of frozen broccoli from the freezer and held it up to Jeff. "Self-steaming." She put it in the microwave and tapped the required two minutes. "The Katzes. What do think of them as suspects? Him? Her? Together?"

The microwave beeped. She used a hand towel to remove the steaming broccoli, replacing it with another frozen fettuccine dinner. Jeff reached over the kitchen bar to retrieve the broccoli. He blew on it to cool it, then opened the bag and dumped half of it on his fettuccine. "I still can't see either of them pulling a solo act to kill Baker. But together is interesting. Something cold and Macbethian about it, which fits right in with a Hollywood marriage, from everything you've told me."

Dee dumped the rest of the broccoli onto her own fettuccine and mixed it in with the pasta. Still unsettled by her set-to with Serena, she stood to eat rather than take a seat at the kitchen bar. "What's sad is if they were in on it together, I think it may be the only bond they share. The couple that kills together . . ."

"That's not where I thought you were going when you said the word 'sad.' But speaking of bad Hollywood marriages, I took a break from cop shows last night to watch the new episode of *Vengeance: Year 3004* and your ex has revealed that your alter ego, Lee Flern, is the actual devil."

Dee let out a groan. She pushed away her meal, no longer hungry. "That's even more motivation to find Michael's killer. I refuse to give Ian the satisfaction of my motelier career going in the dumper. Knowing him, I'm sure he'll add a futuristic motel to the series, run by Lee Flern, that's really a portal to hell." She paused. "Which would make a great spin-off series."

"Pitch it to him," Jeff said with a sly grin.

"Shut up," Dee teased, tossing a pot holder at him.

Jeff rose from his stool. He let out a mournful sigh. "I better go. I need a solid night's sleep. I have to be on my game tomorrow with O'Bryant."

"Do you want me to come with you?" Dee asked, worried for Jeff.

He shook his head. "Thanks, but not a good idea. I get the feeling O'Bryant is looking to make his ranger bones on this case. If you come with me, we'll be the Macbethian couple he's got in his crosshairs."

Reluctantly Dee conceded he had a point, and Jeff left.

* * *

"If Jeff slept worse than I did last night, he's in big trouble," Dee told Nugget the next morning after a long, restless night. The affable mutt, curled up at her side, responded with a yawn and a stretch that stiffened his limbs so much, he appeared to be playing possum. He relaxed and nuzzled Dee with his head.

Dee rose and readied for the day. After showering and dressing, she checked her phone and saw a text from Deputy Sheriff Aguilar. The night before, she'd alerted him to Jeff's interview with Ranger O'Bryant, sensing the green blood was attempting an end run around Aguilar's authority by cutting him out of the meeting. She read the sheriff's response: **Thanks for the heads-up. Will be at mtg. End of story. Full stop.**

"I was right," Dee said to Nugget, who was chomping down on a bowl of kibble. "O'Bryant was pulling a sneaky move. And Aguilar is ticked off."

She nuked a mug of hot water and dropped a tea bag of Extra Bold Earl Grey into it. Dee was the rare human being who couldn't stand coffee. She wasn't one of those types who explained, "I don't like coffee, but I like coffee ice cream." No, she hated the taste so much that if she accidentally bit into coffee-flavored anything, she spit it out and rinsed her mouth. This led to much teasing in the writers' room, and envy on her part, when a show sprang for a run of complicated coffee drinks—and Dee's plain old tea.

She parked herself at the kitchen bar and inhaled the Earl Grey's aromatic scent before taking a sip. In keeping with the theory that "the enemy of my enemy is my friend," Aguilar's animosity toward O'Bryant worked in her and Jeff's favor. But Dee knew it could only go so far.

If local law enforcement wouldn't put the effort into expanding their list of suspects, she and Jeff would have to do it for them.

The more she considered the Katzes as suspects, the more far-fetched it seemed. Callan could have made the drive from L.A. within the window of Michael's death, but what if he had to stop to charge his trendy EV? This would have slowed him down enough to push him out of the time frame. Plus, the murder seemed impulsive, not planned. The term "control freak" applied to every Hollywood agent Dee ever worked with. Even if Callan and/or Serena lost it and bonked Michael on the head with the heavy rock, Dee couldn't see them leaving an incriminating crime scene behind. *If nothing else, Callan would have his assistant, Marisa, clean up his mess,* Dee thought. She allowed herself a moment to indulge in an image of the obnoxious assistant scrubbing up after the murder, like a crime scene Cinderella. Then she moved on.

She ran through the names Elmira had listed as having issues with Michael, then opened the Notes app on her phone and began typing:

Shawn Rand-something: personal trainer
Liza Chen: former girlfriend; cheated on
Brian Oakhurst: jealous frenemy
Jonas Jones: mysterious falling-out

She examined the list and debated who to approach first. She landed on Liza, who Elmira had informed her owned the Golden Grub Café. The old saw of hell having no fury like a woman scorned offered clearer motivation than in the cases of Shawn, Brian, and Jonas.

Dee hopped off the kitchen stool. She dreaded any trip to the hostile environs of Goldsgone, but being on a mission to target a murderer in the close community made it more daunting.

She eyed Nugget, snoozing away on the couch, his long tongue lolling from his mouth. If she showed up in Goldsgone with the doggy in tow, the fact she'd adopted the late Jasper's hound might buy her some goodwill, or at least tamp down the overt antagonism toward her.

She removed his leash from its hook and dangled it in front of the dog. The ear that stood straight up stood even straighter. One large brown eye opened. "Nuggetty," Dee said in a singsongy voice. "Who wants to go for a ride?"

CHAPTER 13

"Hi! Hello there! Howdy!" As Dee and Nugget sauntered down Main Street, she dashed off a cheery greeting to anyone who made eye contact with her. Tourists responded in kind. Locals either glared or ignored her. But one or two nodded a reluctant response, which she took as a win. A horse-drawn carriage containing a family of tourists clip-clopped by, leaving a trail of horse droppings and stinky scent in its wake. *Metaphor for my relationship with Goldsgone,* Dee thought as she held tightly on to Nugget's leash to keep the dog from bounding over to check out the droppings.

She and the pooch arrived at the Golden Grub, a charming café housed in, no surprise, a historic brick building. But Dee picked up on some modern touches. Wire baskets of purple freesia and begonias hung from the black wrought-iron fence surrounding the eating areas on either side of the café's sleek glass front door. Taupe contemporary standing umbrellas provided shade for the tables, which had an Eames mid-century vibe versus the cutesy iron bistro sets Dee expected to find.

I hope the killer isn't Liza, Dee thought. *It would be a shame if it was the one person in this town brave enough not to go full* Little House on the Prairie.

Since it was midmorning, there were plenty of empty tables. Not seeing a hostess, Dee chose her own seat at a table next to a big bowl of water on the ground that Nugget lapped from before splaying himself across the patio's cement floor. Dee glanced into the restaurant through the expansive glass window behind her. She saw a young waitress dressed in the requisite old-fashioned garb—even a risk taker like Liza couldn't break all the Goldsgone rules—conferring with a stunning Asian woman around Dee's own age. She was dressed similarly to the waitress, yet with a touch more elegance, her dress being a solid navy with pale blue trim as opposed to the calico of her staff and pretty much every other female Goldsgonedian. She wore her thick black hair pulled back in a messy bun, an au courant style, especially when compared to the beribboned braids of the waitress.

With a worried expression, the waitress gestured toward Dee, and Dee feared she'd be kicked out of the café before she had the chance to engage with Liza. The café owner glanced out the window and happened to meet Dee's eyes. Dee grabbed the opportunity to make contact, waving and mouthing "hello" with a big smile. Liza responded with a nod that lacked the sour reluctance of the other greetings Dee had forced. The restauranteur turned back to the waitress and gestured for her to wait on Dee.

The waitress exited the restaurant's interior and came to Dee. She handed her a menu, a fake smile plastered on her face. "How do. Can I get you a drink to start with?"

"I'd love an iced tea, light ice." Dee perused the menu, which boasted a clean, contemporary font that contrasted with the item's Old West descriptions. Dee appreciated

Liza's careful attempt to find a middle ground between cool and kitschy. "And I'll go ahead and order. I'll take the Miss Sally the Saloon Girl Salad. Dang Good Dressing on the side, please."

"Yes, ma'am."

There's that fake smile again. She hates me, like everyone else in this town. I'm leaving a giant *tip. I need allies!*

"Comin' right up."

A busboy dressed like a miner brought Dee's iced tea and a breadbasket full of warm, delicious chunks of sourdough bread. While she waited for her salad and snacked on bread, slathering it with what tasted like farm-fresh butter, she evaluated the best way to casually engage Liza. Before she had a chance to land on an answer, the waitress brought her salad.

"Wow, that was quick," Dee said. "You're not trying to get rid of me, are you, ha-ha?"

She disguised the real question as a joke. The waitress didn't respond, instead moving quickly to another table, which confirmed Dee's suspicions.

The aroma of the warm grilled chicken emanating from Dee's salad reached Nugget. He sat up and fixed pleading hound eyes on Dee, adding a small whimper for extra-guilt effect. "Buddy," she said, torn. "I'd give you some, but I don't know if you're allowed to eat human food."

The whimpering grew louder, drawing disapproving attention from the people at the next table. "I just adopted him," Dee tried to explain. "I don't know all his habits. He never does this at home. I guess because I only nuke food. No delicious smells like these. Which makes me think, I should turn on the oven at my place and see if it even works."

"Here, Nug."

Dee turned to see Liza standing by her table, holding a large bone. Nugget gave an enthusiastic bark, accompanied by much tail-wagging, and the restauranteur handed it over. He lay back down, holding the bone between his front paws, and happily gnawed at it.

"Thank you so much," Dee said, grateful.

"Jasper used to stop by for bones," Liza said. "Although I can't remember a time when he ate here himself. He was an ornery sort." She scrunched up her face. "Wow, did that sound Goldsgonedian!"

Dee laughed. She silently thanked Nugget for inadvertently engineering the meetup with Liza and vowed to reward him with a lifetime of bones. "Are you busy? Can you sit for a minute?"

Liza scanned her restaurant. "Everything looks good right now. I've got a break until the lunch rush." She took the seat opposite Dee.

"I'm Dee Stern. The new owner of the Golden, with my partner, Jeff Cornetta. But I think you know all that."

"I do."

"Thank you for letting me eat here. I was afraid Verity Gillespie got to you."

"She did." Liza said this without any hint of apology. "But you looked hungry. And she's not the boss of me."

Dee couldn't help grinning at Liza's facetious word choice. The restauranteur was clearly her own woman, which Dee appreciated. She gently segued to the reason for her visit to the restaurant. "She holds me responsible for our guest who died."

"Michael."

An expression Dee couldn't decipher crossed Liza's face. "We worked together on a show. My first, his second.

Someone said you knew him too?" She played innocent, posing this as a question.

"We dated in high school. And a little after."

Convinced Liza was downplaying the relationship, Dee decided a small lie might extract more details about it. "When we worked together, Michael told me about this girl he'd reconnected with from his past and how into her he was. And now here I am in your restaurant. Small world, huh?"

"Are you sure he was talking about me?" Liza said this lightly, but with a definite edge.

"Positive. He described your restaurant and everything." *Yikes, it's a little scary how easy it is for me to lie like this.* "Someone told me you two were a couple again. I'm so sorry for your loss."

"I don't know who told you that," Liza said, her tone casual. "But they're wrong. We did go out a few times over the last few years, but it was never serious. We never expected more from each other and finally decided just to be friends. We agreed it was the best thing for us." She stood up. "The lunch rush is starting. Enjoy your salad."

Liza left. As Dee ate, she went over their conversation in her mind. Dee's television career had taught her the difference between good and bad directors. She'd even shadowed a couple of the good ones when she pondered a career change, only to learn there were even less opportunities for women directors than women writer-producers.

The good directors were able to draw a variety of emotions from the actors, encouraging layered performances. Through them, Dee learned to spot the subtextual emotions under a simple line reading. Which is why she knew Liza was covering her real emotions with a nonchalant façade.

"Best thing for us," my keester. She was furious *at Michael for how he treated her. "Keester." Ha! Now I'm the one who sounds like a Goldsgonedian.*

Dee finished her salad, which was a satisfying mix of designer lettuces, chicken, dried cranberries, toasted quinoa—a mixture Miss Sally the Saloon Girl never would have dreamed of back in the day. Having laid waste to this bone, Nugget indicated a need for a bathroom break, so Dee paid her bill and attached the leash to his collar. She gazed over to where Liza was welcoming customers to the restaurant and felt a pang of sadness. She's felt an instant rapport with the restauranteur. Under other circumstances, she could see them being friends. But until the police arrested Michael's killer, absolving Jeff and her, to a lesser extent, of the crime, she was flipping America's legal script and operating under the presumption that everyone was guilty until proven innocent.

She began herding Nugget toward the patio exit. Suddenly the dog stiffened. He let out a growl that belied his easygoing nature. Wondering what might have disturbed him so much, Dee followed his eyeline to an excessively buff thirtysomething, with a shaved head, wearing a tank top and gym shorts. His skin was so heavily tanned, it conflicted with the tattoos decorating his body.

Liza handed the hulk a huge to-go drink. "Here you go."

The guy pulled a large shake colored a bilious green out of the bag and examined it. "Raw honey? Extra protein?"

"Yes," Liza said. She didn't bother to hide her exasperation, indicating he wasn't a customer she felt a need to impress. "I . . . *We've* been making you protein shakes forever, Shawn. I think we've got your order down by now."

Dee's pulse raced. Muscle Man was Shawn Rand-something, local personal trainer and Michael's former best friend. Another potential suspect.

He opened his mouth to say something, then snapped it shut. He looked at Liza with an expression Dee couldn't decipher. Then he grunted a response that didn't sound like an apology and headed off, walking the walk of a bulked-up hulk, unaware of the woman and dog following him.

CHAPTER 14

Dee and Nugget, who was becoming a valued partner in crime, casually moseyed down the block behind the personal trainer. He disappeared into one of Goldsgone's endless supply of picturesque storefronts. An artificially distressed wooden sign above the door read GYM DANDY. A placard next to the front door listed all the equipment and classes the gym offered, ending with the name of its sole personal trainer.

Dee took Nugget's leash and wrapped it around a parking meter designed to look like an old hitching post. "I have to talk to the man we followed," she said to the dog in a whisper. "Don't worry, I'll be quick. Promise."

Nugget barked what sounded to Dee like *No worries,* and relaxed onto the pavement.

Dee pulled open the gym door. Luck was on her side. The trainer was manning the small gym's front desk, a disgruntled expression on his face.

Dee made a show of perusing a corkboard full of flyers for local events. She picked up a gym brochure from a stand on the desk and studied it. "This is exactly what I've been looking for." She held up the brochure. "I'm inter-

ested in a semiprivate training session with Shawn Radinsky. I've heard great things about him as a trainer."

"He's me." Conversation with Radinsky revealed
tobacco-stained teeth. "And happy to get you set up. Do
you have any potential schedule conflicts?" Dee shook her
head. Radinsky typed on the keyboard with thick, meaty
fingers and studied a computer screen in front of him.
"How's Wednesday, two p.m.?"

"I'll take it."

The trainer tapped on the computer a few more times,
then said, "You're booked for Wednesday, two p.m., Dee."

Stunned the trainer knew who she was, Dee's mouth
dropped open. "How . . ."

"I heard all about you from Verity Gillespie." Shawn
pointed outside. "And I recognized Jasper Gormley's
mangy mutt. Who's trying to mate with the town gossip's
standard poodle."

Dee craned her neck to see what Nugget was up to. The
hound was on all fours straining on his leash in a vain effort to align himself with a coiffed apricot standard poodle, who was playing hard to get. The poodle's pet parent
was busy gossiping, or so Dee assumed, and oblivious to
the dogs' mating dance.

Dee pulled open the gym door. "Nugget," she hissed.
"Down, boy! Down."

She finally got the dog's attention and gestured for him
to lie down. He ignored her. Fortunately, the woman
Shawn pegged as the gossip headed off down the block.
Thwarted in his quest to get busy with the poodle, Nugget
released a grumpy bark and returned to a prone position.

Dee turned back to the trainer. "Thanks for alerting me
to Nugget's doggy hashtag-me-too moment. The last thing
I need is for him to knock up some unsuspecting local's

pooch. Although that's not really possible, thank God, because I made sure Nugget was fixed."

Radinsky muttered something unintelligible and focused on his computer screen, sending the message he was done dealing with Dee. She, however, was not done with him. "I heard you were friends with our late guest Michael," she said, soldiering on. "I know there's a feeling in this town that as his hosts, we bear some responsibility for his demise." She spoke formally on purpose, hoping it put distance between the motel and Michael's murder.

"I don't care if you offed him yourself." Radinsky shrugged, stretching the grimaces on the faces of the matching Joker tattoos on his shoulders. "I haven't seen Mike in about a year. Not since I helped him move a bunch of stuff to a storage facility in West Camp after he sold his parents' place on Lake Goldsgone."

Dee picked up an edgy undercurrent to his delivery, just like with Liza. Michael's Goldsgone fan club didn't seem to include any of the people Elmira listed as his actual friends.

She was about to press the trainer for more intel on his relationship with the writer, when a fit-looking older man, dressed in a track suit embellished with the gym logo, emerged from the door leading to the workout space. Dee recognized the man as the gym owner, from a framed headshot touting him as such hanging over the community bulletin board. "Radinsky, you're late wiping down the gym equipment," he growled at the trainer. "The bathrooms could use a wipe too." The owner noticed Dee and instantly changed his tone to almost fawning. "Well, hello there. Welcome to Gym Dandy. How can we help you?"

"I'm all set, thanks to Shawn, who's been wonderful," Dee said. She laid it on thick, hoping it would score a few points with the beleaguered employee/ex–Michael Adam Baker amigo. The tactic didn't work, earning her a flushed glare instead of a grateful smile.

Dee knew a dead end when she saw one. She entered the training session into her phone calendar, politely thanked Radinsky, and left the gym. After waking up Nugget, who lay snoring on the sidewalk, the duo headed to the side street where she'd parked her car. They passed the Church of the Forty-Niner, a lovely edifice built of redwood in the nineteenth-century Carpenter Gothic style. Gingerbread trim painted white adorned the church entry, as well as all the windows, even framing the stained-glass triptych above the entry.

A man who appeared to be in his late thirties handed plastic letters to an older woman, who inserted them in an announcement on the message board, which sat front and center on the church's small, but verdant, front lawn. The letters were big enough for Dee to read. Her heart sank when she saw they announced a memorial service for Michael Adam Baker.

The woman finished adding the letters and wiped her eyes with a ribbon dangling from her bonnet. The younger man gave her a comforting pat on the back, but Dee couldn't help noticing the dark expression on his face didn't match the gesture. He helped the woman to her feet. As she adjusted her starched white apron, she glanced toward the sidewalk. Dee froze. She recognized the churchwoman as the nasty clerk from Verity's gift shop.

She and the woman briefly locked eyes. Dee unfroze and broke eye contact. "Come on, Nugs," she said to the mutt, who was busy sniffing a questionable pile left by another animal. She tugged on his leash. "We have to go."

"Miss! Oh, miss!"

The woman waved to Dee. Caught, Dee gave a weak wave back. "Howdy!" She gave Nugget's leash another pull, but the dog stubbornly refused to move.

"Wait! Please."

Trapped, Dee stood there, bracing for a Goldsgonedian tongue-lashing from another Baker acolyte. The woman lifted her skirt above her ankles, revealing an anachronistic pair of Skechers Go Walks. She made her way down the lawn's slight hill to Dee.

"I owe you an apology," she said, much to Dee's surprise. "I'm sorry I was so rude to you when you stopped by the gift shop where I work. I don't know what got into me."

"I do," said her companion, who had followed her from the message board. "Verity Gillespie." He said with with a sour expression. "The Wicked Witch of Goldsgone."

Finally sensing an ally in the time warp of a town, Dee brightened. She glumly dismissed this as wishful thinking when the man introduced himself. "I'm Brian Oakhurst and this is my mom, Millie."

Dee recognized the duo as Michael's idolized English teacher and her son, friend to the late writer. "If you didn't like me before, you'll like me even less now." Worn out by the morning of subterfuge, Dee went with total honesty for a change. "I know how much Michael meant to you. Everybody in town thinks either I didn't do enough to save his life or I killed him myself. Same goes for my business partner at the Golden, Jeff. We didn't. But until we can prove that, I've come to accept that everyone in Goldsgone is going to hate us."

She waited for the Oakhursts to confirm this, adding their voices to the chorus of haters. Instead, Brian said, "I don't think you or your partner friend killed Mike. But if either of you did, you probably had a good reason to."

Millie clutched the high, ruffled neckline of her eyelet lace white blouse. "Brian Oakhurst, what a terrible thing to say. Poor Michael is gone. Show him respect and move on from whatever happened between you in the past." She addressed Dee. "I apologize for my son. He hasn't been the same since his friend died."

"Former," her son couldn't keep himself from muttering.

His mother ignored him. "I'm sure Deputy Sheriff Aguilar will track down whoever did such a horrible thing to Michael. But in the meantime"—she shifted position, an uncomfortable expression on her face—"it's probably best you don't come to his memorial."

"Understood," Dee said, relieved beyond belief at the decent exchange between her and the Oakhursts. But missing the memorial meant missing out on an opportunity to scrutinize potential suspects all gathered in one place and suss out possible clues in their reactions and interactions.

She exchanged civil goodbyes with the duo. They returned to the church, and she finished the walk to her car, made leisurely by Nugget's frequent greeting of other dogs and occasional sexual attraction to them. As the two strolled, Dee used her nascent director's eye to analyze her conversation with mother and son Oakhurst. Regarding Michael's murder, Dee noted Millie Oakhurst carefully framed her response in a way that didn't absolve either Golden Motel proprietor of murder: "I'm sure Deputy Sheriff Aguilar will track down whoever did such a horrible thing to Michael" wasn't a ringing endorsement of either Dee's or Jeff's innocence.

But two other snippets of the conversation struck Dee

as more telling. Millie had excused her son's behavior by saying he hadn't "been the same since his friend died." Brian couldn't resist spewing out the qualifier "former," as in a *former* friend. His mother insisted he needed to get over the past and move on.

Which begged the question: What happened in the past that Brian Oakhurst was so obviously unable to move on from?

CHAPTER 15

Upon returning to the Golden, Dee found Jeff at the kitchen counter in her apartment, intent on whatever he was doing on his computer. His eyes were shadowed, and his lightly freckled skin was paler than usual, if that was even possible.

Dee felt for her friend. "Hey," she said softly.

Jeff started, which startled Dee. She yelped. Nugget barked his concern.

"Sorry," Jeff and Dee said simultaneously. They acknowledged the moment with a shared rueful laugh.

Dee went behind the counter and removed a water bottle from the mini fridge, where they stashed them for guests. She then took a seat on the kitchen barstool next to Jeff.

"How did the interview go?"

Jeff grimaced. "Bad. O'Bryant was doing that thing I saw a lot on the cop shows I watched to prep for the interview. He tried to wear me down so I'd confess to killing Baker."

"Didn't the sheriff deflect any of that?"

"Aguilar? He wasn't there."

Dee mentally cursed the Goldsgone law enforcer for being a no-show and vowed to confront him on it.

Jeff took a slug of the water bottle he'd already opened. "What have you been up to?"

"Doing some amateur sleuthing in the creepy time warp that is Goldsgone." She shared the details of her conversations with Liza and Shane, as well as the mother-son Oakhurst duo. "I think the personal trainer shows the most potential as a killer. And I just heard myself. That sounds like a comment on the bottom of a report card from a school for murderers."

Jeff pointed at her with his water bottle. "Potential TV pilot. Bank it."

"I keep telling everyone I'm out of the business," Dee said, exasperated. Jeff gave her a "Who are you kidding?" look and she buckled. "Argh! You're right. Banking it. In case I ever do go back. Anyhoo, there's something off about him, although it could be the steroids, because you know he's on them. It may take both of us to figure out what went down between him and Michael and how badly it ended. I booked us a semiprivate training session with him, so blow the dust off your exercise togs."

" 'Dust' is right. I joined a gym near me to meet girls and bought a bunch of insanely overpriced exercise gear. I got there, put it on in the locker room, saw how dumb I looked, and never went back." Jeff took a sad sip of water.

"We'll deal with your lack of confidence at a later date. Right now, with Aguilar being MIA and O'Bryant being an O'A-hole, it feels like it's up to us to figure out who really offed Michael. 'Offed.' Now I sound like a mobster."

"I do like 'O'A-hole.' That's a keeper. It's too bad we can't go to the memorial. All the suspects in one place."

Dee gave a vigorous nod. "That's exactly what I thought."

"Great minds." Jeff tapped his head and winked. "You know the killer won't miss it. It'd be too obvious. He'll want to blend in with everyone." He thought for a moment. "Or she. Liza . . . the restauranteur. Any 'scorned lover' vibe there?"

"Maybe. I feel like I would have picked up anger *and* hurt if that was the case. But I only picked up anger. Whether there was enough of it to motivate murder, I don't know." She hopped off her stool and went around the counter again, bending down to pull two bags of potato chips out of the cabinet below. "God, investigating is exhausting. I don't know how anyone does it as a career. I thought nothing would be harder than writing the 'Couple of Coco-nuts' episode of *Duh!* where the teen band gets stranded on a desert island and has to sing loud enough for a passing cruise ship to hear them and send a rescue party. I was wrong."

She offered a potato chip bag to Jeff, who declined it. "Thanks, but no thanks. I don't have much of an appetite these days."

"I get it," Dee said, sympathizing with her beleaguered bestie. She returned to her stool, stopping first to glance at his computer screen. "I'm afraid to ask, but . . . any new bookings?"

Jeff shook his head. "I've been playing with a few social-media campaigns. What do you think of 'Enjoy a platinum stay at the Golden'?"

"It's . . . something."

Jeff winced. "Yikes. Not helping my self-confidence."

"I'm sorry. I want to make things better, not worse for you. For us." She glanced at the bag of chips in her hand. Her appetite was gone too. She put the bag on the counter. "Let's do something productive, but not murder-y."

She walked over to the stack of prints from motel rooms, motioning for Jeff to join her. They each took a print and then a rag, which they spritzed with glass cleaner. As the moteliers cleaned the frames, they pitched and tossed a variety of market campaigns, some serious, a few purely silly. Dee was happy to see the task had the desired effect of relaxing them both.

She held up her print frame up to the sunlight pouring in through the large room's windows. The glass was so sparkly-clean that her own image smiled back at her. She added it to the growing pile of prints ready to be rehung in the motel rooms. "I love this painting."

"You reminded me," she said, "I still have to do a search to see where the original is."

"Definitely. It's like a hidden treasure."

Jeff stopped cleaning. He stared at Dee. Then his face broadened with a wide smile. "That's it. Our campaign. 'The Golden Motel—a hidden treasure nestled in the Sierra foothills.'"

Dee gave an enthusiastic nod. "I like it."

"I can create a graphic where I use this painting as the background and insert a photo of the motel." Jeff swiped the air with his hand, indicating Dee should visualize the scene. "I'll include a finished version of the pool and pop in a few extra pine trees to make the Golden look more hidden."

"I don't like it, I *love* it!" Dee responded with glee.

Inspired, Jeff rose to his feet, pacing as he spouted ideas. "I'll design it to look like a vintage postcard from when the Golden was built. We can print real postcards we give our guests and make a small mailbox where they drop them for us to mail. Publicity for the price of a postcard stamp."

Dee rose and paced alongside Jeff. "We can put the image on different souvenir items to sell."

"Yes! Mugs, mouse pads, key chains. Notepads we put in all the rooms that guests can also buy, along with pens that say, 'The Golden Motel: A Hidden Treasure in the Sierras.'"

"Whoo-hoo!" Dee threw her arms around Jeff in a jubilant hug. "We finally have something to celebrate!"

Jeff hugged her back, then pulled away. "Does Elmira sell champagne? She must. If you can buy it at a gas station in California, you have to be able to buy it at a general store. I'm gonna go buy us a bottle, then get to work on the graphic."

"I'll come with you. I can't wait until we tell Elmira about this. Ooh, I just had another idea!" Dee bounced up and down, her go-to move whenever she was super excited. "Forget my historic trail idea for Foundgold. We can do a 'hidden treasures' map instead, where we lay out all the same stuff, only in a different, more fun way. When you think about it, Foundgold itself is a hidden treasure. We totally lean into that."

"Awesome." Jeff fist-pumped. "We *rock*."

"Yes, we do," Dee said.

She grabbed a jacket sporting the logo of a long-forgotten sitcom she'd worked on, and flung it over her shoulder, then sauntered to the front door with a jokey swagger. She flung upon the door. To her and Jeff's shock, Deputy Sheriff Aguilar stood there with his fist suspended in the air as if about to knock.

Aguilar lowered his hand. When he spoke, his tone was somber. "I'm here for Jeff."

CHAPTER 16

J eff turned white as a sheet. "Is this what it feels like before you pass out?" he croaked, keeping one hand on
the doorframe to steady himself.

"I'm not here to arrest you," the sheriff quickly corrected. "I'm here to apologize for not making it to your interview with O'Bryant. A tourist in Goldsgone thought his
car was stolen. Turned out he had a few too many hard
sarsaparillas last night and forgot where he parked it."

Dee released a slightly hysterical giggle of relief. "I guess
hard sarsaparilla packs a punch. I'll remember that next
time I get a hankerin' for it. OMG, why do I keep talking
like I was born in 1850?"

"Local hazard. Happens to all of us. You should hear us
at our weekly poker game. It's like a scene from an old
Western." Aguilar took off his hat and fiddled with the
brim. "Um . . . you mind if I come in?"

"Of course not," Dee said, speaking for her and Jeff,
since he was still recovering from the one-eighty of fearing
he was jail-bound to at least a temporary reprieve. "Come
on in, Sheriff." She ushered Aguilar into the room and
showed him to the couch. He flicked the sides of his duster

coat so they spread out on either side of him and sat down. "Water?" Dee asked. "Un-hard sarsaparilla? We don't actually have any. I thought I'd ease the tension with a small—extremely small, more like minuscule—joke."

This got a smile from the law enforcement official. "I'm good. And instead of 'Sheriff,' let's go with Raul."

"Okay . . . Raul." Dee exchanged a look with Jeff. Being on a first-name basis with their law enforcement visitor boded well.

Raul leaned back against the sofa and crossed one long leg over the other. "I wanted to give you guys a little insight into my relationship with Ranger O'Bryant. We hate each other."

Instead of saying, *That's blatantly obvious to anyone who has eyes,* Dee went with "Thank you for the insight. Go on."

Raul did so. "O'Bryant treats me like an annoyance, not a colleague. It gets to me."

"Sounds like he's jealous," Dee said.

"Of what?" Raul shook his head, perplexed.

Dee eyed the smart young officer at the beginning of his career and thought of the paunchy ranger inching toward retirement. The contrast gave her a good inkling of why O'Bryant was jealous. But maybe it was something more obvious to a woman, because Jeff also looked mystified.

"The Goldsgone substation is small," Raul continued. "I rotate with one other deputy sheriff, Gerald Tejada, and there's a civilian office manager. It's meant to handle crimes like drunk-and-disorderly conduct, petty theft. Sometimes we tackle bigger crimes, like theft or domestic disturbance. And drugs. No matter how small a station is, that's a chronic problem. The main sheriff's station is in West Camp, the county seat. They work with Majestic

Park law enforcement on bigger cases, like this one. They're only letting me stay on it because they figure O'Bryant's doing the heavy lifting. And it frees up all the guys in West Camp to focus on cases like busting meth labs and illegal grows in the backcountry."

Hearing this, Jeff leaned forward. Dee knew him well enough to assume they were thinking the same thing: Michael's murder might be tied to an illegal marijuana operation. The deep country of the state's national parks was peppered with the operations, often run by dangerous cartels. "Maybe Baker was looking for a new source of funds," Jeff said. "It's possible he got on the wrong side of an illegal grow."

Raul appeared doubtful. "I grew up on Mirror Lake. My family ran a bait-and-tackle shop and rented boats. At least during the summer. During winter, my parents led cross-country ski tours. But we barely got by. So Dad took over a plot of land in the backwoods and grew weed. Before it was legal. That is, until a cartel threatened to do away with him and his crop. Baker was older than me, so I don't remember much about him. But what I do remember tells me he'd be too scared to get involved with a cartel."

The sheriff had a point.

"You're right," Dee said. "Baker could be a bully, but he was also a coward. He'd be terrified of making up a fake cartel for a script."

Raul adjusted his duster. "This flipping coat is a pain. I wish they'd let me wear a bomber jacket, like a normal sheriff." He addressed the others. "I know you've been nosing around town trying to find other suspects in the murder. I get it. You need to clear your names and save your investment in the Golden. I can't actively condone amateur sleuthing, but I'd like to solve this case and prove to certain people—okay, Ranger O'Bryant—that I'm an actual law enforcement officer and not some kind of cartoon character. If you come across any promising leads, feel free to share them. On the down-low. This is between us."

Dee and Jeff responded with nervous nods. "Got it," Dee said.

"Good," Raul responded. "So, have you come across anything worth a closer look?"

Dee relayed what she'd garnered so far from inserting herself into the business of Liza Chen, Shawn Radinsky, and the Oakhursts.

"Be careful with Shawn," Raul warned. "He's got a temper on him. Brian Oakhurst is another story. He never liked Baker, because he felt like he could never live up to him in his mother's eyes. Millie is okay, but she works part-time at the mercantile, and anyone who spends too much time with Verity Gillespie starts absorbing her poison. And forget about Liza. She's good people."

"From what I hear, Michael treated her badly," Dee said. "She could have snapped."

"*Never.*" Raul spoke with such vehemence, it took Dee aback. "Liza's an incredible woman. She's so much better than that piece of sh . . . that piece of dirt . . . deserved. Even if she was angry with Baker, she'd never give him that kind of power over her. Snoop elsewhere. She's a dead end."

It took enormous willpower on both Dee and Jeff's parts not to exchange another discreet look.

Raul stood up. "You've got my number. If you run into anything that'll put this case to bed, text me."

Dee and Jeff let Raul out with a promise to do so.

"Wow," Dee said as soon as she was sure the sheriff was out of hearing distance. "He is *so* in love with Liza."

"From what you said, she's beautiful, she's nice, and she's a good businesswoman." Jeff grew wistful. "Sounds like my type."

"Nah." Dee shook her head. "She doesn't seem psychotic."

"Shut up," Jeff said. But he said it with affection.

Dee wrinkled her brow as she pondered their conversation with the sheriff. "If Michael's death wasn't related to an illegal grow, it still could be related to money in some way. It's very possible he was looking for a new source of income. His career was in trouble. He burned enough bridges to make it tough to get a staff job or even a one-off pilot deal. A lot of writers like him are too full of themselves to think they have to worry about offers drying up. They assume they'll work forever. But unless you have a hot credit, one that's evergreen, every sitcom writer's career has an expiration date."

Jeff glanced at her with a quizzical expression. "And you went into this business, exactly why?"

"Because you're in the trenches with the funniest people you'll ever meet. You hear your words coming out of the mouths of actors you can't believe you get to work with. And when someone out there has a bad day, you hope that when they turn on their TV, the script you wrote will give them a break from it. And, hopefully, they'll get to laugh." Dee felt herself choking up. She coughed to clear her throat and contain her emotions. "With all the dysfunction and terrible hours and competition, I don't regret a second of it. I'm so lucky I got to have the career I did. But I'm ready for a change and the Golden Motel is my future. *Our* future."

Dee strode into her bedroom. She pulled open the whitewashed oak door of the closet and took out her carry-on suitcase. Jeff watched confused as she opened the dresser drawers and began extracting clothing she placed inside the suitcase.

"Whoa. What's going on? Where are you going?"

"Los Angeles. Which means that instead of a semi-private training session with Shawn Radinsky, you now get a one-on-one with him. Dig up whatever you can on him, or from him. But be subtle about it. I second what Raul said. Radinsky reads like a guy with a very short fuse." She went back to the closet and dug around for her sundry bag. "I'm going to hit up a few acquaintances of mine and Michael's to see if I can find out anything about his financials." She hunted for her phone, which was buried under a T-shirt. "I better call Dad and tell him I'm coming down for a night. Maybe two."

"Are you sure about this?" Jeff asked, concerned. "With what happened to your mom . . . your relationship with your dad . . . going to the studios—it's a lot of triggers for you."

Dee stopped her whirlwind of activity. She gave Jeff a hug. "Thank you for worrying about me," she said with a smile. "I'll be fine."

She spoke with a confidence that belied her own fears.

CHAPTER 17

Dee texted the emergency contact Michael Adam Baker listed as his emergency contact on his motel registration form, a woman named Pria Hart. Having no idea what kind of relationship they had, she kept her message succinct. After she offered condolences, she used the return of Michael's clothing—law enforcement was still holding tight to his electronics—as an excuse to meet in person and have a brief chat.

She then texted Mindy Baruch, a sitcom writer friend she'd made while working in the trenches at *On the John,* and then worked with on *Duh!* Mindy had also done punch-up for Michael on two pilots he wrote, which were shot but never picked up to series. Dee hoped Mindy, who knew Michael better than she did, could offer insight into his recent behavior and mindset.

Finally Dee texted the one person she found it hardest to communicate with: her father. He texted back a GIF of a cartoon ship's captain clinging to the mast of a boat rocking on a high wave and the message: **It'll be great to "sea" ya!** Dee expected the goofy response. Sam Stern was a voice actor who'd created so many cartoon characters in his long career that he'd earned the nickname "The Man of a Million Voices." Dee loved him dearly, but as she read the meme, she thought with sadness that she could always count on her dad to hide his emotions behind a GIF, a meme, or a goofy cartoon voice.

Her phone pinged a return text from Mindy, a string of happy emojis and a promise to arrange a drive-on for Dee at New Century Studios, where *Duh!* filmed.

Dee put her suitcase in the Honda trunk, then checked her cell phone again to see if Pria had responded. To her disappointment, she hadn't.

Dee trotted Nugget over to Jeff's cabin. After covering the care and feeding of the amiable mutt, and again assuring Jeff she'd be fine in Los Angeles, she hugged man and beast goodbye and set off on the five-hour road trip to La-La Land.

Dee began the journey with a stop at the All-in-One for snacks and beverages. "You want a treat for the road?" Elmira asked. She gestured to the bakery case like a spokesmodel. "I made brookies. They're a brownie *and* a cookie."

"Mmmm," Dee responded, knowing both would taste equally inedible. "I'll take a half dozen. I'll share them with friends."

"Spreading the word beyond Foundgold," Elmira said with pride. "I like it." She rang up the brookies, along with Dee's more palatable snacks. "How's the investigation into Michael's murder going? Any good leads?"

"Not really," Dee admitted. "That's what I'm going to L.A. for, to see if I can find any links there."

"Am I still a suspect?"

Dee turned to see Serena Finlay-Katz emerge from the baby aisle, stroller and baby sling in tow. The charcuterie artist failed to hide her hurt under the facetious tone.

"Serena!" Feeling guilty, Dee went overboard with delight at running into her. "I'm so sorry about that. I'd really like it if we could start over and be friends."

"Okay." Serena took a dog treat from the jar on the convenience store counter and fed it to the being in her baby sling, ID'ing the inhabitant as Oscar. "I heard you tell Elmira you're going to Los Angeles. I'm doing a huge grazing board for a wedding at the casino in West Camp this weekend. My assistant in L.A. sourced a lot of the ingredients and they're ready and waiting at Les Fromages in Beverly Hills. If you could pick them up for me, I'd be super grateful."

"Sure. Happy to." *Shrewd move, Serena.* Every time Dee was tempted to write the woman off as a vapid flake, she managed to defy expectations.

Dee left the store with her supply stash, which she placed on the passenger seat for easy snacking access. She felt her phone buzz in her back pocket and extracted it from her jeans. She was glad to see that Pria had gotten back to her, but with a message that generated a raised eyebrow: **Happy 2 chat. U can burn his clothes.**

So many questions, Dee mused. She texted back, confirming the date and time.

A scenic drive through the Sierra foothills eventually led to the 99 Freeway, which sliced through the flatlands of California's Central Valley. The 99 dumped into the 5 Freeway, the merge doubling, tripling, and quadrupling the cars on the road. Dee transitioned from the 5 to the 170, which also answered to the grandiose name of the Hollywood Freeway. Dee exited at Riverside Boulevard, taking local streets to the family home in Studio City.

I so do not miss this, Dee thought while waiting at a stop sign and watching a woman walking a goldendoodle interrupt her cell phone call to scream at a man running the stop sign in the opposite direction from Dee.

She made a right onto a side street lined with palm trees and parked in front of a compact ranch house painted a comforting sea green with white trim. The street had once been lined with the small homes built as a postwar subdivision. Almost all were gone, victims of the Los Angeles teardown craze. In their place were McMansions, whose stratospheric price tags belied their cookie-cutter construction.

Dee parked in the narrow driveway behind her father's twenty-five-year-old navy Volvo sedan. She retrieved her carry-on from the car trunk and walked up the driveway, stopping to pick up her father's mail, which mostly consisted of WE BUY OLD HOUSES! flyers from rapacious real estate dealers looking to score the decades-old house for cheap. She continued to the home's front porch, stopping to yank a WE BUY OLD CARS! flyer out from under the Volvo's windshield wipers.

Dee gave the front door a gentle tap to alert Sam to her arrival. Then she opened the door, which her father refused to keep locked, even in the face of Los Angeles's rising crime rate. She stepped into the living room and was immediately struck by the lingering scent of the 1970s citrusy perfume that was her mother's favorite. The scent seemed baked into the walls and traditional furniture of the room. Tears welled up in Dee's eyes.

Sam Stern glanced up from where he sat, straddled on the floor, surrounded by STOP THE NOISE! posters. Her father had thrown himself into convincing the local airport to rejigger the flight path it had arbitrarily changed without giving notice to local residents. Dee knew it was a quixotic quest, but at least it gave her dad something to focus on besides grieving his wife of over forty years.

Sam's face lit up at the sight of his daughter. "Deedle Dee! My girl." He clumsily rose to his feet. Dee extended a hand to help steady him and they hugged. She couldn't help noticing how her father had aged since her mother's death. He still had the salt-and-pepper hair that suited him and a well-defined bone structure to his face, which Dee regretted not inheriting. But his slim, fit frame, so suited to his five-nine height, felt boney. After years of being told how much younger he looked than his given age, Sam now wore every year of seventy-one on his face and body.

They broke apart. Sam eyed his daughter with approval. "You look good. More than good. Healthy. Rested. Even a little tan?"

"Yeah, the funeral pallor you get spending 24/7 in a writers' room is gone," Dee said with a grin. "How are you doing, Dad? You look good too." She didn't share her concern about his appearance, knowing he'd deflect it.

"I am jiminy jim-dandy," Sam declared in the voice of Tweety Sweety, one of the legendary cartoon characters he'd acted. "I wish I could have dinner with you, but we have a Stop the Noise meeting at Art's Deli. I can bring you home a sandwich. You can eat one of those for days. Won't have to worry about another meal while you're here."

"Ha, so right. You know what, I'll take you up on that. Turkey and bacon on rye, mayo, tomatoes, no lettuce."

She went to take her wallet out of her backpack, but Sam stopped her. "Oh no you don't," he said in a gravelly voice with a heavy Southern accent. "The day I can't buy my own daughtah a sandwich is the day I don't deserve to be a fathuh."

"Thanks, Colonel Cluck," Dee said, recognizing the voice behind the character of an ad campaign for a local fast-food chicken chain.

An airplane roared by overhead. Sam clicked a clicker

Dee didn't realize he was holding in his left hand. He held it up triumphantly. "Tenth complaint registered in the last hour. We're gonna win this thing."

Dee left her father to his clicking and poster making. She exited the living room's sliding door and walked through the spit of a backyard to the "she shed" Dee called home for the several months following her mother's unexpected death. Sybil "Sibby" Stern had suffered a fatal heart attack in her sleep. Waking up next to the still body of his beloved wife was the only thing that ever silenced The Man of a Million Voices. Sam Stern barely spoke a word for weeks after Sibby's traumatic and heartbreaking passing.

The she shed was a fully functional ADU, more studio apartment than shed. The furniture was IKEA utilitarian. The room's most prominent feature was the large table, where Sibby and friends met weekly to do needlework and crafts while enjoying "wine o'clock." The table was on wheels so it could be pushed out of the way when it was time to lower the Murphy bed disguised as a closet. A love seat upholstered in a fading black-and-white toile fabric backed up against the wall facing the small kitchen area.

Dee collapsed onto the couch and closed her eyes, worn out by the drive and the emotional strain of coming home. Her phone rang, startling her. She yelped. It fell out of her jeans pocket onto the carpeted floor. She retrieved it while maintaining her prone position.

"Jeff?"

"You know what's extinct? The word 'hello.' "

"Hello."

"Howdy!"

Dee winced. "Uh-oh. Someone's gone full-metal Goldsgonedian."

"With good reason. You know how we can't go to the

memorial that'll be packed with suspects? Well, I found something we *can* go to, and it'll be much more fun. The Goldsgone Annual Howdy Hoedown. According to Elmira, it's a fundraiser for local charities that's basically a big square dance with a lot of potluck food. It's happening tomorrow night. Everybody in both towns goes, along with tons of tourists. Sometimes there's even a real-live barn building." There was a long pause. "You're not saying anything."

"I was waiting for you to get to the fun part."

"It beats a memorial, especially one for a jerk like Baker. There's also an auction. We can donate a weekend at the Golden, along with some of our new swag to generate publicity, while we mingle and suss out clues to Baker's murder."

"You're right. It's a good event for us to attend."

"Thank you. FYI, there's a note on the flyer saying proper costume isn't required, but is encouraged."

"Which is the passive-aggressive way of saying it's required. Fine. I'll do-si-do over to the house at some point during my trip here to see if Grammy had a square dance dress." After retiring from decades as a kindergarten teacher, Sam's widowed mother had launched a second career as a film and TV extra. The extras who could provide their own wardrobe booked more jobs, so Grammy Stern had amassed a wide range of outfits, some of which the Sterns held on to for sentimental reasons.

"I'll mosey on over to the mercantile and buy a man's square dance shirt. I'm sure Yes-*that*-Donner's selling them. Wouldn't hurt to score some points with her."

"You have a better chance at that than I ever will, especially if you bat those baby browns and fluff your copper curls for her."

"You make me sound like a 1930s vamp." Jeff grew serious. "How'd the drive go? You okay? How's your dad?"

"Getting here was your typical Hell-A freeway ride. A self-driving car passed me doing eighty while the driver texted. Dad is . . . Dad. We all handle grief differently. I cry. Dad goes into the voice of Tweety Sweety."

"One of his best characters. But not appropriate, considering."

"It's not fair of me to judge him. He lost the love of his life. He's also aging out of his career, which I know is painful for him. It's a tough time for Dad. I can tell he's a little lost." Dee yawned. She rubbed her eyes. "I'm pretty wiped out. I think I'll crash early."

"Good idea. Rest up for tomorrow. Let me know if you learn anything I need to act on."

"Will do."

The two signed off. Dee's eyelids began to flutter. She forced herself awake and texted Sam to let him know she was calling it a night and he should refrigerate her turkey sandwich. She then wheeled the table out of the Murphy bed's path and pulled down the bed. After a desultory face wash and teeth brush, she climbed into bed.

Dee fell asleep, hoping that her conversations the next day would garner much-needed insight into the motivation behind Michael Adam Baker's murder.

CHAPTER 18

Fueled by nervous energy, Dee woke up early. She decided to capitalize on this with a hike on a popular trail in the Studio City hills.

After throwing on workout clothes, Dee left the she shed. On her way to the car, she stopped to peek into her dad's house. All was still, which she expected. Sam had never been an early riser, as opposed to Sibby, who confounded husband and daughter with her morning zip and boundless cheer.

Dee continued to her Honda. She climbed in, backed out of the driveway onto the street, and started toward the trail. She noticed that the few older homes still standing on the block had a dispirited look to them, as if resigned to their fate as teardowns. There was more activity in the McMansion driveways, where young moms in yoga togs were strapping sleepy children into car seats for the drive to school.

Dee's hike got off to a bad start with a fifteen-minute wait for a spot in the small lot that offered the trail's only parking option. Tired of finding used diapers on their lawns and being woken up by fanatical fitness coaches screaming at their boot camp hiker clients, the residents of the celebrity-riddled surrounding neighborhood had instituted permit parking, effectively banning day trippers from the environs.

After she finally scored a spot, Dee began the steep climb that constituted the trail's initial approach. The first ten minutes were strenuous in the extreme, but then the dirt path leveled out to a more gradual climb. With scrubby vegetation and few trees to provide shade, there was no escaping the Southern California sun beating down on Dee, and she found herself missing the thick woods and deep green of Foundgold.

A few women hiking together outpaced her on the trail. As they disappeared around the bend, she heard one of them say to the other, "A couple million doesn't cut it anymore." Dee considered this. The hiker wasn't wrong, at least when it came to living the good life in Los Angeles. The comment was particularly true of the showrunner circles where Michael Adam Baker aspired to travel. Dee felt surer than ever that the TV writer's desperate attempt at story theft was financially motivated.

She finished the hike with much huffing and puffing and vows to exercise more, once she returned home. *Home,* she thought. *That's what Foundgold is to me now.* The realization made her happy. She headed back to the she shed, where she showered and changed into an outfit of black leggings, black ankle booties, and a drapey purple tunic top.

Dee got to the coffee shop, where Pria had asked to meet, right on time. She snagged the one table not occupied by people on laptops hogging a spot for the day. A woman in her late twenties entered and glanced around. She was petite, with fine features, and glossy black hair, which hung past her shoulders. Even though Pria was obviously of East Indian descent, she reminded Dee of Liza. Taking a chance, Dee waved to her.

The woman acknowledged the wave and walked toward her. "Dee?" she asked.

Dee nodded. "Hi, Pria. Thanks so much for meeting with me. Can I buy you a coffee?"

"I'm good." Pria took the seat opposite her. "And meeting with you is my pleasure. Especially if it's a chance to talk smack about Michael."

"Okay, then," Dee said, taken aback by Pria's honesty, but appreciative of it. "I assume you know by now he was murdered."

"Oh yes. I had a chat with a ranger named O'Bryant."

Dee managed not to say *Ugh!* "I hope I'm not going to make you repeat yourself."

"I wouldn't worry about that. The conversation was short and pro forma. The minute I verified my alibi, he lost interest in me."

Dee fumed. She was positive O'Bryant was merely going through the motions until he gathered the proof he needed to arrest Jeff. "Since Michael listed you as his emergency contact, you must have been close."

"Very. But why he listed me as his emergency contact, I'll never know. Either he had no other person to put down or it was wishful thinking." Dee picked up a note of sadness in Pria's voice. "We were living together until I found out his 'research trips' to Goldsgone were BS," the ex-girlfriend explained. "He was cheating on me with an old girlfriend. I saw the same number come up a few times on his cell phone when he left it out. I wrote it down, called it, and had a very interesting chat with the woman who answered."

"By any chance, was it Liza Chen?"

"Yup. I see that look on your face. If you're thinking Liza and I joined forces to off Michael, here's where I was the night of his murder." Pria scrolled through images on her phone. Landing on one, she held it up to Dee, whose eyes widened. Michael's ex-girlfriend stood posed on a movie premiere's red carpet, her arm entwined in the arm of the film's megastar, Jace Anders. "My current boyfriend. I traded up. I'm not talking financially, although that too. But definitely a kinder, more supportive guy—and one who's not a serial cheater."

"About the financials. Do you know anything about Michael's?"

"Considering he still owes me for the last two months of rent I covered before I kicked him out, I can tell you he was in deep debt. He bought a house at the top of the market and was underwater on the mortgage. His scripts weren't selling and his overall deal with New Century Studios ended. He burned through his savings and was living off his credit cards. Once he burned through the limits on those, I don't know what his plans for survival were."

"I bet I do," Dee said, her tone acidic. She shared his plan to rip off her career transition.

"Oh, that's bad," Pria said. "But I'm not surprised. It's very Michael." She placed her phone inside her Fendi purse.

Knowing Fendi purses cost four figures or more, and that Pria's career as a script supervisor didn't afford such luxuries, Dee assumed it was a gift from her new boyfriend. In which case, Pria, the below-the-line crew member, had definitely traded up.

"I can't think of anything else to tell you right now," Pria said. "If I do, I'll call you. Are you talking to any of his coworkers? He spent more time with them than he ever did with me."

"That happens in TV."

Pria stood up. "Good luck. I have no idea what Michael's future would have looked like if he hadn't died. But no one deserves to be murdered."

She left after promising Dee tickets to her boyfriend's next movie premiere. Dee might feel conflicted about Hollywood, but even she couldn't resist a shot at attending one of the town's glamorous events.

Dee bought a chai tea and an almond biscotti and returned to her table, fending off another laptop-wielding interloper. She alternated crunching on the biscotti with typing notes on her phone from her meetup with Pria. In general, the conversation confirmed what Dee suspected about Baker's financial straits, but Pria had provided details ratcheting up how dire they were. Underwater on a mortgage, excessive credit card debt, being kicked out of the apartment he shared with Pria—Michael Adam Baker was spiraling from successful career to homelessness.

There were a few hours between her appointments with Pria and her friend Mindy Baruch, so Dee used the time to hang out with her father, which meant joining him in a protest against the FAA's noxious new flight pattern. They caught up between waving posters at drivers on the corner of Laurel Canyon and Ventura Boulevard, encouraging them to honk their support for the cause. Dee noticed women hovering around Sam and felt torn between wanting him to find happiness again and resenting any woman who thought she could fill her mother's shoes. Sam responded to the flirting with charm, but zero interest in romance, rendering the issue moot . . . at least for the moment.

After the protest, Dee went back to her father's house,

where she made quick work of the turkey sandwich he'd saved for her. She left him practicing various takes on the voice of a trash bag for an upcoming commercial audition and headed to New Century Studio.

She was happy to see Manny was the guard at the gate. Rotund and jovial, Manny was a studio fixture. "Weird to be giving you a visitor drive-on," he said, handing Dee the pass. "We miss you."

"I bet you say that to all the unemployed writers," Dee said, placing the pass on her dashboard.

"Only the ones I like."

"Aww," Dee said. She had a feeling Michael Adam Baker didn't fall into this category.

Manny leaned out of the guardhouse. "A couple of execs are on a retreat," he said in a conspiratorial tone. "I booked you into one of their spaces by the soundstage instead of the visitors' lot."

"Bless you, Manny. You're enough to make me reconsider quitting *Duh!*"

Manny let out an exclamation of mock alarm and waved his arms back and forth. "God help us, no! I would never wanna be responsible for that." He dropped his arms and went back to speaking in a stage whisper. "Although from what I hear about how lousy the new episodes are, they could use you."

Dee blew the guard a kiss and drove onto the lot. She maneuvered around an obstacle course of golf carts zooming back and forth, costume racks being wheeled across the narrow lot streets, and tour groups taking selfies in front of the soundstages where their favorite shows were filmed, either in the present or the past. After narrowly missing a couple of actors dressed as aliens who suddenly decided to play catch with one of their second heads, she pulled into her designated parking spot, which sat right in front of the *Duh!* soundstage.

She showed her pass to the set guard, who was new to her, then wended her way through the hallways behind the show's sets to the empty dressing room where Mindy asked to meet. Mindy was already there.

"Dee!" She threw open her arms for a hug.

"Min." The two friends shared a warm embrace.

Dee glanced over Mindy's shoulder and, to her surprise, the dressing-room mirror reflected the image of someone else in the room—a man, within the ballpark of her own age, clad in the typical writers' room attire of T-shirt and jeans. He'd given up the fight against baldness and gone with a shaved head. Like most staff writers, he'd also given up the struggle against the ten or twenty pounds that came with a lifestyle short on exercise, but long on free food.

Dee released Mindy. The unexpected visitor stood up and extended a hand. "Hi, R.J. Morrin. We haven't met, but I know your work."

"I know yours too," Dee said, shaking his hand. She'd never been on staff with R.J., but she knew friends who had and they spoke well of him.

"I hope you're okay with R.J. being here," Mindy said, apologetic. "He replaced Michael after he was let go."

"Wait, what?" Dee wrinkled her brow, confused. "From where? Here? Michael worked on *Duh!*?"

"Yes," Mindy said. She tilted her head, also confused. Her mass of brown curls tilted left with her. "After you left the show. I thought that's why you got in touch with me. He didn't tell you when he showed up at your motel?"

"Nope. He never mentioned it. I guess there wasn't any reason to. Still, kind of odd he didn't bring it up."

R.J. spoke up. "When Mindy told me you were coming to get some intel on Baker, I had to be in on it. I have a lot to say about him. A *lot*."

From the malice in the voice of a writer deemed in general as a stand-up guy, Dee intuited that none of what R.J. had to say about Michael Adam Baker was good.

He confirmed this with his next statement: "I'm not surprised someone offed him. I'm only surprised it took this long."

CHAPTER 19

Dee took a seat in the chair at the makeup table and swiveled to face Mindy and R.J., who were both sitting on the dressing room's ratty old sofa.

"I'll go first," Mindy said. "I don't have that much to tell you other than that Michael now was hugely different from the Michael we worked with at *On the John*, and the pilots I did with him. He was still really superior and arrogant on the pilots. You know, all 'I've got an overall deal and that makes me a writing god.' When I heard Dan wanted to bring him on here," she continued, referencing the *Duh!* showrunner, "I brought this up, but they insisted he'd changed. And they were right. Talk about being humbled. He tried so hard to be nice to everyone, it was uncomfortable. And he'd lost any writer mojo he ever had. He barely pitched anything, and what he did almost never made it into the script. He spent a lot of time out of the room taking calls. He said they were about new deals, but we didn't believe him, because he'd come back all sweaty and nervous. Dan fired him after only a couple of weeks and brought in R.J."

"My turn." R.J. rubbed his hands together, if not with

glee, then with a definite dose of satisfaction. "I had history with Baker. We worked on the first season of *Besties* together. Way more of my jokes got into the script than Baker's, which made him jealous and insecure. He told Shawn, the showrunner, I was bad-mouthing him, which was a total lie. But Baker was two levels above me, so Shawn took his word over mine and didn't pick up my option. I didn't get hired anywhere the next season. My career never completely recovered. I mean, I'm here."

R.J. did a sweep of the room with his hand. Dee got it. Working on a show like *Duh!* was a job of last resort for writers whose prior careers had been spent on network and streaming shows. There were solid comedies created for kids. *Duh!* wasn't one of them. "Anyway, I play poker, like a lot of writers."

Dee and Mindy exchanged a knowing look. Poker games were the hanging-out equivalent of trips to the men's room where guys bonded and women rarely got past the door.

"And I know what Baker's calls were about," R.J. continued. "The ones that made him sweat."

. Dee sat up straight, giving him her full attention. She had a feeling he was about to share the kind of scoop she hoped her trip would deliver. "What were they about?"

"Mostly the games were for fun. Small pots. Nobody was ever out more than a few hundred dollars."

Having grown up in a family that was frugal to the point of being parsimonious, Dee couldn't imagine tossing off the loss of "a few hundred dollars." But she kept her judgments to herself. "I know there are high-stakes games too," she said, then took out her phone. "Do you mind if I make a few notes? This is really valuable information, and I don't want to forget anything."

"Go for it," R.J. said. "The big games are where you can get into trouble. And Michael did. I know from friends that he went from casual to illegal high-stakes games run by guys you don't want to owe money to. He racked up major debt, which was what the calls were about. He needed money so badly, he began making 'How to' videos about writing for television that he tried to sell online. It's not a terrible idea, but apparently the videos sucked. Even if they were good, they were never going to deliver the kind of money he needed to pay off what he owed."

Dee, head down, thumbed away on her phone. R.J. sneezed.

"Bless you," she said, still typing.

"Thanks. Allergies. The ratty old couches and chairs in these dressing rooms are dust condominiums."

"Could be a cold," Dee said, still typing. "Writers' rooms are like preschools. One cold gets passed around to everyone. If you come to work, everyone gets mad at you for spreading germs. But if you stay home, you're a wuss."

"Ha," R.J. said, blowing his nose with a rumpled tissue he extracted from his pocket. "Truth."

Mindy's and R.J.'s phones pinged simultaneously. Mindy checked hers. "They're about to shoot the first scene. We need to go. Dee, you good?"

Dee finished typing. "Yes. Thank you, both of you, so, so much. This has been really helpful."

She put away her phone and followed the writers out of the dressing room to the set. A stand-up comedian was warming up the studio audience, while instructing them on the rules of watching the sitcom shoot. Not wanting to disrupt the process, Dee hung back. Mindy kept her company. They watched as the actors were introduced, one by one, to applause and whoops from the audience. The show's star, sixteen-year-old Justin Jeremy, finally waddled out, unhappily imprisoned in a giant roach costume. The audience screamed and cheered, which did nothing to improve his mood.

Dee swallowed a laugh. "A roach costume?" she whispered to Mindy. "Whoa. What did Jeremy do to tick off Dan?"

"His agent called and said Jeremy feels he's not being served well by his material," Mindy whispered back. "He demanded more jokes for him and threw in a few threats about Jeremy walking off the set. So now Jeremy's in a roach costume with no lines at all, stuck listening to the other characters make jokes about *him*."

"A lesson smart actors learn early on," Dee said. "Never get on the bad side of a showrunner. Unless you're into roach costumes."

Jeremy took a pratfall, landing flat on his back. Shaniq Flass, the show's breakout star, who played Jeremy's best friend, snickered, then declared, "I guess roaches check in, but they don't check out. At least not to this party."

He sauntered past the party set's velvet rope, with a teen girl on each arm, as Jeremy flailed helplessly to roars of laughter from the studio audience.

"A roach motel joke?" Dee whispered to Mindy. "How old and stale is that? And it doesn't even make sense. The whole point of the bit is that Jeremy can't check *in* to the party."

"If you want, I'll tell Dan you'd love to join us in coming up with a new joke," Mindy said, baiting her friend.

Dee paled. "I will drop to my stomach and combat-crawl out of here if it means getting out of doing that. Bye."

"Bye," Mindy said, laughing. She grew serious. "And keep me posted on the Michael thing."

"Will do."

Dee made her escape. She was almost at the stage door when she heard a particularly loud roar from the audience. She glanced back to see Jeremy had lost his balance and was once again flailing on his back as the costume designer and her assistant tried to pull him to his feet. Dee pushed open the door and hurried out of the soundstage, more confident than ever in her decision to trade a TV career for a barely functional, retro motel in the middle of nowhere.

The minute Dee returned to the she shed, she conferenced Jeff and Raul to share what she'd learned. "It's a whole passel of new suspects." She heard herself and grimaced. " 'Passel.' I sound old-timey again."

"No worries. We've all been there." Raul spoke reassuringly, although she could hear Jeff chuckle in the background. "Walk us through what you're thinking."

"Michael's killer could be a disgruntled writer. Or a disgruntled poker player from a game where he cheated, because I'm sure he did. Or it could be a disgruntled mobster he owed money to. Or maybe he cheated on Pria with more than one woman, which means the killer could also be a disgruntled lover."

Jeff emitted a frustrated noise. "You said 'disgruntled' so much that the thing where a word doesn't sound like a word anymore is happening to me."

Dee broke open a bag of Cheetos she'd snuck off the crafts services table of a show shooting outdoors on the studio's fake New York street. She popped a few in her mouth and commenced crunching. "Sorry. Bottom line, Michael Adam Baker left a trail of dis . . . contented people behind in L.A."

"I'll contact LAPD and see if they can look into the

poker angle," Raul said. "And do a general look-see at anyone in his life who might have held a grudge against him for some reason. Like R.J., for instance."

"I think R.J. is okay," Dee said through a mouthful of Cheetos. "He got payback by replacing Michael on *Duh!* after he was fired, crummy show or not. But I know there are other writers out there who Michael undercut and hate him for it. I just don't know exactly who they are."

"That's for LAPD to find out," Raul said. "You done good. Now it's their turn."

The three signed off. Dee licked Cheeto dust from her fingers, then washed up and readied for bed, eager for morning and her return to the Golden.

At 7:00 a.m., Dee was blasted awake by a cacophony of leaf blowers from the McMansions on either side of her dad's house. She staggered out of bed and into the shower, then dried off and slipped into sweats and an oversized T-shirt, comfort clothes for the drive home. Once dressed, she packed her carry-on and left the she shed.

She found her father in the kitchen, which smelled of fresh coffee. "How can something that tastes so bad smell so good?" Dee asked with a sigh. She filled a mug with water for tea and placed it in the microwave.

"I got bagels," Sam said, pointing to a spread of bagels, lox, cream cheese, and tomato slices.

"Yum. Thanks."

Dee picked up a sesame bagel and dropped it into the bagel guillotine base. She shoved the sharp cutter into the bagel, splitting it in half, then did the same to a bagel for her father. She heaped fixings onto the bagels, setting one at her place and the other at her dad's, then made her cup of tea. Sam sat down across from her at the retro green-and-gray dinette set Sibby had rescued decades earlier from a neighbor who'd consigned it to oversized trash pickup.

Dee watched her father meticulously assemble a loaded bagel, layer by layer. Whoever said daughters look like their fathers was dead-on when it came to the Sterns. Except the annoying lack of cheekbones, looking at Sam was like looking in a mirror for Dee. She'd inherited the almond shape and hazel color of his eyes, the slight upturn of his nose, along with a smatter of freckles on the bridge of it. The oval faces of father and daughter featured full lips and fair skin that only burned and never tanned.

After breakfast, Dee went through her grandmother's costumes, which were stored in the guest room closet. "*Yes.*" She triumphantly held up a square dance dress to show her father. "I should see if there's anything else useful in here." Dee pushed aside one hanger after another. "Nurse's uniform. Victorian dowager. Old-lady outfit. Ha, here's one." She pulled out a lacy red-and-black saloon girl costume. "If I wore this around Goldsgone, maybe they'd like me better."

Sam struck a pose, planting his fists on his hips and furrowing his brow with comic exaggeration. "What in tarnation?! Someone not likin' my li'l girl? Well, durn those folks."

"You'd be surprised how much you sound like a Goldsgonedian," Dee said, her tone rueful. She placed the saloon girl costume back in the closet and the two left the guest room.

Sam walked his daughter outside the house to her car. "Safe drive home, sweetie."

"Thanks."

Dee hugged her father. A plane soared overhead, and he clicked the clicker she didn't know he was holding. He held it up to the sky and cried out in a flawless English accent, "We shall fight in the beaches, we shall fight on the ground. We shall never give up!"

"Fight on, Sir Churchill," Dee said.

She gave her father a pat on the back and got into the car. She glanced at her rearview mirror and could see Sam cursing the disappearing airplane as she drove off.

On her way out of town, Dee stopped at Les Fromages in Beverly Hills to pick up the large quantity of hugely expensive cheese and meats Serena had asked her to pick up. She then took Wilshire Boulevard to the freeway, her stress level decreasing as city driving transitioned to freeway and then the two-lane blacktop toward Foundgold.

The road wound past rolling golden hills dotted with live oaks and outcroppings of craggy granite, along with the occasional pocket of bright green, a remnant of the unusually wet winter. As the elevation increased, the oaks ceded the landscape to white fir, cedar, and ponderosa pines, with periwinkle wildflowers providing a pop of color. A stream meandered alongside the road, then headed off in another direction. Dee rounded a bend to a breathtaking view of a valley surrounded by the grandeur of the Sierra Nevada mountains. She drank in the spectacular sight and said a silent prayer of thanks to the Fates that had brought her to this part of the world.

She continued the drive toward her new home, following the gentle curves of the road. Not far from the Golden, she found herself growing sleepy thanks to waking up too early. Her eyelids fluttered. Fearing she might fall asleep at the wheel, Dee pulled over onto a wide patch of dirt next to a dense patch of forest. "Five minutes," she murmured as she put the driver's seat all the way back.

She was about to doze off, when the car began to shake. "Earthquake!" Dee yelled, jolting up to sitting. "Please don't damage the Golden, please don't damage the Golden," she prayed out loud as she quickly raised her seat back to its proper position.

The shaking stopped, replaced by a sort of thumping noise. Confused, Dee looked around and behind her. Her eyes locked with another's, and she let out a scream. *"Bear!"*

The large animal stared at her, then resumed his quest to break into the trunk of the car, where Dee had stashed Serena's charcuterie. Dee started the car engine and, with a shaking hand, flung it into Drive. She peeled out of her spot, leaving a sulking bear in her wake.

Her heart raced as she drove, but she calmed down by the time she parked in Serena's driveway. Serena had texted to let her know she wouldn't be home, but Dee could leave the ingredients with Callan's assistant, Marisa.

Dee texted Marisa that she was there. A moment later, the garage door opened. Callan's assistant appeared in the doorway leading into the house, a resentful expression on her face.

She marched toward Dee, who got out of the car and popped open the trunk. "We better get all this inside. I finally met Stoney the bear on my way here. He dropped by when I was parked on the side of the road, hoping to help himself to a snack."

"Whatevs. I don't care about Serena's stupid pretend job. I have real work to do."

Marisa roughly grabbed a shopping bag from the trunk. Dee took hold of the other two bags and followed her into the house and up the stairs to the kitchen, struggling with the weight of the bags. They deposited them on the room's giant island. Marisa's bag tipped over and a Brie wheel rolled out. She ignored it. Dee managed to stop the roll before the high-end *fromage* wound up on the floor. "I think Serena's boards are wonderful," she said. Despite her own skepticism about charcuterie artistry as a career, she felt compelled to defend her quasi friend.

Marisa made a face. "Oh, please." Her voice dripped with disdain. "L.A. has these women who, I swear, were created in labs just to be wives to rich guys. Callan deserves *so* much better. Like, so, *so* much better."

Dee took note of the starry-eyed expression that went along with Marisa mentioning her boss's name. She hadn't realized how deep Marisa's devotion to her boss ran— possibly to dangerous levels. She wondered how far the assistant would go to support and protect him.

"I think Serena genuinely loves and appreciates Callan. Not like Michael Adam Baker."

It was a stupendously clunky transition, but Marisa didn't seem to notice. She smirked. "Oh, Baker got his. I made sure of it."

Dee adopted a gossipy tone. "You did? How?"

Marisa leaned her elbows on the kitchen island and rested her chin on her palms. She beamed with self-satisfaction. "I know everything about Callan's clients. *Everything.* All I'll say is that someone, wink wink, might have told a guy running an underground poker game that Michael wasn't going to pay off his debt. The guy confronted Michael and scared him so much, he left town. He was desperate for money. *Desperate.* But someone, wink wink, also spread word that Michael totally lost it as a writer. He was *ruined.*"

"Wow . . . that's . . . Wow!" Dee congratulated herself

at managing to hide her horror at Marisa's ruthless machi-
nations.

Marisa's cell buzzed with an incoming text. She checked
and her face lit up. "It's Callan. He needs me."

"I have to go anyway. I want to get the meat smell out
of my car before it gets dark. This way, Stoney the bear
won't come back looking for treats."

Dee made a quick exit. She drove off with her question
answered.

How far would Marisa go in service of Callan?

Very, wink wink.

CHAPTER 20

Dee made it to the Golden as twilight shed its own golden light on the silhouetted Sierra Nevada mountains. She got out of her car and took a moment to fill her lungs with the deliciously fresh air. After a few intoxicating, deep breaths, Dee removed her carry-on from the trunk and was about to go into her apartment, when a glow from the west corner of the property caught her eye. She took a tentative step forward to see what was casting the glow and let out an exclamation of delight.

The pool's refurbishment had been completed in Dee's brief absence. The contractor Jeff hired had worked magic, replacing the old pool paint with a rich, sparkling yellow. Coupled with the reflection of the sun on the newly filled pool's surface, it gleamed like the gold nugget its design paid homage to.

Dee picked up her carry-on, locked her car, and ran into the motel lobby, where she found Jeff manning the reservations counter. "The pool! It's gorgeous!" She ran around the counter and hugged him. He winced and groaned, and she released him. "Sorry. What's wrong?"

"Shawn's 'private session.' But I'll get to that. You really like the pool? I wanted to surprise you with the finished product."

"I love it. All we need now is to get the sign fixed and our curb appeal will be leveled up to the max."

"Yes!" Jeff fist-pumped, which prompted another groan. He massaged his shoulder.

"Okay, I need the story behind all this pain. Let me put my bag away and get the meat smell out of my car and I'll be right back."

"Meat smell?" Jeff, confused, said this to Dee's back as she hurried off.

She deposited her bag in her apartment, where she gathered up cleaning products and a pine-scented car air freshener she'd received as a sample promotional item for a possible complimentary guest gift. Dee wiped down her car trunk and added the air freshener for good measure. Judging by the heft of Stoney, or whatever bear had hungered for the charcuterie ingredients she'd escorted to Serena, Dee wanted to make sure any scents emanating from her car were a turnoff, not a turn-on. Once satisfied with her work, she returned to the motel lobby.

Jeff sat on the lobby couch, his feet up on the white-washed oak coffee table. He nursed a beer. Another sat on the coffee table across from him, in front of a matching oak lounge chair. Dee plopped down and opened the beer. "Sorry your session with Shawn was a literal pain. Did you pick up any helpful intel?"

"Basically, no. He did reinforce our theory that whatever friendship existed between him and Michael was long gone and replaced by full-on animosity, at least on Radinsky's part. The one takeaway from the workout is that I think he went extra hard on me to send a message: Back off. Or else."

Dee took this in. "That's scary. He's a strong guy. He could seriously hurt someone."

Jeff grimaced as he adjusted his position. "Don't I know it."

Dee sipped her beer. She mulled over the information Jeff had imparted. "We can't back off. We can't afford to."

"I know. But I think we need to take a more subtle approach. Make it look like we're not investigating, even though we are. Like, tonight at the hoedown. We should look like we're just there to have fun."

It was Dee's turn to groan. "That'll take some acting on my part. And, unfortunately, the acting gene missed a generation in my family."

"You found a dress, didn't you?"

Dee nodded. "Trimmed all over with rickrack, which I bet is the first time anyone's used that word in this century."

"Good. I got a shirt from the mercantile, which scored points with Verity." Jeff rose to standing, with much difficulty. "I bet when we're 'in costume,' like you showbiz people say, we'll find our square-dance-loving characters."

Jeff's assumption proved right. The next night, once Dee slipped into her late grandmother's dress—a becoming shade of sage green, with a sweetheart neckline and a full skirt that twirled out when Dee spun around in front of the mirror—she found herself looking forward to the dance. She loved how the green of the dress complemented her hazel eyes and the nipped waist accentuated her small waist, while the skirt and petticoats hid the hips and bottom where she carried about ten extra pounds.

She arrived at the hoedown on the arm of Jeff, who

looked dashing in his black Western shirt, black jeans, and purple bolotie. The energy in the barn was infectious and Dee found herself bobbing along with the bluegrass tunes being sawed out by the fiddler, banjo player, and guitarist, who comprised the event's small square dance band. "This is like that old TV show *Hee Haw,*" Dee said. "And I mean that as a compliment. I've seen clips of it and everyone looks like they're having such a good time."

The folksy space was lit by strands of incandescent string lights, which bathed the festivities in a warm light. One side of the barn featured a lineup of wooden tables laden with donated dishes prepared by the locals. Beverages, including a giant punch bowl, sat on tables lining the opposite wall. The dance floor took up most of the center space, with tables for dining clustered at the barn's far end.

"Well, hey there, you two!"

The mystery of this cheery greeting coming from Dee's archenemy, Verity Gillespie, was instantly solved by the flirty smile the shopkeeper bestowed on Jeff.

"Ooh," she fawned. "Didn't I tell you that shirt was made for you?"

"You did," Jeff said, puffing out his chest.

Dee managed to squelch an eye roll. "You look very pretty," Dee said to Verity, going with the moment. "I love your nails. And your dress."

"Thank you." Verity twirled. Her bright orange dress, trimmed in lace and gold rickrack, splayed out, revealing layers of color-coordinated petticoats. Then she held out her hand to give Dee a closer look at her nails, which were a blinding orange with miniature gold rickrack painted on each tip. "It's like the kids say, 'Go big or go home.'"

"Well, you sure went big," Dee said.

"Um-hmm." Verity's vague response sent the message she wasn't sure this was a compliment. She hooked her arm around Jeff's free arm. "You mind if I steal your business partner? I made my famous cowboy casserole and I want to make sure he gets a serving before it's all gone."

"Go for it." Dee gestured for the two to take off, and Verity escorted an annoyingly willing Jeff to the buffet.

Dee scanned the crowd. The dance hadn't begun, so most partygoers were several people deep at the food and beverage tables. She saw Elmira and Raul, who waved to her. She returned the wave with a smile, then eyeballed a cluster of familiar faces hovering near the punch bowl. Restauranteur Liza, trainer Shawn, contractor Brian, and real estate agent Jonas were deep in conversation. Each wore a different expression, none pleasant.

Jonas happened to glance toward Dee. The look of concern he'd worn a second earlier disappeared, replaced by a smile. Dee doubted it was sincere, but didn't care. She grabbed it as an invitation to join them, whether they liked it or not. And judging by Shawn's glower when she waved and started toward them, at least one of the four did not.

On her way over, she passed Marisa. The agent's assistant, who was typing on a tablet, had apparently not received the dress code memo. No square dance clothing kitsch for her; she was attired in funereal black from head to toe.

"Hi, Marisa," Dee said. "I didn't expect to see you here."

"I'm here for Callan," she said without looking up, per usual. "He wants to move from agenting to producing and asked me to check this out to see if we can turn it into something. I'm thinking maybe a horror film."

Dee heard a half giggle/half cackle and turned to see

Verity ratcheting up the flirting with Jeff by twirling so hard she exposed her lace square dance panties. "I think you might be onto something," she said to Marisa.

Dee arrived at the punch bowl to find only Liza still there. The women exchanged greetings and sincere compliments on their outfits. Liza looked stunning in an aqua dress that was as simple as a square dance dress could be.

"Do you want some punch?" she offered. "It's alcohol-free, but there's a big selection of booze under the table if you want to spike it."

Dee laughed. "I'll pass on spiking it, but I'll take a cup."

"You got it."

Liza dipped the ladle into the bowl and filled a cup. The crowd around the beverage table grew larger. Someone jostled her and the liquid in the cup sloshed over the edge. "Darn. I overfilled it. Sorry."

"Not a problem. You can't have too much punch."

As Dee took the cup from Liza, she felt herself crowded in on both sides and almost lost her grip on it. "Maybe we should move away from here."

"Good idea. They're about to start the dancing anyway."

Dee and Liza left the beverage area and stood at the edge of the dance floor. The caller had positioned himself on the stage. Dee's good mood took a hit when she saw the caller was none other than Chief District Ranger Tom O'Bryant. He wore a Western shirt in two shades of brown, with pearled snaps holding on for dear life against his potbelly. His jeans were held up by a belt featuring a giant buckle shaped like a steer's head, and a ten-gallon hat sat atop his round head.

"Can I get a *yeeha*?" he roared into the mic.

"*Yeeha!*" the crowd roared back.

Dee joined in the fun, but the thick air in the barn was

beginning to get to her. She felt clammy and slightly woozy. "You sure that punch wasn't spiked?" she asked Liza.

"Positive," the restauranteur responded. "Verity would issue a lifetime ban on me if I disobeyed the rules."

The band struck up a lively tune and O'Bryant called the dancers to the floor. Jonas Jones appeared at Dee's side. "You up for dancing?"

"Sure," Dee said, making a halfhearted attempt to convince herself she was saying yes because it offered an opportunity for one-on-one time with a suspect, and not because the real estate agent was ridiculously handsome.

Jonas glanced Jeff's way. "I'm not gonna get in trouble with your boyfriend, am I?"

"He's not my boyfriend," Dee said. "He's basically my brother from another mother. And props to you for extracting that info from me, even if the approach was a little clunky."

Jonas threw back his head and laughed, then took Dee's hand and led her onto the dance floor. They joined three other couples, one of whom was Verity and Jeff. Dee shot him a look that said, *You're having too much fun to actually be investigating*, but he ignored her.

The fiddler launched into a peppy tune and the other musicians joined in. "Dancers, honor your partner," Ranger O'Bryant called. Jonas bowed to Dee, who responded with a curtsy, which she assumed was the old-fashioned move on the woman's part. "Now, honor your corner," O'Bryant instructed.

Dee curtsied to Jeff. "I wish I had a picture of this, my feminist friend," he joked. "I'd blackmail you with it."

Dee stuck her tongue at him and turned back to Jonas.

"Dancers, circle to the left!" O'Bryant called out.

The dance floor became a sea of groups circling to the left. Dee felt dizzy and swayed slightly.

"Are you okay?" Jonas asked.

"Yes. Just not used to circling, I guess."

"Now circle to the right till you get back home!"

The dancers circled to the right until they assumed their original positions. O'Bryant began barking out square dance orders like a drill sergeant. "Do-si-do! Forward and back! Sides, up to the middle and come right back!"

The music sped up and the pace of dancing suddenly increased. Jonas held on to Dee, who felt increasingly light-headed.

"Are you sure you're all right?" he asked, concerned. "You're perspiring and you look pale."

"Swing your partner!" O'Bryant call-ordered.

"I'm not feeling great," Dee confessed to Jonas as he swung her.

"Now, swing your corner!"

Jonas passed her on to Jeff. They swung; then she returned to Jonas. She flashed on R.J. sneezing in the *Duh!* dressing room and said to Jonas, "I think I may have picked up a bug in L.A. I met with a writer who said he had allergies, but it was probably a cold."

"Promenade all till you get back home!"

Dee and Jonas crossed arms together and promenaded in their square. Dee tripped over Jonas's feet. "Sorry."

The apology came out slurred. The barn began to whirl. Dee's vision blurred. She heard a ringing in her ears. She pulled away from Jonas and staggered backward.

And the world went black.

CHAPTER 21

Dee regained consciousness to find herself lying on a pile of hay in a stable attached to the barn. The worried faces hovering over her came in and out of focus. Her head filled with a whooshing sound. She saw mouths moving and struggled to make out what people were saying.

". . . Hasn't eaten."

Jeff said this as he held out what was either a roll or a rock. Dee couldn't tell. She also wondered why he had the body of a bear.

"Stoney?"

She managed to get that out, but her tongue felt thick. She had no idea if anyone understood her.

"Give her water."

Whoever said this spoke in slow motion. A glass of water floated in front of her. She tried reaching for it, but kept missing. "Stop . . . Can't."

She saw two bears exchange a look. The baby bear resembled the sheriff Raul. The papa bear's girth was contained by a belt sporting a buckle with Ranger O'Bryant's face on it, but with stag horns instead of ears. She heard one of the bears say something that sounded like "balance" before she lost consciousness.

* * *

Dee slowly opened her eyes. Light streaming in through an unfamiliar window made her wince. She felt like she'd had the world's worst hangover, which made no sense. She'd only had a sip of beer the night before and virgin punch at the hoedown.

She slowly brought herself to sitting and saw she was in a hospital room. "Whaaa?"

She rubbed her eyes and then realized a nurse stood at the foot of her hospital bed. "Where am I? Who are you?" Panicked, she clutched her chest. "Did I die? Am I in heaven? Please tell me I'm not. I want it to be so much more than a hospital room."

The nurse chortled. "Hon, I'll be the first person to tell you this place ain't close to being heaven."

"Where exactly am I?"

"Gold County Medical Center." She wheeled over a portable blood pressure monitor. "I gotta check a few things on you." The nurse wrapped the blood pressure cuff around Dee's left arm, then slipped a pulsometer on Dee's finger and ran the tests. "Looks good. All normal." She removed the pulsometer and unwrapped the cuff. "Some people wanna talk to you. First, breakfast."

The nurse left as an orderly brought a simple breakfast of scrambled eggs, bacon, and toast, along with water and orange juice. It hit Dee she was starving, and she scarfed down every drop of food. Exhausted and feeling weak, she leaned back on the hospital pillow. She heard a light tap on the doorframe.

"Come in."

Raul and O'Bryant entered the room, wearing uniforms and matching serious expressions. "How are you feeling?" Raul asked.

"Better . . . I guess." Dee massaged her temples, which didn't help the headache she feared might never go away. "To be honest, still not great."

O'Bryant lowered himself into the room's one chair. Raul stood at the foot of Dee's bed, arms crossed, legs spread a foot apart.

"There's a reason for that," the park ranger said. "You were drugged."

"I recognized the symptoms," Raul said, making sure O'Bryant didn't take full credit for the diagnosis. "Very weak, in and out of consciousness, loss of speech and motor skills, altered mental state. The fact you still have symptoms more than twelve hours later—"

"Wait, what?" Dee sat up straighter and winced from the migraine-like pain that shot through her. "Exactly how long have I been out?"

"Since eight-thirty last night," O'Bryant said. "It's eleven-thirty a.m., so—"

"Fifteen hours." Raul did the math.

"Yikes." Shivering as much from shock as from the room's chill, Dee pulled the thin hospital blanket up to her chin. "Do we know for sure?"

"About the drugging?" Raul eyed her. "Yes. You don't remember doing the test?"

Dee closed her eyes. "I remember two bears taking me into the forest."

"That was a nurse and doctor taking you into the bathroom to pee into a cup for a urine sample," O'Bryant said with characteristic bluntness.

Dee opened her eyes.

"We assume someone dropped Rohypnol into your punch cup at the hoedown. Forensics is going through the discarded punch cups to see if they can find anything—

the doctored cup with the perp's fingerprints on it is the hope—but they're understaffed, so it could take a while. In the meantime, tell us what you remember about when you got the drink."

Dee scrunched her eyes closed again and replayed the moments surrounding her punch bowl visit. "I saw Liza Chen, Shawn Radinsky, Brian Oakhurst, and Jonas Jones talking and went over to say hello." She hoped that framing her sleuthing expedition as a bland bit of socializing would fly. Neither officer said anything. Relieved, she continued. "There were tons of people at the hoedown, so it took me a while to get to them. By the time I did, I only saw Liza there. She poured me a cup of punch, which she said was nonalcoholic and tasted that way. The beverage area was four or five people deep and someone jostled her when she gave it to me, and then I got jostled too."

"Could you see who bumped into either of you?" Raul asked.

Dee shook her head with regret. "No. I wasn't paying attention. I was only thinking about how much fun I was having at the hoedown." *Here's hoping they buy that.* She snuck a look at Raul. The expression on his face told her he didn't.

"All righty, then." O'Bryant stood up. "We spoke to your doctor. She'll be by shortly to check on you, but thinks you should be ready to leave by later this afternoon. We'll keep you posted on the investigation on your end. But you need to eighty-six your amateur sleuthing. It's gonna get you in even bigger trouble than it already has."

"Yes, sir," Dee said, cowed. O'Bryant hadn't bought her disclaimer either. She grudgingly gave the man credit for being sharper than she thought.

The officers left. Dee picked up her cell phone, which was awash with worried messages. Too tired to talk, she texted Jeff an approximate pickup time, then laid her head on the pillow. As she drifted off, she pondered over who might have roofied her. And why? Her last thought before her eyelids fluttered shut: *If they thought they'd scare me off, they were dead wrong. Oops. Poor choice of words.*

Jeff picked her up at 5:00 p.m., along with floral arrangements sent from well-wishers, including a few Goldsgonedians, which touched Dee.

"It makes me feel like I'm starting to make friends here," she told Jeff as he pushed her out of the hospital in the wheelchair the hospital insisted she ride in order to exit. "Although if there's a way to check and see if any of the flowers have been sprayed with a poison that will kill me if I inhale it, it wouldn't be a bad idea."

"Nothing comes to mind, so maybe sniff them from a distance," Jeff said.

She arrived home to delirious jumps and licks from Nugget. "There's also a gift from Serena," Jeff said, pointing to the refrigerator.

Dee opened the fridge and took out a large wooden platter laden with a huge variety of meats, cheeses, dried fruits, and nuts. "This is so sweet. Look! She spelled 'Feel better' in rolled-up slices of prosciutto."

Jeff helped himself to a few slices. "Now it's 'eel etter.'"

"It's practically dinnertime. We might as well eat."

She and Jeff pulled up stools to the kitchen counter and set upon the board. As they ate, "accidentally" dropping an occasional meat or cheese morsel on the floor near Nugget, Dee tried again to remember any suspects who were in the vicinity of the punch bowl.

"Argh," she said, frustrated. "It's like my brain's got a foggy film over it."

"That's the drug," Jeff said. "It's gonna take at least another day to get it completely out of your system. Maybe longer."

Dee scowled. "Terrif. What am I supposed to do until then?"

Jeff stopped eating and faced her. "Delilah, someone drugged you." He spoke with an intensity she'd never heard before. "This time, you were knocked out. The next time, you might die. You need to step back from even thinking about investigating Michael's murder. We both do."

Dee gaped at him. Then incredulity turned to anger. "No! No way am I going to scurry off like some scared rabbit. The Golden is on the line here, *Jeffrey*." She threw his whole name back at him, like he'd done with her. "Plus, a human being was murdered. On our property. If there's anything I can do to expose him or her, I'm going to do it. Full stop."

Jeff casually popped a few almonds in his mouth. "So am I."

Dee screwed her eyes shut and placed her hands on her head, trying to make sense of his about-face. "What? You just gave me a whole speech about not doing anything. Is this opposite day? I'm so confused."

"My speech was a practice speech. The killer wants to scare us off. We're going to let them think they have."

"*Ooh.*" Dee relaxed. "I get it. I may not have gotten the acting gene, but someone in this partnership did." She applauded, then stopped and shook a finger at Jeff. "But you didn't have to scare *me* like that. Not fair."

"I do think you should take it easy. And I have plenty of motel promotional work to do. If we lay low, it'll send the message we're backing off."

Dee yawned. "I have to admit, I'm not feeling a hundred percent yet. I wouldn't mind resting until I'm fully operational."

"Good. We have a plan."

"Yes. But this case has to be solved before someone else is killed. Like me."

Jeff hopped off his stool. "Do you want me to spend the night here?"

"No, it's okay. I doubt anyone's going to try anything so soon after my drugging. Plus, I've got my guard dog with me." She gave Nugget an affectionate pat on the head.

Jeff wrapped up charcuterie to take with him as a midnight snack and left after making Dee promise she'd text him if she felt any concern for her safety. Dee put away the rest of the food board, then took Nugget for a quick walk.

While waiting for the doggy to do his business, it occurred to Dee that she'd yet to watch any of Michael's writing "tutorials." Nugget signaled he was done, and they returned to the apartment. She rewarded him with a bone, then powered up her laptop.

A pretentious website popped up at the top of the search she entered for "Michael Adam Baker." The landing page featured a list of his how-to videos—none of which she could open unless she paid twenty-five dollars to subscribe to Baker's channel. Dee reluctantly typed in her credit card information and joined nineteen other viewers who paid for the privilege of hearing the writer pontificate.

If Michael thought these videos would be a cash cow with thousands of subscribers clinging to his every word, wow, was he wrong, Dee thought. She clicked on one and the late writer filled the screen from his shoulders up.

He flashed a smile that was more of a smirk and then launched into his spiel. "Hey. I'm writer-producer Michael

Adam Baker. I'm not gonna bore you with my credits. You can look me up on IMDB for that. And I'm not gonna share my screen with some BS PowerPoint listing the steps to great writing and a successful career, blah blah blah. I'm just gonna talk to you. About work. About life. About *my* work. *My* life." He flashed another smarmy smile. "My writer life, that is."

Dee managed to stay awake during the first video of Baker bloviating. She forced herself to watch clips of two more. She paged through the rest. One titled "Those Who Can't" sparked her curiosity. But assuming Michael would never out himself as "one who couldn't," she kept going until she landed on a video titled "How the Past Creates a Successful Present." *Maybe there's something here about his experiences in Goldsgone that could provide a lead,* Dee thought as she pressed Play.

A half hour later, she woke up with her head on the computer keyboard. "Thanks for an hour of my life I won't get back," she said to Baker's frozen image on the screen. Dee turned off the computer. Still feeling the aftereffects of her drugging, she decided to shelve sleuthing and turn in for the night.

After the discomfort of the hospital trappings, Dee welcomed the warmth of her own bed. But to her frustration, sleep proved elusive. Her mind kept flipping back to the moments before and after she drank her cup of punch. Still, no faces formed out of the memories. She decided to tread a new path. It occurred to her she hadn't given much thought to when she found Michael sneaking around her apartment. He must have been looking for something. But what? She'd assumed he was hunting down information that would come in handy when he transposed her life into a pilot script. But what if that wasn't why he was snoop-

ing? Could the reason be hidden in one of Jasper Gormley's trunks? She remembered something he'd said when
she was giving him a tour of the Golden: "Jasper was a
weird guy." He'd added that the gas attendant had told
him this, but now whe realized it was a lie. Michael's history in the area meant he knew Jasper Gormley—or at
least knew of him.

Dawn had barely broken when Dee, still wearing her
sleep tee, resumed hunting through Gormley's belongings.
Two hours later, she was surrounded by piles of worn
clothes destined for the dustbin, half-empty chewing to-
bacco packets, an assortment of loose screws, and a couple of mismatched shoes.

"I give up," a defeated Dee said to Nugget. "There's
nothing valuable here and now I need a shower in the
worst way."

The dog snuffled and stuck his snout into the final
trunk. He nosed around and began whimpering. "You
found something you want, buddy?" Dee asked, wiping
dust and sweat from her brow. "Let me get it for you."

She bent over the trunk and rifled through its contents
until she found an extremely chewed-up baseball. Nugget
barked joyfully. Dee tossed the ball, and he bounded after
it. Successful in his quest, he deposited himself on the rug
with the ball between his front paws and commenced
gnawing at it.

"I'm glad one of us got lucky today," Dee said, amused.

She was about to close the trunk lid, when she noticed
something. In his mission to retrieve the ball, Nugget had
knocked the top off a small box. Curious, Dee removed
the box from the trunk and peered into it. She let out a
gasp.

Inside lay a mesh bag filled with shiny gold nuggets.

CHAPTER 22

Jeff examined the shimmering nugget he held in his hand. He let out an impressed whistle, then carefully placed it back in the bag. "I think we found what Michael Adam Baker was looking for."

"I know!" Dee hopped from one foot to the other with excitement. "We need to get these appraised. Jeff, think of what we could do with the money. Fix every leak in the roof. Upgrade all the appliances. Finally fix the neon sign. No more OLD Motel. We can truly welcome guests to"— she made a theatrical gesture with her hands to paint a picture—"the GOLDEN."

Jeff handed Dee the bag of gold. He pecked away at the search engine on his phone. "There's a jewelry store in Goldsgone that buys and sells gold and weighs nuggets and flakes tourists find."

"Let's go." Dee clutched the bag in her hand. "This may be the reason Michael was murdered. We need to get it appraised, then stored in a safety deposit box at the bank."

They took Dee's car to Goldsgone and lucked out by finding a parking spot right in front of the Gold Mine Jewel and Gold Exchange, which they quickly identified by the ersatz nineteenth-century wooden sign dangling from black iron hooks, which Dee assumed were fashioned by the current town blacksmith.

The duo parked and entered the store. "Yay, a store in Goldsgone that doesn't smell like sarsaparilla," Dee murmured to Jeff.

"God *forbid*," a male voice declared.

Dee glanced around to see who spoke. A cheery, chubby-cheeked man in his late thirties stood behind a row of wooden display cases running the length of the shop. He wore the costume of a prosperous nineteenth-century jewelry store proprietor. A patterned vest sat atop his crisp white shirt, with a black cravat tucked into the collar. A gold chain draped across the front of the vest, connecting to a pocket watch tucked into the vest's front pocket. His leaning-toward-doughy frame stopped a few inches short of Jeff's six-foot-plus height.

"So much for thinking I was whispering," Dee said, embarrassed.

The man waved a hand to dismiss her concerns. "Please. I love my hometown, but even I can't stand that horrid scent." He rounded the corner at the near end of the display case row and came to them, making sure not to bump into the additional cases creating an island in the center of the shop. He extended a hand first to Dee, then to Jeff. Dee noticed the cuff links on his shirt were small red hearts. She also registered the anachronistic touch of three rows of piercings on each ear. "Owen Mudd Junior. Went under another name when I lived in S.F. because 'Mudd.' Ugh." He shuddered dramatically, then grinned. "But I'm owning it now that I'm back in the 'Gone."

"You lived in S.F.?" Jeff said, lighting up. "Me too."

The two compared geographical notes, while Dee impatiently tapped her foot and cleared her throat. The message she was trying to send went unanswered until Owen finally asked, "So, what brings you here today?" He flashed a coy smile. "Ring shopping?" He held up his left ring finger and winked.

"No, no," Dee said, eager to prevent a rumor from starting and spreading. "Jeff and I are just friends."

"We tried the marriage thing. Did *not* work out." Jeff made a comical face and pretended to hide the finger he pointed at Dee. She glared at him.

Owen chuckled. "Whatever you're here for, I'm glad you stopped in. I've seen you both in passing and wanted to introduce myself. My boyfriend and I are beyond thrilled there's some new blood in town. At this point, everybody in Goldsgone and Foundgold is probably related to each other."

Being welcomed rather than ostracized by a local made Dee almost giddy with joy. "We're glad someone in Goldsgone is actually happy to see us. Getting acclimated's been kind of a rough road."

Owen gave a sympathetic nod. "I can imagine. I grew up in Goldsgone, so I know all about the cult of Michael Adam Baker." He wrinkled his nose in distaste. "I never got it myself. He always seemed the legend-in-his-own-mind type to me."

"On-target description," Dee said. She lowered her voice. "We have to show you something."

"It's valuable," Jeff said, matching her tone. "Probably best to show you in private."

"Not a problem. I'll lock the door and we can go to my office in the back."

Owen secured the front door and adjusted the clock sign dangling from the doorknob to read BACK IN TWO SHAKES OF A LAMB'S TAIL. He motioned to Dee and Jeff to follow him. The three walked to the back of the shop, where he lifted a curtain that separated the main area from a small office. A gold-weighing scale sat center stage on the room's desk.

Dee and Jeff sat on wooden Shaker chairs facing the desk. Owen took a seat opposite them. "So let's see what you have."

Dee reached into her fanny pack and pulled out the bag of nuggets and gave it to Owen. She clutched Jeff's hand as they waited to hear his estimate of its value.

The jeweler pressed a button that illuminated a magnifying lamp. He held a nugget under the magnifying glass and studied it intently. "Amazing. I haven't seen one of these in years."

Dee's heart thumped. "What are they worth?"

"They're priceless," Owen said. Dee and Jeff squeezed each other's hands. "In terms of memories."

Dee and Jeff dropped their hands. *"Memories?"* Dee echoed, beset with a sinking feeling.

"Jasper Gormley used to give these to his favorite guests as a token of appreciation. They were his 'solid-gold guests.' He'd give them to us kids too, sometimes." A warm smile crossed Owen's face as he reminisced. "He was a good guy. Ornery on the outside, but his heart . . ." Owen, emotional, tapped his chest. "That was 'solid gold.'"

"Uh-huh," Jeff said. "What are the nuggets worth in money terms?"

"Oh. Nothing. Financially, they're worthless. They're not gold, they're brass." He held one up to the magnifying glass and motioned for Dee and Jeff to check it out. "See that dark spot? Tarnish. It's on a couple of them." Owen picked up another, smaller nugget. "These are what we panned for in his sluice."

Dee and Jeff reacted with blank stares, and Owen explained. "Pretend panning for gold is a big thing in these parts." He rolled his eyes. "'These parts.' Listen to me! I've been back way too long, and it's only been six months."

"You were saying," Dee prompted.

"Yes, sluices. I guess you haven't noticed, because you don't have kids, but a lot of the tourist spots in Gold County have fake sluices so families can 'pan for gold.' They love it."

"Do you remember where Jasper's was?" Dee asked, hoping to salvage something useful from the epic fail of a day.

"Of course. You know how there's a long overgrowth of vines between all the bushes on the far side of the pool? The sluice is under the vines. I'm sure you can resurrect it." Owen placed the nuggets back in the bag and handed it to Dee. "I'm sorry I don't have better news. Visitors show up all the time with a nugget or a flake of real gold, thinking they're going to be zillionaires, and I have to deliver the bad news that they won't be able to buy a candy bar with what their 'haul' is worth. I'm constantly disappointing people. It's the hardest part of my job."

He stood up and Dee and Jeff glumly followed suit. Owen lifted the curtain and they exited the office for the store. "Thank you for being so patient with us," Dee said. "Verity nailed it when she labeled us citiots."

"Ugh, Verity." Owen mimed gagging. "You are not citiots. But she *is* a beeyotch."

He unlocked the door and removed the clock sign. Dee and Jeff left the shop with promises to let Owen know when they'd be free for dinner.

"At least we made a friend," Dee said once they were outside.

Jeff responded with a dissatisfied grunt. He squinted in the harsh midmorning sun as he gazed across the street at the Golden Grub Café. "You up for some day drinking?"

"Sure." Dee held up the bag of worthless nuggets. "You think they'd let us pay with these?"

They crossed the street to the hostess stand. Since no one was manning it, and the café was almost empty, Dee and Jeff seated themselves at an outdoor table. A teenage waiter took their order of two lagers from a local brewery, along with an order of the café's homemade potato chips.

"That was a whole lotta nothing," Jeff grumbled after the waiter left to place their order. "Although"—he lightened up a bit—"I think bringing the sluice back to life is a stellar idea."

"Agreed. We can make our own nuggets. Or," Dee added, warming to the idea, "we can give out those cute little sacks of gum that look like gold nuggets."

"Nice," Jeff said, offering a thumbs-up of approval. "And less expensive too."

To Dee's surprise, Liza appeared at the table with their order. "Dee, I'm glad you're here." She handed beers to each of them and placed the chips on the table. "I was worried. How are you?"

"Better." Dee helped herself to a chip, which was extra thick and delicious. "Approaching a hundred percent, but not completely there yet."

Liza shook her head. "I cannot believe someone would do something like that. In Goldsgone. It can't be a local. It has to be some sketchy visitor."

Dee, who was about to take a plug of beer, put down the bottle and eyed her. When she spoke, her response brimmed with sarcasm. "Really? You don't think it was one of the wonderful Goldsgonedians who've welcomed us with *such* open arms and haven't remotely given us all kinds of attitude for trying to figure out which one of you killed our first guest? And please don't tell me you think *that* was the act of some 'sketchy visitor.'"

Liza had the decency to look ashamed. "No matter how I personally felt about Michael—how any of us did—his death—"

"His murder," Dee interrupted, not in the mood for excuses or to let Liza off the hook.

"His murder . . . was a tragedy. I don't think any of us have reacted well to it." Liza stood up. "Eat and drink as much as you want. It's on the house."

Liza left and went inside the café. Dee watched her go. She pursed her lips. "I didn't hear an apology, did you? And you know what else? She never asked if the police had any idea who drugged me. Everyone else who checked in to see how I was doing asked that. But she didn't. Interesting."

Jeff didn't respond.

"Jeff?" She turned to see Jeff staring after Liza with puppy dog eyes. Dee groaned. "Come on! Seriously?"

"She's beautiful. And sensitive. And smart. Has to be, to make a success out of a restaurant, especially out here in the country. Restaurants have a high degree of failure. Something like thirty percent." Jeff released a lovestruck sigh.

"She also might be a murderer."

"Don't care," a moony Jeff said.

"Raul's into her too. Raul Aguilar. The sheriff. Who's on our side."

"Oh." Jeff instantly snapped out of it. "He may be all that stands between me and San Quentin, so moving on." He drained his beer. "It's just nice to take a break and think of something else besides murder. Like sex. Or a relationship."

Dee chortled. "I love how that's an 'or' for you. Like they're mutually exclusive."

"You know what I mean. Don't you want more than work and a dog, awesome as Nugget is?"

Dee toyed with her beer, beset with conflicting emotions. "Truthfully, I'm not sure. If I want something besides work or Nugget, I think I'll look for a hobby, not a relationship. I'm o-for-two with marriage. And watching the toll Mom's death has taken on Dad, I can't imagine loving someone so much and then losing them. Dad hides behind his character voices and his causes, but . . ." She noticed Jeff wasn't listening. His attention was focused across the street. Annoyed, she waved her hands in front of his face. "Hello . . . I'm baring my heart here."

"Sorry," Jeff said, his gaze still fixed elsewhere. "But there's a convo going on among three of our murder suspects and there's a fourth person, who's not saying anything, but doesn't look happy about whatever's going on. Don't stare! You'll send out energy that makes them look over at us."

Dee picked up a menu the waiter had left on the table in case they wanted to order more than chips. She held the menu up so it covered her face, then lowered it slightly so she could peek out over the top.

Jonas, Brian, and Shawn stood outside Goldsgone Realty, which, she assumed, was real estate agent Jonas's place of business. He appeared to be explaining something to the others. All looked dour as they took in whatever he was telling them. Brian's mother, Millie, stood slightly to the side of the group, fidgeting with the handle of a basket full of flowers she carried.

"This isn't the first time we've seen those guys huddled together like they're planning a Hail Mary pass in the last seconds of the game," Jeff said. "But Hovering Mama is a new touch."

Jonas said something that elicited a nod from Brian and a glower from Shawn, which Dee had come to consider his go-to expression. The conversation ended and the three started on their separate ways. Millie put a hand on Brian's arm. He brushed it away and tromped off. Millie, face creased with worry, took a step to follow him, then changed her mind. She crossed the street toward the café.

Dee ducked behind her menu. "She's coming this way," she said to Jeff, sotto voce. "And I bet she could use an ear."

She made a show of studying her menu as Millie approached the café, then feigned delighted surprise at sighting the retired teacher. "Millie? Hi."

"Hello." Millie's response was polite, but strained.

"Are you having lunch? Don't eat alone. Come join us." Dee motioned to the table's empty seat. Jeff flashed a warm, welcoming smile.

Millie hesitated. She resumed her apparently nervous habit of playing with her basket handle. After a moment, she came to a decision. "Some company would be lovely. Thank you."

She joined them at the table, bringing a sweet perfume from the basket of flowers with her. The young waiter came over to take her order. "A bowl of Chow Call Chowder, please."

"That sounds delicious," Dee said. She addressed the waiter. "I'll take a bowl of the chowder too."

"Make that three," Jeff said. "Along with a basket of Rascally Rolls and butter. Thanks."

The waiter left. Millie placed her basket at her feet. She seemed to have relaxed slightly, and Dee sensed an opening.

"Are you okay?" she asked, feigning concern. "I get the feeling something's bothering you."

The teacher's worried expression reappeared. "Is it that obvious?"

Dee and Jeff simultaneously gave sympathetic nods. "Whatever it is, it might help to talk about it," Dee said.

Millie's brow creased. "I don't want to bother you with my problems."

"It's no bother," Dee said. "Really."

"You need to talk, we're here for you," Jeff added.

"Thank you," Millie said. "That's very kind. Especially since people in town haven't been the most welcoming to you." She paused, then said in a quiet voice, "It's Brian. He got into some kind of business deal instigated by Jonas. Brian won't tell me anything, but from the bits and pieces I've picked up, I gather it's not going well."

"Ah," Dee said. "That must be hard on you as a mother. Feeling like your son is in trouble and not being able to help him."

"Yes." Millie's head bobbed up and down. Her expression darkened. "It's that Jonas, I'm sure. I don't trust the likes of him one bit."

"Have you picked up anything specific about the business?" Jeff asked as she hid her disappointment at hearing another person, in addition to Elmira, reveal they had doubts about Jonas. "Maybe Dee and I could look into it for you."

"All I know is it involves a run-down old building in West Camp. I heard Brian say something about storage."

The word jogged a memory for Dee and she bit her lip to keep from letting out an exclamation as she linked it to the current conversation. The waiter brought their chowder, and Dee managed to control her eagerness to pursue the possible clue. She and Jeff made small talk with Millie as they ate. She didn't reveal anything else that might be helpful, but the moteliers earned goodwill they hoped she would share with other locals, especially after they told her the cost of her soup was covered.

"I've had these flowers out of water too long," Millie said, rising to leave. "This has been lovely. I can't thank you enough for lunch and for letting me share my concerns with you." She again appeared worried. "Although I probably shouldn't have said anything. Please keep our conversation between us."

"Absolutely," Dee said.

"Cone of silence." Jeff mimed a cone over his head.

Assuaged by their promises, Millie left. Dee made sure she was far out of earshot, then leaned into Jeff. "Millie doesn't know it, but she dropped a big clue for us. You know how she mentioned an old building and said she heard the word 'storage' come up? When I brought up Michael to Shawn Radinsky, he said he hadn't seen or talked to him since he helped move belongings from Michael's family's lake house into a storage facility in West Camp."

Jeff put down the sourdough roll he was about to bite into, which would have been his third of the meal. "The run-down building Millie mentioned could be the facility Radinsky was talking about. And whatever business deal Jonas Jones roped the others into could have something to do with Baker's family's stuff."

"*Exactly.*" Dee buzzed with an energy she hadn't felt since she and Jeff had embarked on their amateur sleuthing. "We need to find that storage facility."

CHAPTER 23

The café proved to be the perfect location, allowing Dee and Jeff to keep an eye out for Jonas while searching the Goldsgone Realty website for a West Camp storage facility currently on the market.

"Nothing's coming up," Jeff said, scrolling through the agency's listings.

"Either Jonas is representing it on his own or it's a back-pocket listing," Dee said. "You know, one of those listings that's not being made public for whatever reason."

"Everything about this business deal Millie mentioned seems stealth, so my money's on the former."

Dee wrinkled her brow as she contemplated a course of action. "If we're going to find this building, we may have to follow Jonas and hope he leads us there."

Jeff looked doubtful. "Sounds like the waste of a day and gas. Or electricity if we take my car. He could be going anywhere, and we could end up nowhere."

"I know it's a reach. But I'm trying to lay this out like a storyline." Dee broke it down for Jeff. "Scene: Three guys huddle together talking over a business deal. They break apart. All look unhappy. Concerned. It's not going well.

Based on what Millie said, along with Shawn's comment to me about a storage facility and Jonas being a central figure, I think we're safe assuming the deal involves real estate. If I were scripting this, I'd give Jonas the drive of trying to salvage the deal. I'd send him to the site to search for any angle he might have missed."

"That's fiction," Jeff said, still doubtful.

"Yes," Dee acknowledged. "But good fiction is inspired by honest and believable human behavior."

Jeff drummed on the table with his fingers, mulling this over. Then he stopped drumming. "Sure. Why not? It's not like we've got guests to check in."

"Okay, then." Dee thought the plan through in her head. "We hang out here until we see Jonas leave."

"What if he doesn't?"

"From my experience in Studio City, where everyone and their mother is a real estate agent, they're always on the move. Once he heads out, we wait a beat, then follow him in my car. Keeping out of his eyeline will be a little tricky on these empty country roads, but luckily I drove, and a white Honda Civic is practically the state car of California. We won't stand out."

"Sounds like a plan," Jeff said. "If a far-fetched one."

Having agreed on a course of action, they sat back to wait out Jonas. An hour and a bathroom break later, he exited Goldsgone Realty, as predicted by Dee. He got into a black hybrid BMW SUV parked in front of the building and drove off. Dee and Jeff waited a few seconds, then raced to her car, jumped in, and took off after him.

Dee was careful to maintain distance from Jonas, occasionally allowing a car to drive between them. The real estate agent first stopped at a charming Victorian cottage with ornate gingerbread trim painted in an array of colors.

He walked up the steps to the front door and rang the bell. An elderly woman answered the door. She lit up at the sight of Jonas and the two shared a hug. They conferred for a moment; then she went back inside. He stopped at the large FOR SALE post hammered into the front lawn and filled the empty plastic box with a batch of one sheets about the property, which he pulled from his briefcase.

The agent's next few stops repeated the same pattern.

"I've learned a couple of things from our spying efforts," Jeff said after a few hours had passed. "One, this guy has to be the most successful agent in town, because he's got a lotta listings and every client has been happy to see him. And two, Chow Call Chowder isn't filling. I could eat one of the oxen that brought the settlers to Goldsgone right now."

"I'm hungry too," Dee confessed. "Let's go for another hour, and then we can give up."

They resumed following Jonas. He reached an intersection and turned left. Dee forgot her hunger and gripped the steering wheel. "He's heading to West Camp. This is it."

She hung back, but maintained an eye on the black BMW as they traversed the ten-mile route to the county seat. Jonas passed through the town's charming historic district and made a right turn onto a side road. Dee parked a few houses away. She and Jeff watched as he parked in front of an old stone cottage, where another happy customer waved from the front porch.

Dee and Jeff both let out a groan. "You were right," she said, disheartened. "This was a total waste of time."

"Not really," Jeff said. "We know that if we have to sell the Golden, we should hire Jonas as our agent."

"Let's go home. We can finish off Serena's charcuterie board for dinner."

She started the car and made a U-turn, then a right onto Main Street. "We're behind him again," Jeff said.

"Yay," Dee responded, her tone dry. "Maybe we'll get to follow him to his dentist."

They drove through the historic district, then passed through an un-scenic edge of town, which was populated by a variety of auto repair shops and others offering necessities like plumbing and HVAC services.

"We passed him," Jeff said. "Make a U-turn and pull into the driveway in front of the junkyard."

"Why?"

"Because Jones is parked across the street. In front of what looks like a big old warehouse."

Dee instantly did as instructed, maneuvering onto a patch of gravel that allowed her car to be at least partially obstructed by a giant pile of old tires. She and Jeff got out of the car, closing the doors as quietly as possible. They scurried across the street, taking cover behind a rusted hulk of a pickup truck fronting an abandoned gas station.

A faded sign above the front entrance of the enormous brick building Jonas had parked in front of read WEST CAMP STORAGE AND WAREHOUSE. Elated, Dee poked Jeff in the side. "This is it! I know it is. It's the only warehouse in West Camp. We found it!"

"Ouch, and yes. Shh. He's getting out of his car."

The real estate agent walked to the back of his SUV, which opened as if by magic. He removed a large rectangle wrapped in a blanket and struggled to carry the awkward object to the warehouse. The trunk door slowly closed as he disappeared into the building.

A few minutes later, he reappeared sans object. He got into the SUV. The car's light stayed on briefly, allowing Dee and Jeff to see the real estate agent press a button on his computer screen and then appear to be talking to someone. The car light cut out. Seconds later, Jonas powered up and drove off.

As soon as the agent rounded a curve and was out of sight, Dee and Jeff ran to the warehouse. The front door was sealed with a lock box, so they searched the building for another entrance. They found a heavy metal back door, also locked.

"If we can't get inside, we need to at least look inside," Dee said.

"How? There are only a few windows and they're too high up for either of us to see into."

Dee thought for a moment. "Do you think you can hoist me onto your shoulders?"

"Ooh, boy." Jeff gave his head a worried scratch. "I can try."

He crouched down below a high, narrow window, leaning both hands against the building's brick wall for support. Dee flung one leg over his shoulder, then another. Jeff slowly rose until Dee was able to grip the windowsill, pulling herself up to relieve her friend from some of her weight.

"What do you see?" Jeff asked, grunting from the strain of supporting her.

She peered inside the warehouse. A vast space lay before her. A cement floor. Brick walls. In a far corner, she saw several flat bundles like the one Jonas had brought into the space with him stacked on top of each other. That was it. "Nothing. Except for whatever Jonas carried in, and a few more like it, it's empty."

"What about Michael's stuff? Whatever it was from his family's house that Shawn helped him move?"

"Wherever they moved it to, it wasn't here. Or if it was, it's gone. You can put me down."

Jeff lowered Dee and she climbed off him. He winced and rubbed his shoulders. "I don't get what's going on"

"I don't either."

They walked back to the front of the building. Dee stopped to pick up a small item lying by the door. She held it up to Jeff. "A For Sale sign. I guess this is another one of Jonas's properties. A pocket listing, like I said, which would explain why it's not on the company website."

The two glumly slunk across the street to Dee's car.

"So much for sleuthing." Jeff pointed to his stomach. "Me hungry."

"Me wanna drink. A few drinks."

Dee turned the key in the ignition. She was about to put the car into Drive, when her cell rang. She pressed a button on the computer screen to answer the call, which was channeled through the Honda's speakers.

"Elmira?" she said, recognizing the number.

"Thank the Lord I reached you."

The panic in Elmira's voice alarmed the moteliers.

"Are you okay?" Dee asked. "You don't sound it. What's wrong?"

"I don't know where you are, but get back to the Golden as fast as you can. One of your cabins is on fire. With how dry this state still is, the whole motel could go up in flames."

CHAPTER 24

Dee drove faster than she'd ever driven in her life. It was dark by the time they reached the Golden, which made the flames shooting up from the motel cabin stand out in terrifyingly stark contrast to the inky black night.

Her hands shook. She clutched the steering wheel harder to make them stop. "There's no place to park."

The motel's small gravel lot was packed with fire trucks and firefighting equipment. Cars and pickup trucks lined the road, parked haphazardly as if the drivers left their cars in a hurry.

"You can fit in there." Jeff, jaw set tight, motioned to a small space. "You'll be sticking out into the road, so leave your hazards on."

Dee followed his instructions. As they hurried from the car, the flames disappeared, replaced by thick gray smoke. Dee's eyes burned and she coughed.

"This is terrible." Tears mingled with ash on her cheeks. "What are we going to do?"

"It's gray smoke. I think that's the good one."

"How can that much smoke be good?"

"It's the kind that means the fire is burning itself out, I think."

The two pulled their shirts up to cover their mouths as they ran toward the cabin. They passed people they recognized and people they'd never seen before hosing down the other cabins and the motel lodge itself to prevent them from being ignited by sparks still dancing in the air. Dee called a muffled thank-you to everyone they passed, including Elmira, who was dressed in the gear of a volunteer firefighter.

They reached the cabin's smoldering ruins.

"It's Michael's cabin," Dee said to Jeff, who responded with a grim nod.

About a dozen men wearing orange uniforms, helmets, and masks were hosing it down and policing the area around it for errant sparks. A few trained their hoses on hot spots, where the fire had jumped to dry vegetation.

Elmira trudged up the path to Dee and Jeff. "It's out. But the CDC won't go nowhere till they're sure every ember's been extinguished."

The lettering on the back of a firefighter's jacket that read CDC PRISONER registered with Dee: The CDC stood for California Department of Corrections. The Golden had been saved by the state's legendary inmate crew of firefighters.

Elmira led a firefighter wearing a yellow jumpsuit and a different helmet from the others over to Dee and Jeff. "This is Chief Harris. Chief, these are Dee and Jeff, the motel owners."

He nodded a greeting. He carried an ax in one hand and a shovel in the other, negating handshakes. "Sorry you lost a cabin. But it could've been a lot worse. My crew here's given me an all clear for the near area. I've got a couple of guys in the woods making sure nothing flew that way. We're lucky there's no wind tonight."

Dee felt faint with relief. "We can't thank you enough. Elmira, can you help me get water and snacks for everyone who helped out?"

"You betcha. Heloise already dropped off treats from the All-in-One." Dee's fear she'd be rewarding the people who saved her business with Elmira's inedibles was allayed when the shopkeeper added, "I didn't have time to bake today, so I had to bring in from the West Camp bakery."

Jeff stayed behind with the fire crew, while Dee and Elmira set to work laying out a spread of snacks and beverages in the motel lobby.

"Can someone get the door?" a voice called from outside.

Dee hurried to open it, revealing Serena holding a huge charcuterie board. "I heard what happened from my sitter. I figured I wouldn't be much use putting out the fire, but I wanted to do something."

"This is so kind," Dee said. "Thank you."

She relieved Serena of the board and gave her a hug. She threw her arms around Elmira as well. If she could have hugged every volunteer, she would have. Months ago, they were strangers to her. Now she and Jeff owed them their potential livelihood.

More locals continued to show up, some motivated by a desire to help, others more of the looky-loo variety. Even they didn't show up empty-handed. A man who looked vaguely familiar handed her a container of homemade guacamole and a bag of chips. "I'm so sorry you have to go through this," he said with sympathy. "If there's anything I can do, please let me know."

"Thank you . . ."

"Owen."

Recognition clicked for Dee. "Yes. Owen. The jeweler. Hi. Sorry about that, and thank you."

He flicked his hand, dismissing her concern. "Please. I'm being selfish. I don't want some fire scaring you off from living here." He glanced out the window. "Is the fire crew still out there?"

"Yes. They're tending to hot spots."

Another volunteer showed up, distracting Dee. With the fire out and the nearby hot spots contained, volunteers and firefighters drifted into the motel lobby for refreshments. Soon the atmosphere went from tense to convivial. Dee managed not to burst into tears as she distributed hugs and gratitude.

"There are still firefighters working the woods," she told Elmira. "I'm gonna put together treats and drinks to hold them over until they can get down here."

Elmira and Serena pitched in to help fill a box with pastries, snack bags, soda, and water. Dee carried it up the small hill toward the crew. She saw a man hurrying out of the woods and heading down another path, and realized it was Owen. He was gone before she could thank him for his help and excellent guacamole.

She found the fire chief and Jeff conferring by the cabin nearest to the smoldering site of the former cabin.

"Thanks to Chief Harris here and Captain Perez, who's in charge of the crew, we got lucky again," Jeff said to Dee once she reached them. "Because this cabin was far enough away from Michael's and shut up tight, there's no smoke damage."

"Huge relief," Dee said. "Replacing one cabin is going to be expensive enough." She handed the box to the chief. "I brought this for you and the crew up here."

The chief's soot-stained face broke into a happy grin. "Vittles," he said, using the Goldsgonedian term for food. He took the box from Dee. "My guys just let me know they're done. They're on their way out of the woods now."

He turned to where a small clutch of firefighters was emerging from a grove of pine trees, led by the aforementioned Captain Pereze. Next to him was possibly the most handsome man Dee had ever seen, which was saying something, considering she'd spent her career working with actresses and actors, not generally considered a homely bunch. He had the sculpted jawline of a comic book hero brought to life, and brilliant blue eyes that contrasted with his jet-black hair. Dee pegged him as being somewhere in his mid-thirties. She imagined he'd been almost too pretty in his youth. Now he wore his years like the hot firefighter on the cover of an erotica novel.

"Is he walking in slow motion?" she murmured to Jeff. "I swear he is."

Jeff gave her the side eye. "Really? *Now* you decide to crush on someone?"

The crew reached Chief Harris. "We got all the hot spots under control," Captain Perez said, "thanks to Huck here, who knows every square inch of the area."

He patted the handsome man on the back. Huck blushed under the sooty grime that did nothing to distract from his handsomeness. He shook pine needles from his hair, a gesture Dee found endearing.

"Comes from growing up around here," he said, shrugging off the compliment with a bashful smile.

"I'm Dee," she said, taking it upon herself to introduce herself. As an afterthought, she added, "And this is my *business* partner, Jeff." She made sure to emphasize the word "business." "We're the Golden's new owners and we can't thank you enough for helping to save it, Hunk . . . Huck."

Mortified, she prayed he didn't notice her faux pas. But a snort from Jeff let her know it didn't get past him.

"My parents'll keep an eye out for any flare-ups," Huck the hunk said. "They live nearby."

"Wonderful," Dee gushed, earning another snort from Jeff. "I brought refreshments, but since you're all done up here, why don't you come down to the lobby. You can rest a spell." Dee heard herself and grimaced. *"A spell." There I go, sounding like a Goldsgonedian. Maybe he found that . . . sexy?*

"Sounds good to me."

Dee, Jeff, and the firefighters tromped down the low hill toward the reception area. Dee made sure to position herself next to Huck.

"I noticed a big, old pile of bear scat not too far into the woods," he said. "Stoney must've stopped by not too long ago."

"You know about Stoney?"

"I'm the one who named him," Huck said with pride. "Stoney the bear. Like Smokey, Get it?"

"Yes. Funny stuff," Dee said, cringing a little inside at selling out her humor creds over a handsome guy's lame joke. But recalling Elmira's explanation that the bear was named by someone who was part of an illegal grow operation explained why the writing on the legs and back of Huck's orange jumpsuit read CDC PRISONER.

Huck noticed the triangular bell dangling from the roof's edge of the lodge. "Excuse me a minute."

He traipsed over to the bell and banged on it with gusto as Dee watched, confused. A few minutes later, Ma'am and Mister Ma'am emerged from a bank of trees closer to the road. Dee stared in shock as the three exchanged teary embraces.

"I was hoping you'd be on this crew, buddy," Mister said.

"I was ready to start a fire just to get some time with you," Ma'am added. She gave Huck's cheeks an affectionate pinch.

"Are you seeing what I'm seeing?" Dee asked Jeff, who'd caught up with her.

"Yup. They're gonna make for some interesting in-laws."

Dee gave him a poke in the ribs, then approached the family reunion. "There's food and drinks inside, Mister and Ma'am. That's where we're heading. But, Huck, I was thinking maybe you should show me where those hot spots were, so Jeff and I can keep an eye out for them tonight."

She heard a muffled laugh from Jeff and shot him a look.

"I can show you those, miss," a portly volunteer fire-fighter offered. "I was with the woods crew, so I know exactly where they are."

"Oh," Dee said, hiding her disappointment. "Thanks."

"You three come with me," Jeff said, indicating everyone else follow him into the lobby. He waved to Dee. "See you when we see you."

They disappeared into the lobby, leaving Dee with the volunteer. "All righty," he said, hefting his ax over his shoulder. "And while we walk, I'm gonna give you a lesson on maintaining a safe, fire-free environment."

Goody, mansplaining was Dee's glum thought as they reversed course and traipsed back up to the woods behind the cabin.

* * *

By the time the firefighter finished telling Dee everything she already knew, and they returned to the motel lobby, the crowd of volunteers, firefighters, and inmates had dispersed. "Don't worry," Jeff told her. "I told Hunk you might be calling about a fire only he could put out, whacka whacka." He wiggled his eyebrows like a lewd comedian, earning another poke in the ribs from Dee.

The two began straightening up the room, tossing garbage and collecting cans and bottles to recycle.

"Huck was a nice distraction from our ongoing nightmare," Dee said. She tied off a trash bag. "But we've got a big problem. I'm sure someone set that fire. Who and why?"

"While you were in the woods with your Eagle Scout, Raul came by with a crime scene technician from West Camp and an arson investigator from WCFD. As far as I know, they're still up at the cabin. Hopefully, we'll get a report from them when they're done."

When they finished bagging the trash, Dee made them each a plate of leftovers to serve as dinner. Exhausted by the evening's dire event, they ate in silence. Dee was loading the dishwasher as Raul appeared in the doorway.

"You guys still functional? I know it's been a rough day."

"I doubt either of us is gonna get much sleep tonight, so come on in," Dee said.

He did so and the three took seats in the living room after Raul declined their offer of a drink or something to eat. Nugget, worn out by spending the last few hours trolling the living room and kitchen for dropped treats, positioned himself at Dee's feet and promptly fell asleep.

"So, what's the verdict?" Jeff asked. "Arson or accident?"

"Arson," the sheriff said, his tone terse. "The FD investigator instantly picked up the scent of gasoline. He found evidence of it on the foundation. Whoever did this wasn't a pro and didn't do much to disguise their act."

"Jeff told you it was the cabin where Michael stayed, right?" Dee asked. Raul nodded in the affirmative. "Which means someone burned it down either because they thought it contained incriminating evidence or to send us a message."

"I'm guessing it's door number two," Raul said. "O'Bryant has all of Baker's electronics. Laptop, phone, tablet. We went through the place looking for additional clues and it's a sure bet you did the same once we were gone."

"Only because I had to put together all of his belongings," Dee said, feeling a little guilty for following up law enforcement's thorough investigation of the cabin with her own snooping.

Jeff wrinkled his nose. "Sorry to interrupt, but the garbage is really starting to stink. I'm gonna put it in the bear box."

He got up and went to the kitchen, where he picked up a trash bag. He walked over to the side door, which led out of the apartment to the side yard, where the bear box that protected trash from hungry visitors like Stoney was located. He stopped.

"Huh. That's weird." Jeff bent down and picked up an envelope from the floor. "Did you see this?" he asked Dee. "It's addressed to you."

"It is?"

"Only your name. Not your address."

Jeff put down the bag and gave Dee the envelope. Her name was typed on the outside of it. She opened it and removed a sheet of paper. Dee read it and paled.

"What does it say?" Jeff asked. "From the look on your face, nothing good."

"If we're looking for confirmation it's door number two—someone burned down the cabin to send a message—we got it in this note."

Dee handed the missive to Raul. Jeff read its contents over the sheriff's shoulder: *STOP POKING YOUR NOSE IN OTHER PEOPLE'S BUSINESSES . . . OR ELSE.*

CHAPTER 25

"So much for feeling like we were finally accepted by the locals."

Dee's voice shook as she said this. It was one thing to intuit people weren't "fans" of theirs, to use Hollywood jargon. It was another to have a threat hand-delivered.

"Don't write off the whole town," Raul said. "This is from one person. Most likely, our killer."

A frisson of fear coursed through Dee. She gulped. "Which means the killer either was here—like, pretending to be a volunteer—or slipped the letter under the kitchen door." The apartment, which she'd come to feel was a refuge, now felt more like a potential death trap.

Jeff's lips formed a thin line. "We're changing the locks tomorrow. The doors are sturdy. Jasper Gormley probably wanted to make sure they were bearproof. So new locks should do it, regarding better security. And I'm spending the night on the couch."

"I'd say 'you don't have to do that,' but I'd be lying."

Jeff lay a reassuring hand on her shoulder, and she gave it a grateful squeeze.

"I'm holding on to the note," Raul said. "The envelope

too." Dee handed it to him. "And I need a list of everyone you can remember who was here tonight. If you don't know their names, write down what you remember about them. With enough detail, I should be able to identify anyone from Foundgold or Goldsgone."

"I already made a list of suspects," Dee said, hastily adding, "Of course, you have one too. Duh. The expression 'duh,' not the bad show I was on. Are you going to question them?"

"I have to proceed with caution." The sheriff carefully placed the paper back inside the envelope. "Otherwise, O'Bryant will be all over me. Law enforcement can be very territorial, if you haven't noticed."

"We have," Jeff said. Dee gave a vigorous nod of agreement.

"Step one is checking the note for prints. Wearing gloves when you drop off a threat like this is Criminal Activity 101, so I doubt we'll find any besides Dee's. Which reminds me, stop by the station tomorrow so I can take yours."

"I'll come by first thing in the morning."

"Good. Then it'll be on to step two."

Raul stood up. Dee and Jeff walked him to the door, where he stopped. "I don't have to tell you to keep this note business to yourself, but I'm gonna say it anyway. There's another reason why we wanna proceed slowly and carefully and let as little information out as possible. We don't want to put a scare into our prime suspect. A scared suspect is a dangerous suspect. From my experience, someone who's killed once has a whole lot less trouble doing it a second time."

With that ominous observation, Raul departed.

Jeff, who had parked himself on the couch, threw his

head back and splayed out his arms. "I love how when you think things can't get worse, they somehow manage to."

Dee, brow furrowed, tapped her index finger against her lips. "Raul may have to play by the rules, but we don't. The four people hovering around the punch bowl were Liza, Shawn, Jonas, and Brian. Liza is too smart to literally hand me a drugged cup of punch. We know there's something sketchy with Jonas and the warehouse. We need to do a little recon on Shawn and Brian. Not sure how to poke around Brian, but it's my turn to schedule a private training session with Shawn."

"God be with you on that. I don't think my neck will ever be the same." Jeff winced and rubbed the offending body part.

"Let me see if Gym Dandy has a website, or if you have to make an appointment in some old-timey way, like having the request delivered by Pony Express."

Dee left the living room for the bedroom, where she retrieved her laptop from between her mattress and box spring, the rudimentary hiding place where she'd tucked it when volunteers began flooding the motel. She returned and set up shop on the dining-room table.

"Yay, Gym Dandy is twenty-first century when it comes to their business. I can schedule a session right from the comfort of my own home. Let's see what Shawn's avails are for tomorrow." She typed and then examined her screen. "Except for an appointment with none other than Verity Gillespie—who, by the way, I noticed was not part of our volunteer brigade of firefighters and kind, helpful citizens tonight—Shawn's schedule is wide open. I'll book an appointment for eleven, after I get fingerprinted at the sheriff's station."

"Sounds like a fun day." Jeff released a loud yawn. "I'm

beat. I'll go with you and Nugget on his evening pee walk, but I'll let you play Nancy Drew tomorrow. I'll work on coming up with promotional summer packages. Hopefully, Michael's killer will be caught by then and we'll be back to our boring old selves."

In the morning, rather than wear the worn, oversized T-shirt she usually worked out in, Dee went with a more subtly sexy look of tight, teal-patterned crop top and leggings, which accentuated her body's curves. Whether or not Shawn was the culprit who drugged her drink, advertising a little feminine mystique couldn't hurt, even if it went against her moral code. But not wishing to broadcast the look to the Goldsgonedian world, Dee topped off the outfit with an extra-large zip-up hoodie that hid everything.

She stopped by the sheriff's station first, where the office assistant took her prints, since Raul was out on a call. Then she took a deep breath and strode into Gym Dandy.

She found Shawn waiting for her at the front desk. Considering she was a paying client—and from what she could gather, the trainer didn't exactly have a stable of them— she found it telling that he didn't bother to fake enthusiasm about their session. He muttered a greeting, then left the desk for the gym facilities. Lacking instructions, Dee followed him.

Despite its nineteenth-century setting, the gym featured up-to-date equipment. A row of ellipticals and treadmills lined the brick back wall. They faced a glass window that looked out on a lovely patio. Weight machines filled the gym's interior; to Dee's right, a sign above a door labeled the room behind it as STUDIO SPACE FOR GROUP CLASSES.

Dee removed her hoodie, surreptitiously checking for a

reaction from Shawn. She picked up an infinitesimal raise of an eyebrow, which quickly disappeared.

"Hang the jacket in the locker room," the trainer said. He gestured in the opposite direction from the studio space. "We don't like junk on the gym floor."

"Okey dokey." Dee hurried into the women's changing room, where a small bank of lockers covered the wall facing the bathroom and shower facilities.

She left the locker room and met Shawn by a treadmill. "Warm up with five minutes on the tread," he said in a disinterested tone. "Then I'll put together a strength-and-training routine you can do yourself."

"I was planning to book more sessions with you." Dee wasn't, but she wanted the option of future sleuthing and found it curious a man who lacked a sustaining client base was already writing her off as one.

"I'm not taking on new clients. I'm booked solid."

Dee knew this was a lie, but she didn't press him. Instead, she vowed to milk whatever she could out of the trainer in the time she had with him.

If only.

Every time Dee steered the conversation toward Michael's murder or the hoedown, Shawn deflected, tacking left to her right and right to her left. While he didn't deliver the brutal session he'd inflicted on Jeff, by the time they were done, Dee felt every muscle of her body. *That's more about me being lazy when it comes to exercise than Shawn's workout,* she thought, feeling guilty about the number of times she'd stopped at In-N-Out Burger on her way to the Studio City gym and then decided it was "too late" to work out.

Shawn handed her a sheet detailing the exercise routine he'd worked out for her and ushered her to the Gym

Dandy front door. Figuring it didn't hurt to be polite, Dee thanked him for the session.

"You're welcome," he responded. "And just so you know, I didn't set Baker's cabin on fire." He smirked. "I didn't need to."

He gave Dee a push out the door and slammed it shut. She heard him turn the door's locks. Then she was left to ponder his odd closing comment: *"I didn't need to."*

Shut out of further snooping at Gym Dandy, Dee debated her next move as she strolled down Goldsgone's scenic streets. She walked past Gold Rush Contractors and Carpentry, then backtracked.

As long as I'm in town, I might as well get an estimate for replacing Michael's cabin, she thought. *Here's hoping we don't need a gold rush to pay for it.* Jeff had checked their insurance policy and arson wasn't covered. Dee said a silent prayer their provider would accept a claim if they could prove they weren't the ones who set the fire for the insurance money.

She scampered up the few steps to the business's front door and stepped into the reception area, which was furnished in what Dee had come to think of as Goldsgonedian Victorian. To her surprise, she found Millie Oakhurst futzing with a large floral display behind the carved walnut table.

Millie beamed at Dee. "Well, hello there. I figured you'd stop by at some point, although not quite so soon."

"You did?" asked a thoroughly confused and more than slightly weirded-out Dee.

"Yes." The older woman's smile faded, replaced by compassion. "I heard about your fire. I'm so sorry. It leaves a scar on your property, doesn't it? We're the only contractors in town, which is why I knew you'd drop in, at least to get a quote."

"We?" With all her repeating, Dee was starting to feel like a befuddled parrot.

"This is my son Brian's company. Once I retired from teaching, I joined him in the business. When I'm not working at the mercantile, I'm here."

"Ah." Dee finally got a sense of what was going on. "And you're very prescient. I stopped in to get a quote for replacing the cabin."

Millie smoothed the starched apron covering her calico maxidress and stuck a strand of hair that had come loose back into her gray bun. "Brian is in the back building cabinetry for a summer home he's renovating. Give me a minute to finish this and I'll take you to him."

"It's a stunning arrangement," Dee said, admiring the colorful mix of sunflowers, calla lilies, hydrangeas, and roses, all in shades of peach, orange, pink, and yellow. A white flower with tiny petals similar to baby's breath filled out the arrangement, adding an airy, cloudlike touch to it. The scent of lilies perfumed the air.

"Thank you so much. Flower arranging is a hobby of mine. I tried quilting, but like the saying goes, when you've made one, you've made them all." Millie stepped back to admire her work. "There. All done."

She squirted sanitary gel on her hands and rubbed them together, repeating the process a second time. She gestured for Dee to come with her and they headed down a long hallway, past a couple of small, empty offices and a larger one housing both a conference and drafting table.

Millie made small talk as they walked, eventually segueing to Dee's relationship with Jeff. "I've heard you and your fellow motel owner are just friends. Is it true?"

"Very." Dee wasn't sure if she was flattered or discomfited by the fact locals gossiped about her and Jeff. It was to be expected in a small town—something else the citiots would have to get used to.

"No man in your life?" Millie's gray eyes twinkled with curiosity.

Huck's handsome face floated through Dee's imagination, then drifted off. "No. Not right now."

"My Brian is single too," Millie said, getting to what Dee realized was the point of the conversation.

Wary of being dragged into some kind of matchmaking venture on Millie's part, Dee responded with a vague "uh-huh."

The strand of hair with a mind of its own came loose again, and Millie tucked it back, this time with more force. "He and Liza Chen dated. They seemed to enjoy each other's company. I don't know why it didn't work out."

Dee had a good idea of why the restauranteur's relationship with contractor Brian Oakhurst went south—the rekindled romance between high-school sweethearts Liza and Michael. She wondered how Brian felt about the relationship. Could he have been jealous enough to commit murder?

She and Millie exited out the back door to a cement flat pad covered with a metal roof—sort of a huge shed with no walls. Carpentry equipment filled the space. At the moment, Brian, wearing a face shield, was pushing a piece of wood through a table saw, whose loud whine made Dee's ears ring.

Millie stood in front of her son. Seeing her, he turned off the saw and lifted his shield. "Bri, sweetie, look who stopped by," she said, making it sound like Dee had dropped in for tea.

"I'd love to get a quote from you on the cost of replacing the cabin that burned down," Dee said, getting right down to business. Brian was an attractive man, with a nose that stopped at sloping too much and a thick head of hair whose color matched his brown eyes. But either he had no personality or he was keeping a lid on it until he met the right person, which Dee knew she wasn't.

"Got it," the contractor said. "I'll take a look and send you an estimate. You can give your contact info to Millie."

He flipped the mask down, turned the table saw back on, and resumed work. Dee found it interesting that he referred to his mother by name. Mostly likely, he did it to maintain a semblance of professionalism. But she also wondered if it indicated a strain between them and a desire to detach himself from the kind of mother who might border on being a "smother."

"Brian, honey, don't forget you have to pick up the flowers I need for Sunday's arrangements at church," Millie yelled over the din from the saw. She sniffled. "I still can't believe that special boy is gone. Heartbreaking."

Dee and Millie headed back to the office area, but Dee glanced back in time to see Brian Oakhurst shove a two-by-four through the saw with increased ferocity.

Dee left her cell phone number and email address with Millie, but only after enduring ten additional minutes of the retired English teacher extolling the miracle that was her star pupil, Michael Adam Baker. By the end of it, Dee's sympathies were with Brian.

If he did kill him, his mother should be indicted for driving him to it, she thought when she finally made her escape.

She arrived back at the Golden bummed out that she didn't have any valuable new clue to run by Jeff.

It turned out she didn't need one.

Dee found Jeff waiting for her in the motel lobby. "Finally," he said when he saw her. "There's been a development. I didn't want to call you about it, because I didn't know where you'd be. It's intense. I have to say, I didn't see it coming."

"What's going on?" Dee's anxiety level ticked upward. "What happened?"

Serena emerged from the lobby's restroom. Tears streaked her face. "The horrible park ranger O'Bryant arrested Callan's assistant, Marisa, for the murder of Michael Adam Baker."

CHAPTER 26

Dee's jaw dropped. While Marisa was on her list of suspects, the news of the assistant's arrest still came as a shock. "Seriously? When? Why?"

"This morning. She was helping me load a cheese board into the car, when the ranger appeared with a bunch of other police cars. Thank God my babies were inside with the sitter when they showed up. It was awful."

The distraught woman dropped her head into her hands. Jeff guided her to the lobby seating area and she collapsed into the couch. He took a seat next to her. Dee claimed the other side. "Do you need water? Something to eat?"

Serena shook her head. "I knew Callan was on the list of suspects because of his falling-out with Michael. Callan turned over his phone logs to the police. His cell business calls from when he was up here and not in L.A., where he mostly used his office phone, matched Marisa's." She lifted her head. "What most people don't know is that assistants listen in on pretty much every call an agent makes. It's a way of verifying conversations and also saving the agent the time of repeating any information the assistant needs to follow through on."

Dee, veteran of several agents, did know this, but she could see from Jeff's appalled expression that this was news to him. He folded his arms in front of his chest. "And no one complains about this blatant invasion of privacy?"

"No," Dee said, "because in the time it would take for an agent to share the details of a conversation with their assistant, another agent could have reached a showrunner and gotten their client the job you wanted. Go on, Serena."

"Marisa is extremely loyal to Callan. To be honest"—Serena put to words exactly what Dee was thinking—"she was in love with him and considered herself a way better match for him than me." She wiped away a tear that had slipped over her lower lid onto her cheek. "There have been days when I thought she might be right."

"She's not," Dee declared. While she had her own doubts about the agent's relationship with his wife, she had no doubt Callan would never trade Serena in for a power-hungry recent college graduate. A hot, non-power-hungry recent graduate, maybe. But not for someone whose own ambition posed a threat to his.

"Callan could never do better than you," Jeff said, his ire raised. "You deserve better than *him*."

Seeing Jeff slip into hero mode, Dee shot him a subtle message to tone down the testosterone. "You haven't told us what led to the arrest," she said to Serena.

"They found incriminating texts from Marisa to Baker on his cell phone. She threatened to kill him—on the night he was murdered. They found her fingerprints on his cell phone. The police think she killed him and tried to wipe the phone clean, but got scared off by Stoney the bear or something."

"That's it?" Jeff stroked his chin, currently home to

trendy beard stubble. "It doesn't sound like much to go on. Then again, any take I have on this is based on watching TV cop shows and not an in-depth knowledge of the process." His phone sounded an alert. He checked it. "I get notifications from the local TV station. O'Bryant's holding a press conference."

He held up his phone so the women could watch with him. Ranger O'Bryant was front and center behind a podium. Raul Aguilar was only half visible in the background, and the half Dee saw looked miserable.

The ranger shared his update via prepared notes, but a tone of self-satisfaction still managed to underscore his stiff reading of them. " 'We applaud our law enforcement team for the diligent efforts that led to a suspect's arrest in the heinous murder of TV writer-producer Michael Adam Baker, and we can assure the citizens of Foundgold, Goldsgone, and the surrounding areas that with the perpetrator apprehended, there's no present danger to the community. We won't be taking questions at this time.' " He took his notes and left the podium, a trail of law enforcement officials in tow; Raul, head down, brought up the rear.

Serena burst into tears. "I can't believe this is on the news. Every entertainment site and blog is going to pick it up. It's going to destroy Callan."

Dee did her best to comfort Serena. "We should get her home," she murmured to Jeff. "She should be with Callan right now. If he's not in Foundgold, we'll figure out a way to get her, Emmy, and Oscar down to L.A."

Jeff went to his cabin to get his car fob. Dee and Serena met him in the Golden's circular driveway and the three took off for the short ride to the Finlay-Katz abode.

To Dee's relief, Callan's black Range Rover sat in the couple's driveway. Jeff parked in front of the house. Serena threw open the car door and raced up the home's front steps, with Dee and Jeff close behind. She used an app on her smartphone to unlock the front door and the three went inside.

"Callan?" Serena called, anguish in her voice. "Callan?" Panicked, she clutched Dee's arm. "Oh, God, he's not answering."

Dee peeled Serena's fingernails from her wrist, where they were beginning to draw blood. "Don't worry, Serena. I'm sure he's—"

"In here, babe!" called a chipper voice from the kitchen.

Serena, Dee, and Jeff raced to the kitchen. Callan stood in the room's center, leaning against the long, granite-topped island. He was attired in jeans and a V-necked black cashmere sweater, whose combined cost, Dee was sure, belied the casual air they gave off. He'd obviously been working the phones; he held a cell in each hand.

Serena threw herself into her husband's arms. He managed to hug her, while still holding tightly to his phones. "When I didn't hear you, I thought something terrible might have happened." Callan's sweater muffled Serena's voice.

Callan, his palms occupied, gave her hair a stroke with the back of his hand. "Sorry. I was on the phone with my publicist." He held up a phone.

"Agents have publicists?" Jeff asked, flummoxed. "I don't get it."

"Some agents have their own agents," Dee explained. "To handle their personal deals."

"Don't get that either," Jeff said.

Callan held up his other phone. "I've also been talking to my lawyer."

"Now *that* I get," Jeff said. "Considering the circumstances, it's smart to have someone who knows the law in your corner."

"He's an entertainment attorney," Callan said.

"I'm out." Jeff walked away from the others. He lifted an apple from a basket on the kitchen dining table and plopped down in a seat to eat it.

Callan put down his phones. His arms free at long last, he returned his wife's hug. "Hon, not gonna lie. I didn't know which way the wind would blow with this Marisa thing. But get this. According to Katrina and Larry—my publicist and lawyer," he added for the benefit of Dee and Jeff, "it's not a nightmare, it's a gift. An assistant who's willing to murder for their boss. Do you have any idea how good that makes me look? I'm an agent you'd kill for. *Literally.* Who doesn't want to be represented by someone who inspires such intense loyalty? I can't keep up with the calls from potential clients. Mostly because I don't have an assistant right now. But still, I could name-drop some major stars." One of his phones rang and he let go of Serena. "It's Katrina again. *Variety* wants a quote from me. I better take it." He answered the call.

"I'll walk you out," Serena said in a whisper to Dee and Jeff, leading them from the kitchen as an upbeat Callan nattered on with his publicist.

They reached the front door. "You've had a rough day," Dee said to Serena with compassion. "Take care of yourself. And your family. If Jeff and I can help in any way, let us know."

"Thank you both so much," Serena said. "I know a lot of this is weird for you. At least for you, Jeff."

"Amen to that," the techie said with feeling.

"But to have you both there when I needed someone."

Serena choked up. "I thank goddess you moved to Found-gold."

Serena hugged each of them goodbye. Dee and Jeff left the house and walked to Jeff's car in silence. They climbed in and started off. "I can see why you wanted out of show business," Jeff finally said.

"Callan's publicist and lawyer aren't wrong," Dee said. "And that's what's scary."

They grew silent again. The road dead-ended at the Golden's two-lane road. Jeff made a left toward the motel. "I don't know how you feel about Marisa's arrest," he said, "but I have a hard time believing she offed Baker."

Dee let out a sigh that released all the pent-up emotions swirling inside her. "I can't tell you how glad I am to hear you say that. I don't believe it either. I know Serena's convinced Marisa was in love with Callan. And I thought so too. But I've known a lot of Marisas. They've worked the desks of my own agents. And the more I think about it, the more I think Marisa wasn't in love with Callan himself. She was in love with his power. That doesn't create the kind of passion that would lead to murder. An affair, yes, although I don't get any sense that Callan's interested in Marisa in a sexual way, especially when he knows sleeping with her would get him hashtag-me-too'd in a heartbeat, particularly by other agents looking to poach his clients. I think what would have happened eventually is that despite Marisa's obsession with Callan, if she'd seen his power start to slip, she would have quit and glommed on to another hot agent. I mean *business* hot, not *hot* hot."

Jeff slapped a hand on the steering wheel. "Finally someone around here said something that made sense!" He grew quiet again. "So, what do we do?"

"I have no idea," Dee confessed. "I've never been an

amateur sleuth before. And poor Raul has obviously been sidelined in the investigation."

Dee stared out the window. The forest they drove by was so thick with trees, it blocked out all sunlight. What Dee once found beautiful felt dark and foreboding now. "There's also something about the cabin fire that's bothering me, but I can't figure out exactly what. It's only a feeling. Which is totally useless. So I guess when it comes to Michael's murder, what we should do right now is . . . nothing."

While there might be nothing to do on the amateur sleuthing front for Dee and Jeff, there was plenty to do for the Golden. Jeff's marketing efforts targeting families had generated a few welcome reservations, so he set to work clearing and restoring the motel sluice. He also used his tech skills to turn Dee's hidden treasures map brainstorm into the beta version of an app where participants accumulated an online "gold nugget" for each visit they paid to a site on the map. Gamers who visited all the sites could turn in their virtual nuggets for a prize: a small toy bear wearing a T-shirt featuring the Golden Motel logo.

While Jeff worked magic online, Dee immersed herself in physical labor. The new reservations required additional rooms were ready for guests, so she alternated between stripping and refinishing the wooden floors with painting the interior walls a warm beige. She also invested in ordering the new mattresses and linens the rooms required, knocking back a stiff drink after maxing out one of her two credit cards.

By the time the week was over, half the Golden's rooms and cabins were ready to be called temporary home by tourists. Dee's improved spirits took a hit when Brian

Oakhurst emailed an estimate that made rebuilding the late Michael Adam Baker's late cabin a no-go. But a visit from hunky Huck restored her good mood.

Dee joined him, a few inmate crew members, and their supervising captain for a property check to see if there were any steps she and Jeff could take to generally ward off additional fires.

"I recommend creating a perimeter around the property that you keep clear of any potential kindling," the captain advised. "Dry leaves, pine needles, broken branches."

"Uh-huh," Dee said, scribbling on a notepad.

"Huck, can you show Ms. Stern where her property line ends and the Majestic's begins?" The captain gestured toward the forest.

"That would be helpful for any future problems," piped up Dee, who knew exactly where the line lay, thanks to Michael Adam Baker's corpse splitting the difference between the Golden and the Majestic. But Dee wasn't about to pass up the chance to bask in Huck's handsome presence a few extra minutes.

"Sure," the inmate firefighter said. "Old Jasper did everyone a favor when he built a stone fence and put up wiring to separate the properties and blah blah blah blah blah blah . . ."

Huck didn't say this. But for Dee, he might as well have, considering she was too lost in his deep, dark eyes to hear a word he said.

"So, are we good here?" the captain asked.

"Huh?" Dee snapped out of it. "Yes. Yes, sir. Very good." She scribbled a few fake notes to cover the fact she wasn't paying attention, and clicked her pen shut.

"Time to get back to base, boys."

The captain held up a hand and the crew fell in line behind him. They marched through the woods and down the motel's slope to the parking lot. Dee tagged along next to Huck.

"Mom and Dad are glad you're bringing the old Golden back to life," he said.

He held out a hand to help her climb over a cluster of rocks. She took his hand to make the climb, then reluctantly released it. "They're wonderful people. Jeff and I would be in big trouble without them."

"And we're all glad you guys fixed and filled the pool. I must've told Jasper a billion times, you're doing yourself and everyone in town a disservice by not providing an additional water source to take down fires. Although you'll have to gate it. You don't want anything drowning in it, like that poor deer."

They'd reached the pool. Dee squinted to see what Huck was talking about. When she did, she let out a scream.

A body floated in the pool, not a deer. And the Joker's sinister grinning leered at Dee from tattoos on each of Shawn Radinsky's shoulders.

CHAPTER 27

Once again, the Golden was a crime scene. Patrol cars from a variety of law enforcement agencies filled the parking lot and lined the road.

Shawn's body had been fished out of the pool and laid out beside it. A waterproof tarp covered the late personal trainer. Dee and Jeff watched, senses dulled, as sheriffs, rangers, and unidentified officers conferred with each other. Ranger O'Bryant appeared to be throwing around his weight, per usual, barking orders at mystified representatives of other departments, as well as his own.

"This sucks," Jeff said.

"Agreed." Dee watched O'Bryant lumber over to the inmate crew members, who were huddled together with their captain. "I want to see what's going on over there."

She grabbed Jeff's T-shirt sleeve and pulled him with her a few feet closer to the crew, where crew captain Perez was purple with rage as he confronted O'Bryant.

"Instead of calling my men suspects, you should be thanking the Almighty they're willing to risk their own lives for your sorry butt. I can vouch for every one of 'em being in my eyeline our entire time here." He got in O'Bryant's face. "So you accuse them, you accuse me."

O'Bryant literally backed off, taking a step away from the furious captain. "Get statements from all of 'em," the ranger instructed one of his underlings. Then to Dee's dismay, the park ranger made eye contact with her. But she summoned up the strength she needed to deal with him.

"Don't even *think* we did this," she declared as he approached. "We're spending down our life savings to bring back the Golden. We want to attract guests, not drive them away."

O'Bryant shrugged. "Could be a desperate ploy to book true-crime podcasters."

"I could see that," Jeff said.

"Citiot!" a frustrated Dee yelled at her friend.

"But not us," Jeff quickly amended. "We're not that desperate . . . yet." He added the qualifier under his breath.

O'Bryant glanced over to where crime-scene technicians from West Camp were working the area around the pool. "It's not much of a leap to assume Radinsky's murder is related to Baker's. We'll be looking at every possible link between the two."

"The operative word there is 'assume.'" This came from Raul Aguilar, who'd peeled off from his coterie of fellow sheriffs to join them. "Until that assumption is bolstered by actual facts, this death is under my jurisdiction. And it will be referred to as a *death,* and not a homicide, until we have a report from Harry Liu proving otherwise."

O'Bryant began to grumble, then stopped. "We'll keep working our end. If we find a connection between the case, we'll alert you. And I'll count on you to do the same." He gave a slight nod. "Deputy Sheriff."

Raul returned the nod. "Chief Ranger."

With that, O'Bryant walked away, leaving behind an open-mouthed Dee and Jeff.

"What just happened?" Dee asked, staring after him.

"He did his job" was Raul's simple reply. "He may be a pain in my keester, but at the end of the day, he's a professional. We all are."

"'Keester.' Adding that to my Goldsgone dictionary of old-timey words," Jeff observed.

"You mind if me and my men use a few of your rooms for interviews?" Raul asked.

"Sure," Dee said. "Just not the rooms I finished prepping yesterday. They still reek of paint and varnish fumes. Plus, I want to keep them as pristine as possible for our guests. We've got a few booked for this weekend."

Sadly, this proved to be wishful thinking on Dee's part.

After one of the many sleepless nights that had dogged Dee over the recent weeks, she awoke to a loud thump from outside. The sound startled Nugget, who gave an obligatory warning bark, then resumed snoring. Dee cautiously opened her front door and found a bundle of *Goldsgone Gazettes* gracing the doorstep.

She carried the bundle inside and used a serrated kitchen knife to saw through the twine wrapped around the newspapers. The twine broke and fell to the bundle's sides. Dee picked up the top newspaper. She saw the headline and let out an infuriated shriek.

She stormed out of her apartment to Jeff's cabin and pounded on the door. "Wake up, wake up!"

"Huh? What? Hold on."

Dee heard him mutter a few choice words in a sleepy voice.

He yanked open the door. "It's practically dawn. Why the drama? What's the problem?"

"*This.*"

Dee thrust the slender local paper into his hands. Jeff

rubbed his eyes, then widened them as he read the headline: MURDER MOTEL MAYHEM! KILLER STRIKES AGAIN!

"What the f—"

"Exactly." Dee pushed past him into the cabin's tiny main room. She collapsed into Jeff's office chair and it rolled backward, hitting a wall. She used her foot to propel it back to its original position at Jeff's desk.

Jeff, eyes still glued to the newspaper, closed the door. "I flirt like a mofo with Verity 'Yes-*that*-Donner' Gillespie and she pulls this? It's outrageous."

"Oh, it's way worse than that." Dee gestured to the Goldsgone website she'd opened while Jeff was talking. The same headline filled the top half of the site's landing page. "You can bet she's broadcasting it everywhere. Not that a story like this needs a boost. We're talking about a double murder in a tiny town that probably hasn't seen one since two miners got into a fight over a mule in 1849."

Jeff grabbed his cell phone off the coffee table. He thumbed it and cursed. "You're right. Shawn's death has officially been classified as a homicide. It's all over the internet, locally and otherwise. The coroner, that guy Liu, worked quickly. He released his findings late last night. We'd both passed out by then."

"Does it say 'cause of death' anywhere?"

"He ran a tox screen. Poison. Cyanide."

"So someone poisoned the poor man, then dumped his body in our pool, obviously hoping to incriminate us."

"Seems like it. But it was a stupid move. You and I can prove we haven't been near Goldsgone in days. Still . . ."

Jeff checked something on his phone. He made a face, then placed it back on the coffee table.

"What?" Dee asked, filled with dread.

"Nothing," Jeff responded, doing his best to sound casual.

"Wrong!" Dee jumped up from the chair and it flew backward, colliding with the wall. "I know you! You're hiding something!"

"No, I'm not!"

"Yes, you are!"

"No, I'm not!"

"You are, you are, you are!" Dee punctuated this with a foot stomp.

"Okay, fine!" Jeff stopped yelling. He spoke in a quiet, defeated voice. "Our guests canceled."

Dee let out a wail. "No!" She paced the room, distraught. "This is the biggest mistake of my life. Instead of saving the Golden, I'm going to ruin it and I'll drag you down with me. It'll end up on that social-media site I follow about dead motels."

Dee grabbed Jeff's phone from the coffee table and opened an app. She thrust the phone in his face. "Look at the old pictures. The motel is alive. Vibrant. Filled with families and women in those great bathing suits from the sixties. But 'After,' meaning now"—Dee swiped left—"it's dead as our motel careers." She began to hyperventilate. "I'll buy you out, Jeff." She gasped for air. "I don't know how, but I will. Run! Run while you can."

Jeff grabbed her by the shoulders. "Dee, stop! Now! I'm not going anywhere and neither are you. But you *have to* calm down. Close your eyes."

Dee sucked in a deep breath, then followed Jeff's order.

"Now picture yourself on the 405 at six p.m. on a Friday driving back to the Valley after a meeting in Culver City. Are you picturing it?"

Dee gave a small nod.

"Good. Now picture yourself exiting the 99 for 41. You're passing through the outskirts of Fresno. You're in the country. You're on the quiet, rolling road to Foundgold." He paused, waiting.

Dee's breathing slowly returned to normal. She opened her eyes. "Thank you. I'm back."

"Good. We are gonna get through this. Together. Go home and walk Nugget. Inhale some awesome Foundgold fresh air. I'll be by in ten or fifteen minutes. We'll have breakfast together and come up with ways to save the Golden."

Dee gulped back tears. " 'Kay."

"And, Dee"—Jeff held tightly to her shoulders and looked her in the eye—"stop blaming yourself for getting me into this. I'm an adult. I invested in the Golden with you because I wanted to. Everything you said was right. I was sick of paying a fortune for about three feet of living space. I did want to start my own website and consulting business. Except for the murders and fear of bankruptcy, I've never been happier. So thank you for getting me into this."

He released Dee. She threw her arms around him and let the tears flow. "You're the best friend ever," she sobbed.

"Ditto." He peeled her off. "Now go. I'll see you in a few."

Feeling better, Dee returned Jeff's phone to him and went back to her place. She leashed up Nugget and they strolled through the bucolic forest surrounding the old motel, their steps cushioned by the pine needles carpeting the ground, which released a refreshing scent with each step.

Dee took Jeff's advice, relishing every breath of the crisp mountain air she inhaled. She gazed upward at the majestic granite peaks of the Sierras standing sentry over the valley and the villages, like Foundgold nestled below.

I love this place and we will *make it work,* she thought while waiting for Nugget to finish sniffing what she hoped wasn't bear scat.

But what if we don't? the devil on her shoulder hissed. And just like that, Dee's anxiety level trended up again.

The walk finished, she fed Nugget his breakfast and set about making hers and Jeff's, scrambling eggs with mushrooms, spinach, and cheddar. By the time Jeff showed up, the eggs were ready, along with orange juice and toasted English muffins.

"Looks great," he said, taking a seat at the kitchen counter. He held up his tablet. "Since my family packages did actually generate bookings, I think that's the way to go. More crafting ideas for the kids that no one else in the area is doing. Making soap is hot right now. What do you think about a DIY package where guests make soap shaped like gold nuggets?"

"I like it."

Dee took a container of heavy cream from the refrigerator. She poured some into a jar and began shaking it. "I just thought of something. I know O'Bryant hasn't ruled us out as suspects in either murder. But you know who's been around the Golden all this time besides us? Ma'am and Mister Ma'am. And there's something about Mister. I feel like I've seen him before, but I can't figure out where. Maybe it was on a Most Wanted poster at the post office."

"If he was on that list, I think law enforcement would know about it," Jeff said as he tucked into his eggs.

"You're right. Besides, a couple that has a son as handsome as Hunk—Huck—can't be killers."

Jeff dropped his fork and gaped at her. "That's the most L.A. thing I've ever heard you say."

"You're the one who said Serena can't be the killer because she's too pretty," Dee shot back, feeling defensive.

"That's based on fact. Like I pointed out, if Callan's career was going south, thanks to Michael's murder, based on studies of women of similar appearance to Serena who've ended relationships with successful men caught in a scandal, she could easily dump him and either make a lateral move or trade up."

Dee gave him a look. "I don't think you can classify reading online gossip as a scientific study. Still, the Ma'ams are hiding something. I'm sure of it."

She continued vigorously shaking her jar. Jeff watched, curious. "What exactly are you doing?"

"Turning heavy cream into butter," Dee said, her voice vibrating as she shook. "If this works, it could be a family activity for our guests. Everyone gets a jar and heavy cream and they shake it until they make their own butter."

Jeff stared at her, dumbfounded. "You've lost your mind."

Dee ignored him and continued shaking. "I feel like none of our ideas are enough. We need to do more, but I don't know what. Maybe I should learn to play the banjo. Or you should learn to play the harmonica. That's very olden days."

"Right." He added in a dry tone, "I can wear raggedy clothes and black out a couple of teeth so I look like a miner."

"I hadn't thought of that, but great idea!"

Jeff rose. He approached Dee and gingerly removed the jar from her hand. "No more shaking. Sit down and eat."

He guided her to the table and gently pushed her into a chair.

Dee poked at her eggs. "I'm going to take a break from setting up the guest rooms. It only reminds me we don't have any guests. I'll go back to searching Jasper's stuff to see if I can finally find what Michael was looking for."

"Excellent. After breakfast, I'm paying Verity a visit. If I amp up the flirting, maybe she'll back off trying to destroy us."

"Good luck to you. Like Tennyson wrote in 'The Charge of the Light Brigade,' 'Into the valley of death rode the techie.'" Dee picked up the jar and unscrewed the lid. She peeked inside. "Wow, I actually made butter. This could work." She held the jar up to Jeff. "You may not have to black out your teeth after all."

CHAPTER 28

Jeff left, hoping to work some magic with Verity. Dee dragged one of Jasper's trunks out from under the bed. She pushed open the lid and was assailed by the scent of mothballs and mold. Coughing, she shut the trunk. "I'm not feeling this today, Nugs," she said to the mutt, who'd padded in after her.

He rolled over, exposing his tummy for a rub. Dee complied. As she rubbed, the thought crossed her mind that she'd never received an update from Raul regarding the investigation into her drugging. She finished Nug's tummy rub and texted the sheriff to see if he'd uncovered anything. She pressed Send and her phone rang. Dee checked and saw the caller was her father, not the sheriff. She accepted the call.

"Hey, Dad."

"Hey, sweetie. Sorry to bother you, but I wondered if you happened to see my fat black Magic Marker when you were here. I can't find it anywhere."

"No, sorry. It probably rolled under the couch when you were making a protest sign."

"Hmm, I didn't think of that. Hold on." There was a brief pause. "Found it. Thanks, Deedle Dee."

"Glad I made myself useful to someone." The comment came out more acidic than Dee intended.

"Things not going well, huh?" There was a beat of awkward silence. Then he said in a deep voice, "This sounds like a job for Super String Man. Able to tie up villains and problems with a nice, neat bow."

"No." Dee's patience with everything, including The Man of a Million Voices, hit rock bottom. "No voices. I need my father right now, not Super String Man or Tweety Sweety or Colonel Cluck. Please, Dad." She began to cry. *"Please."*

"Aw, Deedle Dee." Struggling with how to respond, Sam tried another voice, this time a deep baritone. "Baby dumplin'." There was a pause. Then Sam spoke as himself. "Delilah Annabel Stern, you are a brave, amazing young woman. I am so proud of you for taking a chance like you did, and Mom would have been too. I'm looking forward to a stay at the Golden, which, I know, is going to be a huge success because *you* are running it, and there's nothing you can't do. Besides, I need a break from clicking that airplane noise complaint button. I'm developing arthritis in my thumb."

Dee burst out laughing. She wiped away tears that had dribbled down her cheeks. "You're the best dad ever. I love you."

"Not as much as I love you," Sam teased. He grew serious. "Sweetie, you do know I'm always here if you need me."

"I do."

Dee ended the call with a promise to keep her dad posted. She leaned back against the bed, taking a moment to replay the conversation. Traumatic as recent events had been, they'd led to an unexpected breakthrough with her father—and for that, she'd be forever grateful.

She got up and went to her nightstand, where she rummaged through its single drawer until she found a mask left over from the pandemic. Dee looped the mask over her ears and flipped open the odiferous trunk's lid a second time, determined to accomplish something, even if all she did was fill up a few garbage bags with Jasper Gormley detritus.

As it turned out, that's exactly what Dee did. But she gave herself credit for decluttering. And once the trunk was aired out, it would add a nice historical touch to the Golden lobby.

Dee's stomach growled. She checked her phone and was shocked to see it was 5:30 p.m. "I worked through lunch," she said to Nugget, whose bark indicated he had no intention of missing a meal. She fed and walked him, then decided to treat herself to dinner at the All-in-One.

Raul called during her drive over there. "Sorry I haven't been in touch. The cabin fire bumped your spiked punch down my to-do list. Apologies for that. But I do have an update. We lucked out on this one. The hoedown barn has security cameras, which were running during the party. Footage showed what looked like Radinsky hitting on Liza Chen. She brushed him off, but he stuck around. When she poured the glass of punch, he bumped her from behind and used the distraction to doctor the drink. He meant it for her. He didn't know she'd poured it for you."

Dee frowned, frustrated by another dead end. "So it had nothing to do with Michael's murder."

"Afraid not. I brought Liza in and she corroborated that Shawn was coming on to her. Apparently, it's been an ongoing problem to the point where his behavior with her bordered on stalking."

"And no clue about who set our cabin on fire?"

"Not yet. Jeff gave us access to the video from your security cameras. Whoever set the fire knew how to dodge them. But the arson investigator is working on it too. He may be able to track down the perp through the accelerant they used."

Dee heard a trumpet blast in the background of Raul's call. "Where are you?"

"Fresno. It's my *abuela*'s seventieth birthday and the mariachi band just showed up at the restaurant. They're pretty loud." Raul sounded embarrassed.

"Thanks for calling. Now go have fun. And wish your *abuela* happy birthday from me."

Dee pulled into the All-in-One parking lot, aggravated by the status of the investigations into both the murders and the fire. She went inside and made a right to the café area. Elmira, who was manning the buffet she'd laid out for the evening meal, greeted Dee with a warm smile. "Well, hey there. I've been thinking about you."

Dee gave her friend a light hug and picked up a plate. "I'm so glad to be here I can't tell you. I'm *starving.*"

Elmira motioned to large trays of food being warmed over Sterno cans. "We've got ribs—pork and beef—roast chicken, mac and cheese, and a token green vegetable." She pointed to a tray of bright green broccoli. "Pile your plate high, honey. It's on the house."

Dee protested, but Elmira shut her down. "It's a slow night, and I refuse to let food go to waste. You'll be taking containers home with you too."

Dee did as ordered. She took a seat at an empty table. Elmira joined her, holding a beer in each hand. She gave one to Dee, whose mouth was full of macaroni and cheese, so she nodded thanks. Elmira might be the world's worst baker, but the woman knew her way around side dishes. If cooking was an art, while baking was chemistry, the All-in-One proprietor was an artist, but no chemist.

"What did you do to this mac and cheese to make it the best I ever tasted?" Dee asked after ingesting another large forkful.

"Used a proprietary blend of cheeses from a recipe handed down through generations of Willikers," Elmira said. "No one can share it under penalty of death." She winked, then realized what she'd said. "Apologies. Very poor choice of words."

"Don't worry about it." Dee picked up a chicken breast, then put it back on her plate. She hesitated. "I need to ask you something. It's personal." The dining area was devoid of other diners, but Dee still spoke in a low voice. "In the past when I was going through tough times, I saw a professional. You know . . . a therapist. I've been thinking that with everything being so chaotic in my life lately, it might help to talk to someone again. My L.A. therapist retired and I don't want to do Zoom with a new person. I wondered if you know anyone in the area I could talk to."

"I understand. You've been through so much. I get how it might help. Hmmm." Elmira thought for a moment. "There is someone in Goldsgone."

"Really?" Dee said, brightening.

"But she's a sex therapist."

"Oh," Dee said, taken aback. "Did not expect that."

Elmira took a slug of beer. "From what I hear, she's got a busy practice. There's not a lot to do around here, so you wanna get that right."

Serena floated down the store's main aisle to the café, stroller in front of her and gauzy, taupe maxiskirt wafting behind her. A tuft of blond hair peeking out from the young mom's baby sling identified its occupant as baby Emmy, which meant Oscar was in the stroller.

"I have news," Serena said in a singsongy voice, once she reached them. She took a seat at their table. "They dropped all charges against Marisa."

"I'm not surprised," Dee said. "Shawn and Michael's murders have to be related. I don't see how Marisa could have physically killed Shawn and dropped his body into our pool. Not without an accomplice. And she doesn't seem to know or even like anyone around here."

"Plus, she's been in L.A. ever since she posted bail," Serena said. "So she alibied out. That's how you say it, isn't it?"

"It's one way." Dee grimaced. "Something I never needed to know until the last few weeks."

"Also," Serena continued, "Marisa was able to prove her fingerprints were on Michael's phone because she borrowed it to make a call when she stopped by his cabin to drop off all his physical materials after he fired Callan. Scripts and stuff. She'd left her phone at our house and wanted to call the Cateau Marmont, where she'd boarded her kitty, and yell at them because their live feed dropped out briefly. The manager confirmed Marisa screamed at her for ten minutes and she's still traumatized by the call."

"Well, Callan must be happy," Elmira said. "He's got his trusty assistant back." Not a fan of Marisa's, she injected a touch of sarcasm into her delivery.

A tiny hand emerged from Serena's baby sling. Serena held out her index finger and Emmy clutched it, emitting happy coos. "Callan's in a terrible mood. You know how having an assistant who would kill for him made him even hotter as an agent? It turns out that even though Marisa's been cleared of the charges, the fact the police thought she *might* have killed for her boss made her the hottest assistant in Hollywood. She got a ton of job offers and quit working for Callan to be a VP of Development for a production company. Callan is super upset, because now he'll have to grovel to her to sell his clients and projects. And you can bet she's going to milk that."

Dee couldn't help but pick up on a hint of schadenfreude in Serena's voice.

Elmira's phone blared an alert, startling all three women, along with Oscar, who responded with a sharp bark to let them know he was on the job if needed. Elmira checked the message and her face clouded.

"There's a fire in the woods above Little Valley Road."

Dee and Serena exchanged concerned looks. "That's on both our ways home."

Elmira stood up. "I gotta close up and put on my volunteer gear." Her phone blared another alert. " 'Volunteers not needed, the inmate crew is there and has it under control,' " she read out loud. "The road is open," she said to the others. "You best head home, to be safe."

Dee and Serena took her advice, rushing to their cars. Dee let Serena exit first, and the charcuterie artist zoomed off in her hybrid SUV. Dee soon followed. She anxiously scanned the sky for flames as she grew closer to the fire's location. About a mile ahead, she saw a plume of smoke shrink and dissipate, confirming the inmate crew's success. Dee released a relieved breath and continued to drive.

She was about to pass the crew's staging area, on the north side of the road, when a compact sedan pulled out in front of her. She couldn't miss the license plate. Encased in a frame bedazzled with rows of sparkling crystals, it read JEWLR. The driver accelerated and roared off, disappearing around a bend in the road.

Dee took this in. She only knew of one jeweler in the area: Owen Mudd Jr. The same Owen she'd seen hurrying down the hill at the Golden on the night Michael's cabin burned down. *Could Owen be an arsonist?* The thought chilled her. She'd genuinely liked the jewelry shop owner when they'd met. But being nice to potential customers didn't rule out a dangerous and lethal secret he might be keeping. What if Michael had found out? And Shawn? He could have killed them both to save himself.

She wondered if she should share the scenario with Raul. She didn't want to risk alienating her and Jeff's law enforcement ally by tossing wild theories at him like a clueless true-crime armchair sleuth. *I'll run it by Jeff first,* she thought as she pulled into the Golden's parking area. *It might be a case of the storyteller in me spinning out.*

Dee got out of the car. She turned on the high-powered flashlight she'd taken to carrying at night and flashed it around the perimeter, making sure Stoney and company weren't paying the Golden a visit. The motel appeared to be bear-free, and Dee was about to start toward her apartment, when the flashlight's beam illuminated something sparkly attached to a leaf in the pool.

Dee bent down at the pool's edge. She put her hand in the water and gently waved it and the leaf toward her until it was within reaching distance. She removed the leaf from the water and stared at the object lying on top of it: a fake nail painted a blinding orange with miniature gold rick-rack painted on its tip. Dee knew exactly to whom the nail belonged: Verity "Yes-*that*-Donner" Gillespie.

Now, this, Dee thought triumphantly, *is a clue.*

She clutched the nail in the palm of her hand and traversed the short path to her front door. She was about to go inside, when she saw the shadow of a hooded figure.

"Jeff?" she called. "If you scare me again, I swear I'll hurt you."

There was no response. Heart racing, Dee beamed her flashlight at the woods. Suddenly a powerful shove sent her sprawling to the ground. The flashlight went flying; then Dee felt excruciating pain as an assailant brought down the force of it on the back of her head.

CHAPTER 29

After briefly passing out, Dee slowly came to. Feeling groggy and nauseous, she reached into her pocket for her phone, but it wasn't there. Her head spun as she felt the ground around her, finally locating it. Dee heard a loud, repetitive sound and tried to place it. After a minute or so, she realized it was Nugget, barking with a furious urgency. She picked up her phone and tried typing in her password. After several failed attempts, she rested it on her chest and closed her eyes, too weak to continue.

Nugget transitioned from barking to desperate howls.

"Nugs?" a familiar voice called. "Dude, you okay?"

Footsteps clomped toward her over dead pine needles. She tried to yell "Help!" but it came out in a whisper.

Jeff's horrified face loomed over her. "What the f . . ."

"Help," Dee finally managed to squeak out.

The next hour was a blur, but by the end of it, Dee found herself back in the unhappily familiar confines of Gold County Medical Center. A neurological examination and CT scan led to a diagnosis of a grade 1 concussion and an overnight hospitalization for observation.

She had a visitor in the morning—Raul. "No Ranger O'Bryant?" she asked the sheriff. She adjusted her position in bed, trying to get comfortable. Her whole body ached, as much from her fall on the hard ground as from the blow to her head.

"He's laying low since the bungled arrest of Callan Katz's assistant," Raul said, failing to suppress a grin. "She's threatening to sue."

"I doubt she will. Knowing Marisa, I bet she'll make a lot of noise to keep the story alive as long as the attention benefits her. Then she'll move on."

"Cold comfort to O'Bryant. He's tiptoeing around Majestic, hoping he doesn't get demoted." Raul took a seat. "Is this the same room you were in when you were accidentally drugged?"

"Yes," Dee said, her tone acerbic. "I always request the room with the view of the HVAC unit on the roof of the second floor."

"The reason you're here this time was no accident." Raul took out his notepad. "Walk me through what happened."

"The fingernail," Dee blurted, suddenly remembering.

"Huh?" The young sheriff stared at her, nonplussed.

"I had the perfect clue and it's gone." Dee slapped her forehead in frustration. Her ears rang. "Ow. That wasn't too bright." She wrinkled her nose, annoyed with herself. "I found one of Verity's fake fingernails floating on a leaf in our pool. I held on to it so I could store it in a safe place in my apartment. When I reached my front door, I saw a shadow. I thought it might be Jeff, because he's scared me before like that. I called to him and shone my light in the woods. Someone came from behind and pushed me down. My flashlight rolled away. It's a really good one—heavy, you know, like, industrial strength. They banged me on the head with it."

Dee gently touched where the flashlight landed and felt a bump. Even a light touch hurt and she dropped her hand. "Maybe Verity realized she lost a nail when she dumped Shawn in our pool and showed up to find it. But she saw *me* find it, followed me, bonked me on the head, and stole the nail back."

"That's a nice story," Raul said, "but your suspect has an alibi. She's in the next room here at the hospital. I saw her on my way to you. Apparently, she's on some weight loss program and went a little too heavy on the laxative tea, which her digestive system didn't appreciate."

"Oh." Dee thought for a moment, the effort not without pain. "What if Verity lost the nail setting Michael's cabin on fire? She hasn't been ruled out as a suspect in his murder, has she?" Raul shook his head.

"Then that's something to consider," Dee said, feeling a little vindicated.

"I'll look into it, along with the security footage from your place. It would help to have the fingernail, though. Physical evidence."

Jeff appeared in the doorway. He held a small bakery box. "Hi. Okay if I come in?"

"Sure," Dee said. "Especially if you come bearing baked goods."

"They're from Elmira," he said, adding with emphasis, "They're *homemade*. By *Elmira*."

"That's code for they're terrible," Dee said to Raul, keeping her voice low.

"You don't need to whisper," Raul said. "We've all almost lost a tooth to one of her brookies. How you can make a brownie-cookie mash-up inedible, I'll never know, but that nice lady found a way." He stood up. "I'm glad you're both here. I owe you an apology. I never should've encouraged you to help me do my job." He sounded chagrined. "Poor judgment on my part. I feel responsible for what happened to you, Dee."

"You're not," Dee said, adamant. "I would have stuck my nose into this investigation whether you wanted me to or not."

"And she would have dragged me along with her," Jeff added.

"Exactly." Dee nodded. "So you can stop feeling guilty."

"I appreciate that," Raul said. "But no more amateur sleuthing. I wanna make sure nothing else happens to either of you. Got it?"

Dee and Jeff remained mute.

The sheriff gave them the side eye. "You're not gonna stop, are you?"

"No," Dee said. "But give yourself credit for trying to make us."

Raul responded with an exaggerated eye roll, then departed, the spurs on his boots jingling.

Jeff took the seat the sheriff vacated. "Sorry I didn't get here sooner. I went and got some big bones for Nugget as a reward for letting me know you were in trouble last night. How are you feeling?"

"Like someone hit me over the head with my own flashlight."

Jeff's pale skin turned red with anger. "When I find out who did this to you!" He made a fist and mimed decking the culprit.

The gesture touched Dee. "I appreciate it, but I hope that whoever did this will be in handcuffs at that point because they've been nailed as Michael's and Shawn's murderer." She leaned back against her pillow and thought for a moment. "Michael's family's house. The one Shawn said was sold. We haven't looked into that angle at all. It might hold some clues about what motivated the murders."

"Good thinking. Do you have any details on it? Like, an address?"

"All I know is it was on Lake Goldsgone. Shawn said he hadn't seen Michael since he helped him move stuff out of the house about a year ago."

"There aren't too many houses on the lakes around here. And it must have been a pretty recent sale." Jeff opened the browser on his phone and typed in a search. He examined the results. "Ah. Here we go. There's a couple of houses for sale, but only one that sold in the last year."

He handed Dee the phone. The listing featured a dozen photos of a charming cottage painted a pale blue and surrounded by a picket fence. A small hill ended at the lake's edge, where a dock extended into the still water, which reflected the charming home.

"What a cute house and gorgeous location," Dee said. "I can see why Michael was drawn back to it."

She returned the phone to Jeff. He stood up and stuck it in the back pocket of his jeans. "You rest. I'll go over to the house and see what I can dig up. Hopefully, the new owners will be chatty and will tell me if anything was left behind by the previous owners. It might mean nothing to them but be a break for us."

He leaned over Dee's hospital bed and ruffled her hair. She swatted him away. "Stop, I hate that."

"I know, that's why I did it. Being annoyed boosts your endorphins." He gave her an affectionate grin and left to pursue the potential lead.

Dee nodded off after Jeff's departure. She slept for a couple of hours, then received a visit from the doctor supervising her case. He approved her release with the proviso she make an instant return to the hospital if any symptoms recurred. When he was gone, Dee reached for her phone to let Jeff know she'd been released. But before she could contact him, her phone rang with a call from him.

"Did you see my text?" He sounded unhappy.

"No, I fell asleep. Give me a minute."

Dee went to her Messages app and opened it to a photo of an empty lot perched on the edge of Lake Goldsgone. A large sign in the middle of the lot heralded a brand-new, state-of-the-art home coming soon to the lot, courtesy of: THE GOLDSGONE GROUP.

"Teardowns even in the country," Dee muttered, disappointed.

"Cheer up," Jeff said. "I think I found something."

Dee's hopes rose. "You do?"

"I researched the Goldsgone Group. And from what I dug up, it's not a group—it's one person. Jonas Jones." Jeff paused for effect. "The same Jonas Jones trying to sell the West Camp warehouse. Where the stuff from Michael's house was taken . . . but has disappeared."

CHAPTER 30

When Jeff showed up to retrieve Dee from the hospital, she insisted he drive by the site of Michael's former home so she could see it for herself. He did so and the two inspected it together. To no one's surprise, they found nothing. "But," Dee said, "I'm positive there's a link connecting the warehouse, Michael's stuff, Jonas Jones, and the murders."

Jeff, who was studying his phone, made a strangling sound. Dee glanced over to him. "What?"

"I looked up the price of the house they're putting up here."

He showed Dee and her eyes widened. "Teardowns *and* gentrification come to Goldsgone. I wonder who profits from the sale."

"If Jonas is the entire Goldsgone Group, he does. But the profits from the home's sale would have gone to Michael and his family. Do you know anything about them? Any potential new suspects?" Jeff's eyes lit up at the possibility.

"Afraid not. He was an only child and estranged from his parents. I know this because of a weird thing that happened when we were working at *On the John*. He left the writers' room to take a call and we all heard him yell 'Yes!' and then let out a hoot. We thought he'd landed a new deal and we were all curious and, of course, jealous, so when he came in the room, we asked if he'd had good news. He got this smirk on his face and said, 'Yes. My father died.' Talk about an awkward moment. It stayed with all of us. I heard from people who worked with him on other shows that he had the same reaction when his mother passed away."

Jeff reacted, appalled. "Ooh, that is dark. I don't know who to feel sorry for, him or his parents."

The two began walking back to Jeff's car. "It makes me so grateful for my mom and dad," Dee said. "Even when Dad's bazillion voices drive me nuts, we never stop loving each other." She halted so suddenly, Jeff bumped into her. "Brainstorm!"

"It better be good," Jeff grumbled, nursing his shoulder.

"It is. I have an idea how we can get intel on Jonas and his real estate dealings. I'll have my dad call him using one of his voices and pretend he's looking to invest in property in the area. He can focus on the lake house and the warehouse."

"That's an excellent idea," Jeff acknowledged.

"Luckily, the blow to my head didn't seem to mess up my brain." Dee squinted at Jeff. "Although I do see two of you."

Jeff yanked the driver's door open. "We're going straight back to the hospital."

Dee put a hand on his arm. "Relax, I'm kidding. Payback for the hair ruffling."

They got into the car. Dee's phone pinged a text. She read it and groaned.

"What? Bad news?"

"It's from Raul. He said the security camera at my place only caught the top of my attacker's head and they had on the hood of a hoodie. But you know why the camera only caught that image? Because a few hours earlier, a couple of squirrels were chasing each other and knocked it out of place. He sent clips." Dee watched them. "I have to say, those squirrels are pretty cute."

After a rapturous reunion with Nugget, Dee called her dad. Sam was elated to make himself useful, especially in a way that utilized his voice-acting talents.

"How's this?" Sam took on the character of Colonel Cluck. "Ah say, ah say, young man, I would like to avail muhself a' your ay-bundant properteees."

"I think you better save that for the chicken chain."

"I could do Rico the Rat from the adult cartoon I voiced. He's a New York tough guy. Might intimidate your real estate agent." He switched into Rico's voice. "Youz got some properties tah showz me, buddy? I gots some bodies to bury, heh, heh, heh."

"Um, a little too close to home with the bodies. Also, I'm not sure how a New York mobster would go over up here."

"Ooh, I know." Excited, Sam switched gears. When he spoke, it was in the smooth, dulcet tones of a British toff. "Hullo, I'm considering a second home in your lovely state and wondered if I might induce you to share a bit of information on the properties you currently have available. You'll meet with me? Brilliant. Ta veddy much."

"We have a winner." Dee smiled. "Remember, we want whatever details you can get out of Jonas on the lake house and warehouse. Thanks so much, Dad. Or should I say—"

"Ian Devonshire Holmes. If you have three names, people totally buy you're a Brit."

"Good luck, Ian. Let me know what happens."

"I'm on it, Deedle Dee. Love you."

"Love you too. More than I can say."

With no other leads to pursue, all Dee could do was wait for a report from her father. Still not feeling a hundred percent, she lay down and snuggled with Nugget for a half hour, then took the pooch on a walk. Even though it was light out, she felt jittery, the trauma from her attack fresh. She kept a constant eye on the woods, and the hand not holding on to Nugget's leash clutched her trusty can of bear spray.

Nugget stopped to sniff a patch of dirt he found particularly odiferous. Realizing the spot was where she'd fallen when pushed by her assailant, Dee clutched the pepper spray more tightly. "You about done, buddy?" she asked, her anxiety level climbing.

Nugget raised his head. Something glittered on the tip of his nose and Dee bent down to see what it was. She peeled off Verity's lost fake nail. "Nugs, you found it!" she exclaimed, hugging the dog. "Right where I must've dropped it. I'm going to be much more careful this time."

She placed the nail in the inside pocket of her bomber jacket and zipped it up. A thought occurred to her. Once her attacker knocked her out, they bought themselves a little time to search the area. Especially since they had her powerful flashlight literally in hand. They could have easily hunted down the nail. But they didn't. *Which means whoever conked me on the head probably wasn't Verity,* Dee realized forlornly. It also occurred to her that the culprit made off with her flashlight, which happened to be an expensive model. "I'm out a weapon that could have ID'd my attacker *and* was a really good flashlight," she groused to Nugget, leading him back inside the apartment.

She fed Nugget and gave him a bone to gnaw on. While waiting for Sam to get back to her, she cleaned off a few more of the Honestadt prints, a task she'd neglected in order to focus on more pressing matters, like catching a killer. But her attention kept returning to her cell phone. "A watched phone doesn't ring." She said this out loud, hoping that would drive home the message. It didn't work. She fell into a rhythm of clean the artwork, stare at the phone, clean the artwork, stare at the phone, ad infinitum.

Of course, it finally rang when she was in the bathroom.

Dee cursed as she hurried to finish her business. She ran out and managed to catch the call on the last ring. "Dad, hi," she said, sounding out of breath. "You got anything for me?"

"I had a very nice chat with Mr. Jones. I can see why he's a successful real estate agent. He's a charmer. At first, I bumped up against the fact he spent a year in London during college. I had to do a little tap dancing there. Good thing we were on the phone and it wasn't a video chat. He couldn't see me pull out your mom's ancient copy of *England on Ten Dollars a Day*. Why she held on to that for all these years, I'll never—"

"Dad, your conversation with Jonas," Dee said, trying to get Sam back on track.

"Right, sorry. Jonas and I went through a list of properties he represents. The house on the lake's gonna be a beaut, but it's out of my price range. Curiously, the very large warehouse is priced much cheaper. I could swing that."

"You mean Ian could swing it," Dee said, fearing her father had gone overboard in committing to his character.

"Yes, but Jonas is so good at his job that he had your very own dad considering an investment. Here's why. Rather than utilize the space as a warehouse, a buyer wanted to turn it into a soundstage. He was storing the contents of a house there, but ran into financial difficulties and had to sell everything and back out of the deal he was trying to put together. A soundstage in one of the most beautiful parts of our beautiful state. Now, that's something Sam Stern *and* Ian Devonshire Holmes could get behind."

"And Michael Adam Baker too," Dee murmured. Her father had stumbled onto a crucial clue; Dee was sure of it. He'd also solved the mystery of what happened to the belongings Shawn helped Michael move.

She could totally see the late sitcom writer pitching the idea of a warehouse-turned-soundstage to Jonas and whoever else might glom on to it. New Orleans and Atlanta both claimed to be the Hollywood of the South. New York was the Hollywood of the Northeast. Bulgaria, Slovenia, and other countries duked it out for the title of the Hollywood of Eastern Europe. So many places wanted to be the Hollywood of something. Why not West Camp and environs as the Hollywood of Central California? If the idea appealed to an industry vet like her father, it would surely be alluring to the residents of the region that stood to benefit the most from it.

Dee was also sure that given Michael's sketchy life track record and gambling addiction, his plan had gone off the tracks. But how? And if so, how had it led to his murder?

"Great job, Dad," she told Sam. "Thanks so much."

"It was a blast. I can't wait to help you out again." His voice brimmed with enthusiasm. "In fact, now that I know I can put my skills to use in investigations, I'm gonna look into getting a PI license."

Hoo boy, Dee thought as they signed off. *I hope I haven't created an amateur-sleuth monster.*

She texted what her father had uncovered to Raul and Jeff. Raul instantly wrote back he'd look into it. Jeff responded with a thumbs-up, adding: **Ran into Serena at All-in-One. Helping her w/ big charcuterie order.**

Dee hoped her friend and partner hadn't transferred his affections to one of the many unavailable women he pined for.

A text alerted her to a package delivery. Since she wasn't expecting anything, Dee's suspicions were aroused. She picked up a broom whose handle could double as a weapon and put an eyeball to the front door peephole.

A gift basket wrapped in cellophane and laden with a wide variety of snacks and beverages sat on the front step. Dee relaxed. She put down the broom, opened the door, and carried the heavy basket to the kitchen counter. She opened the note attached to the basket and read: *From all of us at the All-in-One. Feel better!*

"Aww," Dee said, touched. She unwrapped the cellophane to make sure none of the items needed to be refrigerated. "Nugs, there's even a bag of homemade dog treats for you." She extracted the small bakery box and fed him one of the cookies, which were shaped like paw prints. "I hope Elmira sticks to making these. It's a much better fit for her skill set."

The gift reminded Dee she'd yet to write thank-you cards for the flowers and gifts she'd received after her unpleasant run-in with the doctored glass of punch. From the age where she could only write in block letters with crayons, Dee's late mother, Sibby, had drilled into her that no gift ever, *ever* went un-thanked. Sibby's job as a legal secretary for an entertainment lawyer entailed meticulous proofing of documents, and she brought that home with her. No card or letter departed the Stern house without a rigorous grammar and spell check.

With Raul on the soundstage trail and Jeff busy cubing cheeses with Serena, Dee decided to concentrate on the cards. She took them out of the sideboard drawer, where she'd tucked them. After emptying a bag of locally made potato chips from the gift basket into a bowl, she got to work.

Dee fell into a comfortable rhythm as she wrote, which allowed her mind to occasionally drift. She channeled her mother with every card, proofing them carefully. The task brought back the memory of the threatening note she'd received from the arsonist behind the Golden cabin fire. Something still bothered her about it, but she'd yet to land on exactly what. After wracking her brain for a while, she gave up, figuring it would come to her eventually.

She finished the last card and took a moment to congratulate herself. She glanced upward. "You'd be proud of me, Mom."

She threaded her fingers together, stretched her arms above her head, and hopped off the kitchen barstool. She tended to Nugget, after which he joined her on the couch to watch a British mystery on *Masterpiece*. The feeling they were finally getting somewhere with the investigation into Michael's and Shawn's deaths freed Dee to relax, a sensation she hadn't felt in weeks and greatly welcomed. She finished the night with a glass of cabernet from a bottle in the basket, then settled into bed, where she quickly fell asleep.

In the middle of the night, Dee bolted upright. "That's it!" she cried out, earning a disgruntled grunt from Nugget. Relaxing had allowed her mind to home in on what was bothering her about the threatening note. But Dee knew a theory based on one supposition wasn't enough.

She jumped out of bed and ran to her laptop, where she called up Michael's online video channel. She weeded through what felt like an endless list of pretentious titles for his episodes, searching for one that had tickled her curiosity but she'd skipped past during her last viewing session.

Dee located "Those Who Can't" in the middle of the list. She steeled herself and pressed Play.

Michael's smug face filled the screen. He spent a few minutes extolling his own virtues, then launched into the video lesson's theme. "The Bible says something about false idols." He shrugged. "I don't know exactly what and I'm too busy making bank as a writer to look it up. But I know it's not good. So today I wanna talk about the people you put on a pedestal. And what you should do when you realize they don't belong there."

Dee made it through the entire half hour, which felt four times its actual length. By the time it ended, dawn had broken. She texted an urgent message to Jeff and Raul:

Meet me ASAP! I'm 99.9% sure I know who our killer is.

CHAPTER 31

By the time Raul and Jeff showed up in the morning, the sheriff had received the results of Shawn Radinsky's autopsy. Radinsky's cause of death reinforced Dee's theory about who killed both the personal trainer and sitcom writer Michael Adam Baker.

She pitched her friends a plan to corner the murder suspect. They voiced concern, but she convinced them that with Raul and his fellow sheriff, Gerald Tejada, crouched outside and ready to spring, she'd be safe.

"And I'm pretty sure I can talk O'Bryant into getting in on the action," Raul said, now totally on board. "All I have to do is get him to figure out that if he's not there, he won't get any credit for the arrest."

At noon, Dee showed up outside Gold Rush Contractors and Carpentry, squeezing through the front door as Millie was about to flip around the OPEN.

"Dee, hello," the older woman said. "I was about to close for lunch."

Dee walked to the middle of the reception area, sending the message she wasn't leaving. "I know, but I got Brian's quote to rebuild our cabin and I need to talk to him. It's urgent."

"Brian isn't here right now, he's out on a job." Millie's face wrinkled with concern. "Is it something I can help you with?"

Dee thrust her fists into the pockets of her jacket and nervously tapped a foot. "I don't know. Maybe."

"All right. Give me a minute." Millie adjusted a small arrangement of ivory cabbage roses on the coffee table, where potential clients waited for their appointments. She picked up a heavy bucket filled with unused flowers. Water sloshed over the edge as she carried it to the reception desk, where she placed it on a corner. "All set." She turned to Dee. "Now tell me what's going on. It sounds serious."

"It is." Dee stopped tapping, but kept her hands in her pockets. "I think everyone around here knows the Golden is in financial trouble. Thanks to the murders, we have zero guests. Bills are piling up. I don't know if we're going to make it."

"I'm so sorry," Millie said, genuinely sympathetic. "But how does this tie into Brian?"

"I felt like I couldn't count on law enforcement to catch Michael and Shawn's killer—Deputy Sheriff Aguilar is busy trying to keep tourists safe here in Goldsgone, and Ranger O'Bryant has a whole national park to look after—so I've been investigating on my own. I began thinking, 'Who has the most motivation to off Michael?' And the finger pointed to Brian."

Millie gaped at Dee. "That's outrageous. How dare you even think that?"

"Brian hated Michael. He was jealous of how you fangirled over him. It fractured your relationship, at least from your son's end. I could totally see Michael baiting him and pushing him over the edge to murder. And Goldsgone is a small town. What if Shawn found out? And threatened to turn him in? Brian carries lumber. Transporting Shawn's body to our pool wouldn't be hard. And would possibly incriminate us in both murders. We were already suspects in O'Bryant's eyes. Shawn's murder could drive it home."

Millie pressed her lips together until a thin white line formed around them. "This is the most insulting accusation I've ever heard. My son is a wonderful man. He would never do anything so heinous. *Never.*"

"I figured you'd say that. And you know what? I think you're right." Dee leaned an elbow on the reception table, but kept her other hand firmly in her pocket. "About a year ago, I was at a screening in L.A. where there was a Q and A with the screenwriter afterward. The movie was about a police officer who went through hell to solve a case, and the guy who wrote it was a former detective himself. He said the most important thing he learned on the force was the biggest motivator for murder wasn't jealousy or money or revenge. It's humiliation. Dig deep and it's the root of most murders."

Dee lifted her elbow from the table. She affected a casual saunter back and forth across the reception area floor. She stopped. "I watched a video Michael made: 'Those Who Can't.' He ripped you apart. Your star student totally dragged his 'favorite teacher.' Said he had to unlearn everything you taught him. And he was so mean and snide. I'm sure you couldn't unsubscribe to his stupid channel fast enough. But the thing is, you can't unsubscribe from Comments. You may have deleted yours, but you couldn't delete others. The ones defending you or the ones not so nicely piling on to make fun of you. He posted the video only days before he died. I think you confronted him, and when he refused to delete it or apologize, you blew and killed him."

Millie's jaw tightened, along with the crepey skin on her neck. She forced a smile that was more of a grimace. "What a story. So creative. It's sad you don't have a Hollywood career anymore. I recommend you sell it to a writer who's still working."

"I know it's a lot of theorizing on my part," Dee acknowledged. "But one thing the detective-turned-screenwriter said is that amateur criminals always make mistakes. I think Deputy Sheriff Aguilar will eventually find where you made yours. But he'd find it a whole lot faster if I shared my theories with him. If I don't, though, it'll buy you time. Nicaragua has beautiful flowers and no extradition treaty with the United States."

Millie took a long pause. She toyed with the flowers in her bucket. "I assume you want something in exchange," she said, avoiding eye contact with Dee.

"Brian rebuilds our burned-down cabin for free."

The flora-loving retired schoolteacher, part-time mercantile salesclerk, and construction company receptionist let out a surprised snort. "That's it? My goodness, it almost doesn't seem fair."

Millie yanked a flower from the bucket and thrust it in Dee's face, startling her. She jumped back, but Millie came at her. "This isn't baby's breath. It's water hemlock, one of the most poisonous plants in the country."

She lunged at Dee with the hemlock. Dee pulled her container of bear spray from the pocket where she'd clutched it during the entire confrontation with Millie. She aimed the can at her attacker, but slipped on a puddle of water and fell to the floor. The bear spray rolled out of reach.

Millie pinned Dee to the floor, her gingham dress ripping in the process. She was about to attack Dee with the poisonous plant, when Aguilar and Tejada broke down the construction company door. They trained their guns on Millie.

"Drop the hemlock," Raul ordered. *"Now."*

Trapped, Millie did so. She held her arms in the air and slowly rose to her feet. Tejada cuffed her, while Aguilar dropped to his knees by Dee's side.

"Are you okay?"

"I'm not sure," she said, not making a move to get up. She touched her fingers to her mouth. "My lips are numb. I think a little of that hemlock might have gotten into my system. If it's not too much trouble, would you mind running me by the hospital? Again?"

CHAPTER 32

That evening, Dee, Jeff, and Raul walked into the Golden Grub Café to a round of applause from those gathered there waiting for an update on the day's dramatic events.

"Are you okay?" Liza Chen asked Dee as she led the three to a center table.

"Fine," Dee said. "There was no evidence of hemlock in my bloodstream, so the doctors concluded only a minute amount might have touched my lips. They gave me a fluid intravenous drip, just to be on the safe side. I asked them if I won a prize for most visits to the ER in a month and they made this for me." She held up a surgical glove with the index finger inflated and *You're Number 1!* written on the glove's front in black marker.

Dee took a seat. "I'll get us both food," Jeff said, eyeing a plentiful buffet Liza had set up.

He headed off, trailed by Raul. Jonas and Elmira usurped their seats at the table; a small crowd huddled behind them. Even Ma'am and Mister were there, having joined the impromptu gathering for the free food.

Dee gratefully accepted a bottle of sparkling water from Jonas. Elmira propped her elbow on the table. She rested her chin on her fist and said to Dee, "Tell us *everything*."

"Hoo boy. Where to begin?" Dee took a deep breath and exhaled. "I began to suspect Millie when I landed on what bothered me about the threatening note someone who turned out to be her left for me. It was the word 'businesses.'" The others looked confused and Dee elaborated. "'The note read 'Stop poking your nose in other people's businesses . . . or else.' It sounds incorrect, because it's not how we talk. But grammatically, it's correct. Millie taught English for forty years. She couldn't help herself. She had to use correct English. So did my mom, who was a legal secretary, where the wrong date or word in a document could tank a case."

Dee stopped to take a sip of water, then resumed. "To make sure her message hit home, Millie also burned down Michael's cabin. But I think part of the motivation for that was emotional. Millie was starstruck by her 'star' student, Michael. He knew this and used it to manipulate her. He got her to sweet-talk Brian and a few other locals into investing in his plan to turn the West Camp warehouse into a soundstage, selling how it would attract film and TV production to the area. Right, Jonas?"

Jonas responded with a nod. "To be honest, I still think it's a good idea. The place is sitting empty right now. I use it to store my real estate signs."

Hearing this, Dee mentally ticked off the box that posed the question of what Jonas was doing at the warehouse. "None of you knew about Michael's gambling addiction," she said. "He lost all the money you invested with him and got himself into serious trouble. He thought he could write his way out of it by stealing my life for the premise of a sitcom pilot. And he created a whole online channel of how-to videos. One of which completely tore apart Millie. He called her 'pedantic' and 'rigid,' and said she 'lacked any talent of her own' so she 'glommed' on to her students. It got worse from there. Talk about a fallen idol. She was devastated."

"But to kill because of it!" Liza shuddered.

Raul took over the story. "Millie's one of those people who thinks that if she can just *explain,* everyone will understand why she did what she did. So she talked a lot after we booked her. The first straw was Michael gambling away her investment, along with everyone else's. But she tried to justify that to herself. 'He had a sickness.' 'He needed treatment.' Then she saw the video. And that sent her over the edge. She confronted him, and he was trying to get away from her, which is how they wound up at the Majestic property line," Raul continued. "She says he was coming at her, and she hit him with the rock to defend herself. Unfortunately for her, that defense is a wash, because he took the fatal blow to the back of his head."

The others grew silent. "What about Shawn?" Liza finally asked.

"The coroner's report showed Shawn died from water hemlock poisoning," Raul said. "Served in the tea at Millie's house. As soon as Brian heard his mother had been arrested, he turned himself in as an accessory and explained everything. Shawn, you see, was on his way to confront Michael when he saw Millie running away from the Golden to her car. When Michael was killed, Shawn put two and two together. Angry at Millie for convincing him to invest with Michael, he threatened her, saying he'd go to the police and tell them what he saw if she didn't make him whole with money from her own savings. When Brian found out what his mother had done, he panicked and dumped Shawn's body in the Golden pool. He knew Dee and Jeff were already suspects in Michael's murder. He also conked you on the head, Dee, hoping it would scare you out of investigating."

"Way to welcome newcomers to town," Dee said, pursing her lips. "Back to Shawn. I'd still like to know what Verity's fake nail was doing in our pool."

Elmira chuckled. "I got the four-one-one on that little tidbit. Verity and Shawn had a thing going on. I'm guessing one of her nails got stuck in his hair when they were being intimate during a 'private training session' before he paid Millie a visit, and then the fake nail fell off in the pool."

Dee choked back a laugh. She wasn't the only one.

Their curiosity sated, everyone drifted off except Jonas and Elmira. The All-in-One proprietor stood up. "If there's a better way of ingratiating yourself with our community than helping to solve two murders," she said to Dee with affection, "I can't think of it."

She departed the table for the buffet spread, leaving Dee alone with Jonas. "You know, Millie tried to set you up as a suspect," Dee said.

Jonas narrowed his eyes. "No surprise there. There's not enough gingham and bonnets in the world to hide a racist."

"She said 'the likes of him' when we were at the Golden Grub, but I didn't call her out on it because I wasn't sure if it was Goldsgonedian old-timey or a dog whistle."

"The latter. I hope you didn't play into her accusations."

"*Noooo*, never."

Jonas eyed her with skepticism.

Dee flushed. "Okay, for a minute. But don't take it personally. I suspected everyone. For a brief moment, I wondered if Serena's dog, Oscar, purposely tripped Michael."

Jonas leaned into Dee, his brown eyes twinkling, "This party's fine and all, but I'd like to personally show my appreciation for your amateur sleuthing with a one-on-one dinner date."

Dee hid her surprise at the unexpected invitation. She hesitated. "Jonas, I'm going to be honest with you. Elmira said you're an operator."

To her surprise, he let out a guffaw. "Ha! She says that about everyone who tries to drag these sleepy old burgs into the twenty-first century. Watch." He called out to his cousin. "Ellie, John Harvey from West Camp Office Systems has a new credit card system he wants you to try."

Elmira made a face and called back, "John Harvey? Forget it. That guy's an operator."

Jonas crossed his arms in front of his chest and grinned at Dee, who grinned back.

"Point made. Dinner sounds great. Text me." She gave him her number and gazed after him as he left the table to join the buffet line.

He really is a handsome man, she thought. *Of course, he's no Huck. But who is?*

Dee's stomach growled. She stood up and was about to visit the buffet, when she heard someone say, "Am I too late for the celebration?"

She glanced at the front door to see jeweler Owen enter. What happened next came as a shock.

"There's my future son-in-law," Ma'am cried out. She threw her arms around the jeweler.

"Owen sandwich!" This came from Mister, who embraced him from behind, to much laughter.

Owen noticed Dee gaping at him. "Like my granny used to say, close your mouth, you'll catch flies."

Mortified, Dee did so. "I'm just . . . I didn't know."

Mister and Ma'am released him. "Huck and I are a couple," Owen said. "We have been since high school. We started out dating in secret—"

"I bet," Dee said, sympathetic to what they must have faced in such a rural area.

"It's not what you think," he said. "Huck was from Foundgold. I was from Goldsgone. As you know by now, the towns are archrivals. We were Romeo and Romeo. After high school, Huck got in with some bad characters. He dodged trouble for a while but it finally caught up with him. He's been in jail for the last two years on a five-year sentence but he's shortening his sentence by working on an inmate fire crew." Owen shared this with pride. "Until he's paroled, pretty much the only time I get to see him is when he's on duty with the crew."

Another box ticked off, Dee thought as she recalled the two times she'd seen Owen at the site of fires.

Mister gave Owen a fond clap on the back. " 'Get thee a good husband, and use him as he uses thee.' "

Dee gasped. "Yes. That's it!" She bounced up and down with excitement. "I finally remembered where I know you from. You played the Shakespeare-quoting drunk preacher on an episode of *On the John.*"

"I was wondering when you'd remember," Mister said with a sly smile. Then he grew serious. "The drunk part wasn't acting. A few months after I shot that role, I came up here and went on the bender of all benders. I passed out in my car, figuring I'd never wake up. But I did. Being tended to at a handmade cabin in the woods by her and her son."

He cast a lovestruck glance at Ma'am, who was shoveling rolls into a makeshift cross sack and chatting with Owen and Huck. "I truly found gold in Foundgold." He winked at Dee, then went to join his family.

Jeff appeared holding two full plates. "Sorry for the delay. I was swamped by people congratulating me. Apparently, we've gone from pariahs to local heroes." He couldn't resist puffing out his chest as he set the plates on the table and took a seat.

Dee glanced out the window and saw Verity "Yes-*that*-Donner" Gillespie sneaking a peek into the café. Feeling magnanimous, Dee waved for her to join them. Verity pulled away from the window. She straightened her bonnet and marched off.

"I have a feeling we better enjoy being heroes while it lasts." She sat down with Jeff and eyed his plate. "Wow, to speak in Goldsgonedian, you really tied on the feed bag."

"I'm comfort eating," Jeff said, biting into a pulled-pork sandwich. "Raul's attached himself to Liza. I guess a ten-year age difference doesn't bother him. From the looks she's giving back to him, it doesn't bother her either."

"I told you."

"I know. I'll have to look elsewhere for love." He washed down the bite of sandwich with a chug of beer. "What's your take on the status of Serena and Callan's marriage? Thumbs-up? Down?"

Dee wagged a finger at him. "Nuh-huh. Do *not* go there."

"Got it. How are you feeling, by the way? All better?"

"Yup." Dee speared a forkful of mac and cheese. "I'm at a hundred percent."

"Good." Jeff wiped barbeque sauce off his chin. "Because you may have forgotten, but we've still got one more mystery to solve."

CHAPTER 33

Dee and Jeff collapsed onto her living-room couch. They'd spent hours searching every inch of the Golden to hunt down whatever Michael had been looking for when Dee caught him in her apartment.

Dee glanced down at her T-shirt. Grime and perspiration stains discolored the logo on it from a long-canceled show she'd worked on. "This shirt is cashed. I think it's even too gross to turn into rags." She sneezed. "I've turned into a giant human dust bunny."

Jeff threw back his head and groaned. "This is driving me nuts. I know whatever he was looking for is here somewhere. But where? *Where?*"

He pulled a harmonica out of his back pocket and began blowing into it, trying without success to form a tune. He stopped. "These look easy to play, but I don't get how they work at all. I need to find a tutorial."

"Make sure it's not in German." Dee rose to her feet and stretched. "Time to do something useful. I only have two more Honestadt prints to clean; then we can hang them all back in the rooms."

Jeff resumed teaching himself how to play the harmonica. Dee went to the kitchen to get the glass cleaner, then picked up a print leaning against one of Jasper Gormley's old trunks and set to work wiping decades of grime off it. "Too bad this isn't real. We could add a dozen more cabins with the money we'd make selling it."

She froze. Jeff dropped his harmonica. They stared at each other. "Do . . . you . . . think . . . ?" He spoke slowly, the possibility they'd simultaneously landed on tantalizing.

"Only one way to find out," Dee said, excitement mounting. "Check every single picture."

Brimming with excitement and anticipation, Dee and Jeff examined every print in Dee's place to see if one might be the original missing Honestadt hiding in plain sight for decades. None were.

"We need to check the ones we rehung," Jeff declared.

The two ran from the apartment to the few rooms and cabins decorated with the restored prints. To Dee and Jeff's crushing disappointment, that's what they proved to be: prints.

Disconsolate, the two trudged back to Dee's. Jeff got them each a beer from the fridge. Dee sat on the floor with a thump, resting her back against Jasper's trunk. Too lazy to walk, Nugget inched over from his prone position and rested his head in her lap as if commiserating with her defeated mood.

"I had a terrible thought," Jeff said, handing her a beer. "What if the original painting was in Michael's cabin and burned down with it?"

"I bet that's what happened." Dee grew teary. "It's so heartbreaking. Not just for us. For the art world."

Her cheeks wet, she glanced in Jasper's trunk and saw a rag. She reached for it, but the rag turned out to be wrapped around something. She took the item out of the trunk. It was rectangular. And the same size as the sixteen Honestadt framed prints Dee had so carefully cleaned.

She unwrapped it . . . and gasped. With shaking hands, she held the stunning painting up to Jeff. His jaw literally dropped.

The glorious mountains of Majestic National Park, rendered in oil paint, loomed over a bucolic woodland grove. Deer grazed where the Golden Motel now stood. "With Baker spending a good chunk of his life in the area, he must have heard about the missing painting," Jeff said, gazing at it in wonder.

"And I can totally see him manipulating Jasper into revealing anything he knew about it. Whatever the poor old man told Michael must have led him to assume the painting was somewhere on the property." Dee carefully laid the painting back in the trunk. "We need to keep it in a safe place until we can get an appraisal. I'm calling Owen to see if he'll let us store it in one of his safes for at least a little while."

She called up Owen's number. He answered the call after one ring. "Dee? Hi. Everything okay?"

"More than okay," she said, beside herself with excitement. "Wait until you hear this."

She filled the jeweler in on the marvelous discovery.

"I don't believe it," Owen said. He sounded like he was in shock.

"Believe it."

"After all these years."

"I know!" Dee couldn't help bouncing up and down a little.

"So the rumor was true. Jasper did steal it."

Dee stopped bouncing. She paused. "Steal it?"

* * *

"Smile!"

Dee and Jeff managed smiles as the newspaper photographer snapped a shot of them on either side of *The Sierras in Springtime,* the long-lost Kristof Honestadt painting now returned to its rightful home, the Majestic Lodge. Rather than stuck in the hallway where it once resided, *The Sierras in Springtime* was now front and center in the lodge lobby, offering Ranger O'Bryant more opportunities to milk its miraculous reappearance.

At the moment, he was spouting off about the painting's history to a news crew from Fresno. "Jasper Gormley was a janitor at the lodge for decades. He also ran a beat-up old motel in Foundgold his family built in the early 1940s."

"Beat up, my a—" Jeff muttered.

Dee shushed him.

"Jasper was under suspicion for the theft," O'Bryant continued. "He made a lotta noise about how the painting should belong to his family because it was of the view behind the Golden. But there was never any proof connecting him to the theft. Bottom line: The painting belongs to the Majestic."

The newspaper photographer motioned to the ranger. "Let me get a picture of all three of you with the painting."

"Sure," O'Bryant said, happy to hog the spotlight.

He positioned himself in a way that led Dee to assume she'd be lucky if her arm made it into the photograph. "I've been meaning to ask you," she said to the ranger when they were done, "is there by any chance a reward for finding the painting?"

"There is," O'Bryant said, raising hopes that were instantly dashed. "Two hundred fifty dollars. Standard amount. Most people who receive a reward donate it right back to the park. Funding these national wonders is a real struggle."

"We'll do the same, of course," Dee said, caving to guilt. Jeff gave a weak nod of agreement.

By the time the celebratory reception was over, it was dark outside. "I added the sluice to our website," Jeff said as he drove. "That'll bring a couple families to the Golden. I hope, I hope."

Dee called up the website on her phone. "Nice job. It looks very appealing." She opened another tab and beamed with her first genuine smile of the day. "Good thing we're going to get the sluice up and running, because guess what?" She triumphantly held up the phone. "A class of fourth graders from Sherman Oaks just booked the whole motel for a California history overnight school trip! They love the sluice *and* my historic map."

"Whoo-hoo!" The two hooted.

Jeff took a hand off the steering wheel and high-fived Dee. "We're gonna make this work, Deester."

"We are."

She settled back in the car seat. They rounded the bend. Dee's eyes widened. She grabbed Jeff's arm. "Jeff, look."

"What?" Panicked, he hit the brakes. "Deer? Bear?"

"No. *Sign.*"

His eyes followed to where Dee pointed. The GOLDEN MOTEL sign shone in all its neon glory, every letter lit to perfection. The nugget blinked on and off as if cheerfully winking. The sign's golden light illuminated Serena and Elmira.

Jeff screeched into the parking lot. Dee hopped out before the car even came to a full stop. She dashed over to the women. "What . . . I . . . ." She couldn't form a full sentence.

"Callan did end up signing some new A-list clients," Serena said. She stroked the wispy blond hair of her daughter, Emmy, who was currently housed in the baby sling. "I talked him into fixing the sign as a motel-warming present. Elmira helped me find the company to repair it. Funny how quickly people step up when they hear the words 'money is no object.'" Serena delivered this with a sly grin.

"Ooh!" Dee threw her arms around Serena, then did the same to Elmira. Jeff hugged Serena, lingering until Dee gently pried him off.

"There's champagne and a charcuterie board in the lobby," Serena said.

"And I brought a big box of brookies," Elmira added, "but Serena bumped into me and the box went flying out of my hands and onto the ground."

"My bad. The board was heavy and I lost my balance." Serena exchanged a knowing look with Dee and Jeff.

"Let's go toast." Dee hooked one arm with Serena and the other with Elmira. "To friendship. And the Golden's bright, sparkly future."

Jeff pulled out his harmonica and attempted a triumphal run. The others winced at the off-key notes. "I *gotta* find a good tutorial."

Laughing, the four went inside Dee's apartment.

The forest fell silent. Then there was a crunch of leaves under a heavy foot. Followed by another. And another.

A pair of beady black eyes peered out from between the trees. Then a large black bear lumbered out of the woods.

The bear picked up one of Elmira's fallen brookies and happily chomped down on it. He instantly spit it out. He huffed a few annoyed bear grunts, turned around, and lumbered off until he disappeared completely.

ROAD TRIP TIPS FROM ELLEN

Freeze water bottles. They'll serve as ice packs until they melt, after which you'll have refreshing ice-cold water. Always travel with several empty gallon-sized plastic ziplock bags. You never know when they'll come in handy. We couldn't refreeze our water bottles on a recent trip, so when we stopped for lunch, we filled two of our empty bags with ice from the soda machine, turning the bags into impromptu ice packs.

Always travel with a paper map. GPS is great for point-to-point travels, but a paper map gives you an overview. Plus, if you're traveling in a remote area, there's no guarantee you'll even have reception. A paper map could be a literal lifesaver in that case.

When locals make a face and say a road you're about to travel is very curvy . . . believe them.

COWBOY CASSEROLE

Ingredients:
1 T. olive oil
1 lb. ground turkey, beef, or veggie substitute
1 small–medium onion, diced
1 T. minced garlic
1 28 oz. can baked beans, any style
2 15 oz. cans corn, drained
1 15 oz. can creamed corn
2 cups grated sharp cheddar cheese, divided
26 oz. tater tots, thawed

Directions:
Preheat the oven to 375 degrees.

Heat up the oil in the bottom of a Dutch oven or cast-iron pot on medium heat. Add the diced onion and sauté until tender. Add the garlic and cook together briefly.

Add the ground meat to the onion and garlic mixture, breaking it up as it cooks into small pieces. Once it's cooked, lower the flame slightly and add the baked beans, stirring to combine. Turn off the heat and remove the pot from the burner.

In a medium bowl, combine the creamed corn and regular corn.

Spoon the meat-bean mixture into a greased 9 x 11 baking pan or casserole dish. Top it with the corn mixture, gently spreading the corn to cover the meat-bean mix. Sprinkle 1½ cups of the grated cheese over the corn. Arrange the tater tots in a single layer on top of the cheese.

Bake for 20 minutes. Sprinkle the rest of the cheddar cheese on top of the casserole and bake another 10 minutes. Serves 8–10.

ELLEN'S ROAD TRIP TRAIL MIX

Ingredients:

1 cup raw cashews

1 cup raw pistachios

1 cup raw pecans or walnuts

2 cups Raisin Brain Cluster cereal

¼ cup dried cranberries or other dried fruit cut in very small pieces

¼ cup raisins

2 cup original Puffins (or a similar cereal; even a chocolate or fruity one)

1 cup banana chips (optional)

Directions:

Place all ingredients in a large plastic container with a sealable lid. Shake the container well to combine the ingredients. Measure out ½ cup servings into small plastic bags or containers.

Serves a lot.

NOTE: You'll notice there's nothing included in this mix that could melt, like chocolate chips or M&M's. This mix is meant for car snacking, so you want to avoid food items that create sticky fingers and car stains. If the mix is meant for home, feel free to add whatever sweet treat you'd like to include.

I also make this mix without salty nuts. It's best to avoid salty snacks when you're on the road. Travelers need to down lots of water to counterbalance the salt, which leads to frequent pee breaks. However, feel free to substitute dry roasted nuts for raw in the recipe.

Make sure you store whatever you don't use in an airtight container to prevent the cereal from losing its crunch.

AUTHOR'S NOTE

In the late 1940s, my great-aunt and great-uncle Molly and Howard Seideman relocated from Brooklyn, New York, to Modesto, California, where Howard ran a tomato-packing plant. On my first trip to California in 1975, Molly, whom I adored, took me to Columbia State Historic Park in the southern end of Gold Rush Country. The park is actually a historic village comprising at least thirty extant buildings dating back to the town's founding in the 1850s. It's both picturesque and entertaining, offering a combination of history, shops, and eateries served up by docents and employees dressed in period garb. You can even ride a stagecoach and pan for gold.

The visit made such a lasting impression on me that it inspired the fictional—and facetious!—town of Goldsgone in *A Very Woodsy Murder*. A visit to Yosemite National Park a couple of decades later had a similar impact: it inspired Majestic National Park. When Kensington gave me the fantastic opportunity to write the Golden Motel Mysteries, I merged the memories of the two visits, aided and abetted by a recent research trip where I got to relive the beauty of both parks.

I cheat geography more than a little bit in this series. Columbia and Yosemite are separated by a drive of a couple of hours and several thousand feet in elevation in reality; while in the series, one is but a few miles down the road from the other. I hope you'll forgive my fictional license and eventually visit both Columbia and Yosemite. I'm sure you'll find them as inspiring as I do.

Great-Aunt Molly, how I wish you were here to see the end result of our wonderful adventure.

ACKNOWLEDGMENTS

A huge thank-you to everyone at Kensington for giving me this amazing opportunity, and massive thanks to my agent, Doug Grad, for connecting me to this fantastic publisher. Huge love and thanks for my fellow blog mates at Chicks on the Case, my group mates at the Cozy Mystery Crew Facebook page, and my Fearless Foursome. A special shout-out to fab authors Vickie Fee and James J. Cudney for their beta reads and notes. I owe you both! And thank you, wonderful Marisa Young, for your generous winning bid at the Malice Domestic live auction.

Thanks to Crystal at the Tuolumne County Sheriff's Department for her kindness and help in locking down some law enforcement details. Crystal, if I got anything wrong, remember this is fiction, lol. And to all the rangers and workers at Columbia State Historic Park, the residents of California thank you for your dedication to such an important part of the state's history. I hope you get a kick out of my tongue-in-cheek take on what is an amazing and inspiring site.

As always, a ton of love and gratitude to my husband, Jerry, and my daughter, Eliza, for their patience and endless support. I truly couldn't do this writing thing without you. And to my mom, Elizabeth Seideman, and my late dad, Richard, two voracious readers who passed on their passion for books to all three of their children.

And finally, a special thank-you to my late aunt Molly. I will always love and miss you.